In Camera

By

Graham John

For my father who fought for King and Country throughout WWII in the African and Asian theaters.

This a work of fiction woven into the fabric of known events around the time of the Normandy Landings in June 1944. All flights of fancy are precisely that.

The chauvinistic points of view expressed by some characters are not shared by the author but reflect historic mores which, happily, continue to erode.

If this book helps one iota to preserve the memory of those who fell to preserve our democracy, it will have been a worthwhile exercise.

The right of Graham John to be identified as the author of this work has been asserted in accordance with the Copyright Modernization Act 2011 (As amended).

Copyright © Graham John   2021

ISBN: 978-1-7778437-0-0

Paperback edition first published in 2021.

A catalogue record for this book is available from the Library and Archives of Canada (LAC).

Table of Contents

Prologue *8*

Part One – 24ᵗʰ May 1940 ....*9*

   1.   Belgravia, London...*9*

   2.   Mexico City..*12*

   3.   New Reich Chancellery - Berlin............................*14*

Part Two – 13ᵗʰ June 1942 ....*18*

   4.   Belgravia, London...*18*

   5.   Lady Amelia Brown's Flat, Knightsbridge, London......*21*

   6.   Newmarket Racecourse, Cambridgeshire.............*25*

   7.   Near Gazala, North Africa *32*

Part Three – 4ᵗʰ June 1944 ....*34*

   8. The Dorchester Hotel, London *34*

   9. Dieppe, Normandy..*36*

   10. Southwark Cathedral, London *40*

   11. La Roche-Guyon, N. France - 18:00h *43*

   12. The Dorchester Hotel, London - 22:00h *46*

Part Four – 5ᵗʰ June 1944 ....*50*

   13. Normandy – 09:00h...*50*

   14. Portsmouth Naval Yard, England – 21:00h *52*

Part Five – 6ᵗʰ June 1944 ....*64*

   15. Hayling Island, England - 00:30h *64*

   16. Mid English Channel - 04:15h.............................*67*

   17. Off Le Havre, English Channel – 04:30h.............*69*

   18. Soho, London - 06:00h *73*

   19. Omaha Beach, Normandy - 06:15h *76*

   20. Jig Section, Gold Beach, Normandy – 07:25h *79*

21. Omaha Beach, Normandy - 08:45h.................................. 82

22. Belgravia, London - 13:00h 84

23. Trafalgar Square, London - 15:00h.................................. 85

24. Portsmouth Naval Yard, England - 15:00h 89

25. La Roche-Guyon, N. France - 15:00h 91

26. Portsmouth Naval Yard, England, 15:15h...................... 92

27. Knightsbridge, London - 17:30h 97

28. 85 Fleet St., London - 18:15h.............................. 99

29. Belgravia, London - 19:15h 102

30. 85, Fleet St, London 19:20h.............................. 105

31. Belgravia, London - 20.20h 109

32. 85 Fleet Street, 20:00h 111

Part Six – 7ᵗʰ June 1944.................................... *112*

33. The Royal Crescent, Bath - 01:15h 112

34. The A40 near Reading, England – 08:30h...................... 114

35. La Roche-Guyon - 09:25h 116

36. The Royal Crescent, Bath – 09:50h.......................... 118

37. London Road, Bath – 10:05h.......................... 123

38. The Royal Crescent, Bath – 10:20h 124

39. La Roche-Guyon – 11:00h 129

40. West towards Fishguard – 12:00h 131

41. RAF Rhoose, near Cardiff – 15:05h 137

42. Thirty Miles from Fishguard – 16:40h...................... 140

43. Approaching RAF Brawdy – 16:45h 143

44. Aboard the Rosslare Ferry – 18:45h.................. 150

45. Above St. George's Channel – 19:00h.................... 152

46. The Irish Sea 155

Part Seven – 8ᵗʰ June 1944 .... **187**

47. County Wexford, Eire **187**

48. The Houses of Parliament, London **190**

49. The Ordenspalais, Berlin **193**

50. Wicklow Mountains, Eire **197**

51. The Old Hospital, Wexford **200**

52. Wicklow Mountains, Eire **202**

53. SOE HQ, Baker Street, London **204**

54. A Dublin Safe House **207**

Part Eight **210**

55. Montgomery's HQ, Cruelly – June 12ᵗʰ **210**

56. En Route to Kilburn, North London – June 12ᵗʰ **212**

57. Kilburn, North London – June 13ᵗʰ **227**

58. House of Commons, Westminster – June 14ᵗʰ **238**

59. Kilburn, North London – June 14ᵗʰ **240**

60. The Savoy Hotel – the Evening of June 14ᵗʰ **243**

Epilogue **249**

Prologue

Churchill believed his proper place on D-Day would be aboard HMS Belfast bombarding the Normandy beaches. Likewise his liege Lord for a while, but when cooler heads persuaded King George VI he shouldn't go, he wasn't going to send his Prime Minister in his stead.

So, when Germany's most celebrated warrior made accepted a request to parlay, Churchill would not be deterred. If he couldn't fight them on the Normandy beaches, he would face them in Portsmouth.

His bodyguard, Walter Thompson, thought being on a dockside in the dead of night, within range of more lethal firepower than ever before assembled, was tantamount to being on the front line. But, as so often, he was cajoled by the man he came to love.

As the Nazi regime's most notorious general came ashore, Thompson kept his eyes peeled on the perimeter, intrigued by a catch of moonlight across the basin.

He brought up his field glasses and conned a swarthy fellow in combat fatigues fiddling with some cameras alongside a U.S. transport vessel, the Samuel Chase.

Friend not foe seemingly, but photographs of this gathering could be captioned many ways and change the course of the war. They had to be corralled.

Then came the shot and to a man they took cover; all bar Churchill, who strode towards the shot's origin, chin and Colt .45 jutting out in an apparent death wish.

Part One – 24th May 1940

1. Belgravia, London

Even framed beneath the twelve-foot ceilings of his mansion flat, Brand looked tall, testament to a whip like physique and his 6' 4" frame. He strode over to the radio and switched on a five o'clock news bulletin replete with reports of the Allied retreat to Dunkirk and high hopes of Churchill's new War Cabinet.

Brand sneered at the liplabour being heaped on Britain's neophyte leader whose upbringing, very much like his own, had comprised so little toil and sweat. Having readied the camera and a dozen 4 by 5 cassettes for the shoot, he was sprucing the salon when the intercom rang. At the door stood a model he'd not worked with before, but she came heavily recommended for the images he had in his mind's eye.

Blessed with a capacious memory and many years of work experience he had no need to commit his ideas to paper. While other artists might sketch or paint their desired scenes, he preferred to burn them direct to visual memory.

The agency had told her to speak only if spoken to and go about her business with no fuss. She followed him into a sparsely furnished, shadowy salon and undressed. Her naked feet felt the chill of the marble floor before she stepped forward onto a luxurious Persian rug. Brand wanted some basis to take issue with her so she would project some edginess into the frame, but her appearance made that difficult.

She was a statuesque, natural brunette with barely a blemish on her pale skin having traveled, as instructed, in soft shoes and without underwear under her street clothes. Her facial features were patrician in contrast to the plebeian flecks in her speech which she was happy to shroud in silence.

Brand's long fingers found her limbs compliant but, as he arranged her on a leather chaise longue, the reaction of her body hair betrayed her unease.

"Perfect," thought Brand and quickly got to taking pictures before her discomfort abated and she became comfortable, even worse, chatty.

With the wide-angle lens and skewed back plane elongating her form, he began exposing frames over the girl's left shoulder towards her slender feet and the fading light of the far casement window. Brand was capturing the precise raw material he wanted to take into the darkroom and feed his alchemy of art and light.

He sensed this girl would play her part well, but the acid test awaited her. He walked away from the tripod and over to a mahogany armoire where he kept his props. He took a bundle of braided electrical wire out of a small hessian sack and began unwinding it as he approached the girl's chair.

Her gaze darted from his immaculate manicure to his crystal-clear, hazel eyes. He blinked a reassurance despite himself that, fortunately from his viewpoint, failed to give her any comfort.

Her unease was growing but she was determined to stay put. She desperately needed the generous fee, and the ration stamps she'd been promised as a bonus for this job. Legit work was hard to come by and, though it had been only a few months since rationing started, common place goods had become black market luxuries and priced accordingly.

Brand bound her torso to the chair with the rayon shrouded wire effectively but without any discomforting tension. She pondered whether the pay had been determined by how kinky things could get or how desperate folks were for a bacon bap these days. But as the camphor-infused sack came over her head all conjecture ended, and she resolved to demand a cash bonus if she came through this unscathed.

If she didn't, recourse to the boys in blue would be pointless given her chequered past but she had plenty of friends who could give this geezer a taste of his own medicine.

Brand was getting to what he yearned for. He would have been happier with an untrimmed crotch to make a stronger visual allusion to the tangled wire, but this would do for now. He felt sure she'd come back if booked, perhaps in a few months when she had grown out. He could wait. Once he fixed on a composition, he had no end of patience to refine it in the studio or the darkroom without lazy recourse to the retouching table.

Through the hessian mesh the girl was keeping a sharp eye on Brand. Her legs had been crossed but he parted them slightly now and she felt her sex air. With sight blinkered, she strained to hear flies unbuttoning but neither that nor the rhymic, rising beat of a knob being polished could be heard. This intrigued her as she'd come across only two types of photographer before: lechers and gays and this bird flew into neither pigeon-hole.

His male gaze was normal, that is predatory, but his touch was gentle and his process ponderous but all business. Five more exposures and the odorous sack and wire came off as efficiently as they'd gone on. Brand went back to his camera and the girl took her cue to dress.

As she motioned to go, the photographer held up a finger to bid her pause and he left the room. It was getting dark outside and she hoped he'd hurry. She thumbed a magazine featuring a piece of Brand's mainstream work: a photo essay of London preparing for the expected Nazi blitz. It was a paean to vaunted Cockney spunk which the establishment hoped would resist all temptation to ply for peace once the dreaded rocket bombs came over.

Brand re-entered and she put the magazine down to receive three pairs of silk stockings and an envelope containing a crisp five-pound note. "That'll do nicely," she thought, stepping out gingerly into the damp, encroaching gloom.

2. Mexico City

"What the hell is art anyway?" Rivera asked no-one, least of all the priest seated to his left at the capacious lunch table. "The vainglorious outpourings of indentured monkeys; meant for the proletariat but purloined by the rich!" he said, answering himself.

Frida's eyes went skyward as if to cast off her heavy eyebrows and this hackneyed topic simultaneously. Corbin smiled, curious to see if this spat would set plates flying.

"Who the hell cares?" Frida said, hoping he would sense the futility of the argument rather than expound upon it.

Diego had been in a quandary since being offered a lucrative commission to paint a mural for the Golden Gate Exposition in San Francisco. He was to paint as live entertainment for the attendees, and he'd been given no guarantee where his work would end up after the show, which irked him. Since his well-publicized fight with the Rockefellers, he'd vowed never again to take things for granted when dealing with the American establishment.

Corbin had expected the lunch to be better attended but some invitees had cancelled last minute including David Siqueiros, another artist Corbin wanted to meet. The other guests being fresh to Mexico, including the disconcerted priest, it fell to Corbin to act as referee in the spirited, commonly blue exchanges between Frida Kahlo and her husband.

Frida projected a compelling blend of inordinate willpower and feral sensuality which had sorely tempted many, Corbin included. His restraint reflected a growing realization that life comprised a series of choices, some considered and sensible, others willful. A full-blown commitment to Frida fell firmly into the latter category. She would command far more care and consternation than he was willing to divert from his other ambitions. Whereas a mere dalliance would beggar the interest both she and Diego had shown in his talent.

Besides which her husband was a much better match for her fireworks. Passionate, opinionated and obscenely gifted, Rivera lived life as large as his art.

Corbin's time amidst these electric temperaments enlivened what was otherwise a frustrating sojourn, career-wise. His assignments were interesting enough and his New York editor gave him a long leash. But he longed to be covering the fighting in Europe and the nearest he was getting was the agitation of the Nazi agents in Mexico City, who, by stirring up trouble on America's doorstep, hoped to sustain the U.S. isolationists. Paradoxically he wouldn't be able to leave the Americas until the U.S. authorities granted him a right to stay.

Meantime what would have made Corbin's today - lunch with the exiled revolutionary, Leon Trotsky - wasn't going to happen either he now knew, thanks to Rivera's falling out with his erstwhile houseguest.

Corbin had been a firm fan of Trotsky since hearing him speak so ardently a decade ago in Stockholm. His oration and Corbin's atmospheric images had proved compelling, capturing both his conviction and the death aura hanging over the hunted revolutionary.

They'd also revived official suspicions of a leftist leaning in Corbin that had led to the confiscation of his native statehood and still bedogged his application for American citizenship. Similarly stateless, Trotsky was reduced to laying low in the suburbs of Mexico City, dodging the assassins his archenemy Stalin had sent abroad to silence him.

A phone ringing prompted a temporary truce in the tit for tat between the spouses and justified Trotsky's fears for his own safety. Diego returned his face drawn, exsanguinated.

"Those Stalinist bastards have finally silenced him," he said, "and David helped them do it!"

---

3. New Reich Chancellery - Berlin

As Rommel approached the Führer's private office, Goebbels was leaving, and they exchanged a Heil Hitler salute.

"Congratulations General on your success at Dinant, we are indebted," said Goebbels from his assumed position as the embodiment of German public opinion.

Battlefield reports praised how Rommel, all out of smoke bombs to cloak his vulnerable river crossing, had torched nearby properties instead. Another inspired improvisation to add to his burgeoning list of combat commendations.

"Thank you, Herr Reichsminister but that gratitude belongs to the men I have the honor to command," replied Rommel, wary some thought him too fond of the limelight.

Goebbels hadn't seen Rommel since the occupation of Poland and was glad to hear him honing a keen edge to his public persona. Every regime needed its heroes, especially those who knew their place. If he could resist the temptation to become yet another strutting peacock within the High Command, he could be molded into an invaluable propaganda asset. A warrior revered by the people and feared by his enemies.

There were, of course, chinks that had to be managed. Persistent rumors of an illegitimate daughter bedogged the projection of Rommel as a devoted family man. Goebbels paid particular attention to suppressing, but retaining, any evidence of infidelity, a failing detested by Hitler and shared by himself. Fortunately Rommel's flaws were heavily outweighed by his potential.

Whether in a still image of his chiseled Aryan features, or in a movie striding purposefully amongst men and armour, the camera loved Rommel. Goebbels envied him: beneath his own braggadocio and unflagging optimism was a persona desperate to be liked and respected, most especially by his Führer.

They saluted once more and Goebbels went on his crippled way to another assignation, while Rommel waited to be ushered into the Führer's four hundred square meter office.

At a humungous table Hitler was pouring over plans with Albert Speer and Martin Bormann. After pleasantries the Führer drew Rommel out of Bormann's earshot. Hitler was aware of the grist between the two, indeed encouraged it, as he did with so many of his subordinates' rivalries.

Bormann could barely disguise his dislike for Rommel and eagerly awaited an opportunity to demonstrate to Hitler that his faith in the cock-sure General had been gained by deceit.

For now that faith was seemingly blind and undeniably rewarding. In 1938 Hitler had selected Rommel to command his personal protection unit in Czechoslovakia. Then, just prior to the Polish invasion, Hitler had Rommel promoted to command his mobile HQ, the Führer-Begleitbattalion.

Rommel didn't characterize his relationship with the Führer as close; but then he didn't know of anyone not given to self-delusion who would. But Hitler and Rommel shared a fervent desire to see the inequities of the Versailles treaty redressed and the Wehrmacht's pride restored.

Hitler had cemented Rommel's fealty by giving him command of 7th Panzer for the Belgium offensive, a request denied by Rommel's immediate superiors who, like Bormann, were of the view Rommel was already out of his depth.

Though little more than a year older, Hitler would talk to Rommel like a father to a doted child, never allowing his favoritism to be forgotten. After yet another loudly whispered reminder of his patronage Hitler dismissed Bormann and asked Rommel to provide a minute report of the Meuse offensive.

Rommel thought it odd that the leader of the Third Reich should desire such a close review but delivered a succinct account anyway. He studiously avoided any temptation to play up the role of the 7th Panzer and spared no opportunity to praise his commander, General Hoth. During the presentation Hitler said little and looked at the map even less, preferring to keep his penetrating eyes on Rommel most of the time.

This, combined with the Führer's proximity and bad breath, gave Rommel no reason to relax and he was glad of it. The physical repulsion kept him en garde and keen to discern reassuring evidence of Hitler's leadership qualities. Having already encountered instances of the Führer's tendency to meddle in military tactics, he was yearning for fresh proof of his strategic acumen.

Rommel completed his review and acknowledged more praise before Hitler led him over to a giant atlas globe at the far end of the room. There began a wide sweeping application of game theory to the European and Asian theatres with every permutation of Axis and Alliance juggled.

Rommel was willing to demur to Hitler's political intuition for the plausibility of the various coalitions being conjured. But he was aghast at the Führer's cavalier disregard for the military implications of some of these political combinations.

Intoxicated by recent Axis successes and the Russians' pathetic offensive against the Finns, the Führer was willing, indeed eager to fight on multiple fronts. Rommel now realized why he was the only soldier left there. Hitler wouldn't risk contradiction by a senior Wehrmacht officer during this bonding session.

In present company he could vomit his imaginings with less risk of their flaws being highlighted, not least gaining America as an enemy. If that happened there was no amount of forced labor that could keep the Wehrmacht supplied: they would be banking on Allied mistakes.

After another forty-five minutes of ranting and scatter-gun ranging Hitler appeared spent and becalmed himself back into the present reality. He asked after Rommel's family and his upcoming home leave. Hitler then indulged Rommel with the expectation of an imminent Knight's Cross and asked him to convey a silk scarf for his wife Lucie's upcoming birthday.

Rommel accepted the commensurate gifts graciously and thanked his Führer for the greater indulgences of his time and confidence. With that the general was dismissed and Hitler returned with renewed vigor to his grand building plans and Speer's visualizations.

4. Belgravia, London

Having covered the English Derby once before for this magazine, Brand was pleased to be asked again. His acerbic style was an acquired taste and not all editors took to it. These days though picture magazine editors were tripping over themselves to capture images of a British public going about life nonchalantly despite the bombing and the threat of invasion.

Brand was less happy about being a last-minute replacement; the first choice's 'sickness' likely a sham brought on by the meeting's repeated relocation from Epsom. Regardless, it was decent driving weather, the road to Newmarket was less tedious and he might be able to wangle some petrol vouchers as part of the deal.

The war had provided Brand with scant opportunity to enjoy his preferred form of horsepower, that stabled under the bonnet of his 1939 Alvis Speed 25. What chance there'd been had left him hankering after any excuse for more.

He could also visit any number of internment camps on his journey home. The Swiss Government had seconded Brand to the International Bureau for Education, specifically its Service of Intellectual Assistance to POWs (SIAP) program. This was charged with creating "Internment Universities" within the camps to distract and educate the prisoners. Brand's work devising and staffing the Creative Arts curriculum exempted him from the British draft without monopolizing his available time.

"Righto. I've told Lily Caplan to join you at St Pancras," the editor said. Lily was a young writer Brand had worked with on other "feel good" pieces. Her job was to keep the punters animated for the camera and take notes from which she could compose accurate but droll captions later.

"That won't be necessary Tom," Brand said, "You can rely on me for a few captions, especially with the reduced crowd to cope with. So why don't you save all that extra expense and pay me a little more?" he added, never shy coming forward when it came to his fee.

"Okay, fair dinkums. Now, I need 36 shots. Expect you'll be giving me prints as usual?" the editor enquired, knowing full well the answer.

Normal delivery to this title was exposed film, but Brand had learnt how his images could be manipulated by ineptitude or design and insisted on delivering prints. He still ran the risk of creative cropping by zealous editors, so he presented scenes with as few options as possible to pervert his narrative.

"That's right Tom, wouldn't want to overburden your hard-working subs. 36 pictures eh, is this going to be a double spread?" Brand asked.

"I haven't decided yet, just want to keep my options open," the editor answered disingenuously, uncomfortable with the need to fudge. Shortages of newsprint were shrinking the space available to editors across the industry and Brand doubted this piece would be allotted more than two pages in these austere times.

But he knew another reason why the editor was prevaricating and why he hadn't been first choice for this assignment: his own sardonic view of British society. Brand had difficulty cloaking his disdain for the class-ridden customs of his adopted country, despite his English mother's urging and his illustrious progress through the upper echelons of the English education system.

His dual nationality had proved invaluable, but he preferred his native Switzerland and believed British society was an ugly anachronism ripe for the ructions that would accompany defeat either by the Nazis or the Bolsheviks or both.

Brand's irony was usually subtle enough to elude casual readers and, with thirty-six prints to hand, the editor could excise any blatant expressions of Brand's point of view that might otherwise grin through. But the editor couldn't be sure the distilled output would be enough to warrant multiple pages.

They haggled over price and petrol vouchers until the Editor got to a point where he'd be happy whatever the outcome and Brand felt like he'd had enough sport. The compensation wasn't material to Brand's wealth, rather a yardstick of his professional standing. With the editor's deadline reaffirmed, they rang off.

Brand kept his spare camera, several films and a reporter's pad at the ready in his canvas poacher's bag. With that on one shoulder and his prime Rolleiflex on the other, he dashed across to his garaged Alvis and was on his way north in no time.

5. Lady Amelia Brown's Flat, Knightsbridge, London

The intercom bell woke Corbin with a start, and he rushed over to tell the concierge he was awake and to ask the driver to wait.

"Thank God, it's only 8," he said with relief. Back in bed Lady Amelia Brown could manage only a soft murmur as she sat up and displayed her naked torso. Corbin nicknamed her Kiki after a beloved Parisian friend who had been just as at ease with her body and self-image. Their true beauty and self-assurance emanated from way below the surface.

He'd been looking forward to this day's activities all week and was darned if a thumping hangover was going to nix his plans. He darted into the bathroom, drew his favourite non-alcoholic restorative, a warm bath, and began a quick review of the racing papers.

Today was Derby Day and ordinarily hundreds of thousands of Brits of all classes would be converging on the Epsom Downs for the big event. But this being wartime, the 163rd running of one of the most respected tests of elite equine talent was being run at Newmarket.

Horse racing had been severely curtailed at the outbreak of war, but the restrictions were being eased to help those who depended on the turf to get by. Lords and knaves alike. The Luftwaffe was still a potent threat to the Home Counties and Epsom was being used as an anti-aircraft installation, so the Derby was sent north for the third year running.

A far smaller crop of spectators than usual was expected to travel up to Cambridgeshire but those that did would get close to British royalty. King George VI and Queen Elizabeth had been stalwarts through the blitz; risking early morning visits to smoldering bombsites to bolster morale. Now with the King's stable on the verge of winning four English classics, wild horses wouldn't keep the Royal couple away from Newmarket.

Having waded through the front-page headlines Corbin turned to the racing form searching for a selection of likely winners. As his bright eyes squinted at the dense print his headache intensified. His hangover was owed to a night in the bar at the Dorchester Hotel reuniting with a coterie of combat photographers and reveling in his role as alpha male. After months of clicking his heels in Mexico and an endless stream of lifestyle assignments, he was finally edging closer to the front line.

He was brimming with projects he wanted to pursue in the European theatre of operations and was waiting on his New York chief to bless them. Meantime he was happy if not ecstatic to soak in London life and work on essays celebrating the admirable British resistance to the Luftwaffe's terror.

The Dorchester's head barman, a West Country native named Craddock, domed of forehead, aquiline of nose, and dapper in his white cotton jacket, had concocted a cocktail in honor of Corbin's return, and one was knocked back each time a long-lost friend joined the party.

One part Scotch and one part Drambuie was livened with a heavy splash of fresh lime juice and a dash of Angostura to cut the sweetness. Corbin wasn't sure it'd become one of his favorites, but he was gassed by the barman's gesture and couldn't resist a drink called "The Spike". Especially since Craddock was mercifully diluting Corbin's measures.

Bawdy reminiscences from various battle zones peppered the evening's conversation with a break to listen to a radio bulletin. Churchill and Roosevelt were still basking in the afterglow of the US Navy's victory at Midway and their guarded optimism kept the party spirit barreling along.

The motley crue's quorum was achieved just after eleven with Kiki's arrival. Corbin was mid one of his Spanish Civil War stories when he lost his audience. They and most of the bar's other patrons were rubber necking to catch a better view of Kiki as she strode into the room bedecked in blue satin gown and sable stole. She draped an arm over his shoulders and put a demure peck on his left cheek. Corbin's spirit sailed silently over the moon, glowing with pride in his paramour.

After one last spike to mark Kiki's captivating entrance Corbin was relieved to switch to his preferred celebratory tipple - champagne.

In 1940 when the Panzers were blazing through the Champagne region towards the City of Light, Corbin had wanted to be in Paris with a passion, and not just for the smell of battle. Freshly minted folklore claimed more champagne was drunk that Spring than ever before. Every son of the terroir felt a duty to drain the caves dry, not only to soften the impending ignominy of defeat, but to deprive the Hun of as much of the golden spoil as possible.

"And from which house would the world's greatest war photographer and his good Lady prefer to imbibe tonight?" Craddock asked Corbin. He was skeptical of the alledged luxury of choice given the prevailing climate of rationing and make-do, but he played along.

"A Pol Roger '28 if I may, my good man," said Corbin drawing on the upper crust lingo he'd picked up from the latest Ealing Studios' comedy.

Corbin wasn't expecting even the Dorchester to fill his outlandish order but fifteen minutes later he was watching the cork of the coveted bottle being twisted free. At the restrained pop others might have quaked in anticipation of the heavy price to be paid but that wasn't Corbin's modus vivendi. He lauded the risk-laden lifestyle he'd chosen and to hell with the cost. Tomorrow could care.

Tomorrow was here now with a vengeance and races began at noon so folks could be home by dark and curfew. Corbin tied a half Windsor to the collar of his Turnbull and Asser shirt and took down his Irish linen suit and his Lock & Co trilby. A Cockney cabbie had once told him Churchill was no superhero "cos he puts his trawzers on a leg at a time just like the rest of us". Since when, Corbin had been trying to master a two-legged entry but, prat falling once more, he reconciled himself to being a mere earthling. The absurdity never failed to amuse Kiki.

He took two slabs of toasted white bread and slathered them with black market butter while slurping down a brew from his dwindling stash of Mexican coffee beans. Wiping a stream of molten butter from his chin he said, "You know Goering reckons butter makes the Germans fat, but iron makes them strong. Easy for him to say. I wonder when my mother last tasted butter?"

Corbin's abiding shame at leaving his parents behind on fleeing his native land was never far from his thoughts. He'd anglicized his name from his father's Corbinus to make for easier bylines, but otherwise he clung tenaciously to his Hungarian heritage.

Kiki was sensitive to his ennui so the next dribble of butter on his chin he didn't need to wipe, Kiki licked it off. To his initial chagrin, she was still naked except for silk panties and a subtle mist of Chanel No5. As she straddled his knees and reached down under the napkin on his lap, he reconciled himself to missing the first race.

Kiki was in even less of a hurry. "Now be a good sire and come back to your stall," she purred as she led him back to her bedroom, his necktie serving as a rein.

6. Newmarket Racecourse, Cambridgeshire

Corbin had a soft spot for Epsom and didn't sense the same friendly atmosphere in the snootier surroundings of 'Headquarters', as the seat of England's Jockey Club was known.

The bookies were having a good day though and had soon ensnared the lion's share of Corbin's intended stake money and a good deal more into their swag bags. Tossing his ticket for the previous race over his shoulder for luck he drained a glass of champagne and eased the pain of losing by teasing Kiki.

"How's your beginner's luck holding up?" he asked.

"Might be luck or a good nose for the nags but I've a pretty penny going onto the next," she said in a lousy yet cute approximation of a Cockney accent.

Unbeknownst to Corbin Kiki had sought help with her selections from a relative, the Honorable Dorothy Paget who, unusually, didn't have a runner in this year's Derby. With a hundred horses in training and a penchant for prodigious wagers, Miss Paget had been, almost singlehandedly, keeping the British racing industry afloat since war began.

Despite her largesse, flat racing had been limited to but a fraction of the normal number of meetings per year and the National Hunt season had been cancelled entirely. The racing public were starved of entertainment and the horses themselves were on half-rations leaving them vulnerable to well-fed travelling competition from France and Ireland.

Living most of her life nocturnally, bookies trusted Miss Paget to place bets on races already run, their trust rewarded by her consistent inability to pick winners. But today it seemed Dorothy was on top form. Kiki's Derby pick had become the third leg of a potentially lucrative daily treble but, as they surveyed the paddock, her streak seemed ill-starred. With jockeys up, Kiki's nap, Watling Street was unusually well behaved, parading calmly. But the bookies' 6 to 4 favorite was calmer still, imperious in fact.

Owned by the King and already winner of the 2000 Guineas over the Rowley Mile here at H.Q., the only blemish on Big Game's prospects was the soft going which might expose a lack of stamina over the mile and a half Derby trip. But with the great Gordon Richards on board the bookies' favoritism seemed warranted. Money was piling in for the King's runner given the prospect of the stallion going on to take the St. Leger and emulate his sire, Bahram, by lifting the Triple Crown of the English turf.

"What a monster! If he stays, he'll take some beating," Corbin said. "I need to get down to the rails and feed my bookie some more dosh, I'll see you back at the grandstand, same spot."

"Hello again Mr. Hill," he said to the man standing next to the odds chalkboard sorting a fistful of notes, many of them, till recently, belonging to Corbin.

"Ah Mr. Corbin sir! How may I be of further service?" the man said in a Birmingham accent, pretending to have only just seen one of his best customers.

Corbin stood silently for a moment comparing the prices on Hill's board with those of his neighbors. He'd seen Hill's chalked price rubbed out and shortened even further as his approach had been registered.

So close to the off, all on-course bookies were leery of receiving a large punt without sufficient time to lay it off. But Hill knew his competition would be happy to take a loss leader if it led to the defection of one of his most profitable punters.

With a resigned air Hill had his scribe return the favorite's odds to the prevailing level and waited for the hammer to fall. Corbin smiled and laid a handsome bet on Watling Street instead much to Hill's relief and the disbelief of the neighboring bookies.

On his way back Corbin saw Brand and his Rolleiflex a second time. He admired how he moved unobtrusively, composing his shots with unfashionable care. Compact Leica and Contax cameras had been on the market for over a decade and most photojournalists had switched allegiance to the Contax. The smaller, cheaper 35 mm film format allowed as many as thirty-six exposures on a single roll of film, and the tactile format of the camera was ideal for capturing what would become known as 'the decisive moment' in an action sequence.

"Hi. You're still a Rollei user I see," Corbin said as an icebreaker. Brand creased a smile and tilted his head 5 degrees, remaining fixated on the viewer screen at his midriff.

Undeterred Corbin continued, "Most pros prefer to shoot 35 mill these days, don't they?"

"I don't 'shoot' I'm afraid," Brand said, tired of photographers folding the vernacular of war into their argot.

"Neither do I aim, fire or allow myself to get trigger happy."

Corbin laughed with a heartiness that disarmed Brand who'd expected a riposte heavy with some of the technical bigotry that had plagued photography since its invention. Brand's English was way better than his, but Corbin thought he detected a fellow migrant. The odd word was clipped and given an uncommon emphasis. If Corbin's hunch was correct and this photographer was from the continent, then he'd probably picked up some of his craft in Paris.

"You know, you remind me of my Dutch uncle in Paris. He thinks careful composition trumps split second timing every time," Corbin said.

Brand could appreciate a genuine compliment when he heard one and responded with a full smile this time.

"I'd like to hear about your uncle," he said.

"What about a drink after the last?" Corbin proposed.

"Agreed," said Brand and scooted off to picture the King in khakis and his Queen in lavender.

An obstreperous outsider was refusing to line up for the start which gave Corbin time to get to Kiki just as the wire went up, savoring the eyes, mostly male, on stalks as he approached. Looking as gorgeous as her luck, who could fault their admiration of Lady Brown.

Three minutes later Corbin reckoned she was due over five hundred pounds for her modest stake. Watling Street had won by a neck leaving Big Game to trail in sixth. In the bar Corbin asked Kiki why she wasn't rushing off to collect her winnings.

"Well, unlike you my dear, I savor the journey as much as the destination," she said.

"Whoa, way too deep for this simple journeyman," Corbin said. "Pardon me while I drag my hands over to the bar and get you another drink darling."

"That'll be two and three please dearie," said the most buxom barmaid Corbin had ever seen, and he'd seen plenty. The barmaid had a head on her shoulders too and she'd recognized the up-and-coming war photographer. She was a fan and happy to see he was as attractive in the flesh as the gossip columnists claimed.

Corbin had never had much reason to master English coinage and the barmaid lasciviously scraped his palm with her painted fingernails as she took possession of her due from his upturned hand. Seeing some moths had gathered around Kiki's flame and were keeping her entertained, he was getting to know the barmaid better when Brand came along side.

"And another for my friend the photographer," Corbin said. After some more getting to know you and with a wink of gratitude to the barmaid, Corbin ushered his new friend over to the scrum now surrounding Kiki. Brand raised and kissed Kiki's hand while Corbin dispersed her newfound admirers with some repartee and a few autographs.

"I knew war photographers attracted beautiful companions," Brand said, "but having met you I may volunteer for the front line myself."

Trying not to slip on this ooze, Corbin raised his eyebrows in caricature and said, "You'll have to form an orderly line, I mean, queue, old bean."

"If being a war photographer was all it took, the queue would be anything but orderly," Kiki said, "Luckily my man here has other charms."

"No doubt, but I can dream," said Brand, surprised by how much he was enjoying the banter. Turning to Brand he continued. "So about your Dutch uncle, a man after my own heart?"

"Yeah, he's an exile like me and he took me under his wing while I was in Paris," said Corbin.

"Really and when exactly was that?" Brand asked.

Kiki could tell they weren't going to need her help with these Bohemian reminiscences and excused herself to get to the Tote window before it closed. Corbin's estimate of her winnings had been on the button and the lady at the counter said something about needing to check with her manager.

Or at least that's what Kiki thought she had said through the unhelpful grill. She admired Corbin, with much less exposure to English accents, he understood them far better. Whether it was the anxiety of waiting for this rather large amount of cash to be handed over or what, Kiki didn't feel at ease. She was conscious of a guy behind her standing unnecessarily close and cast a glance over her shoulder hoping he'd back off.

It hadn't worked, so she was gratefully distracted when the lady came back to say she would have to go to her nearest Tote office on Monday for pay out. By the time Kiki had interpreted what the cashier lady was saying, the intrusive guy had disappeared.

Kiki headed back to the bar but, before she could get very far, she saw Corbin and Brand walking towards her. "What's wrong darling?" Corbin asked. "You look like you've seen a ghost?"

"Oh it's nothing really, they couldn't pay me," she said, concealing the true nature of her disquiet.

"What! Why not?" said Corbin.

Kiki laughed. "They didn't have enough cash," she said pausing for effect, "so they told me to come back on Monday." Corbin had never heard anything so bizarre and was on the verge of walking back to the Grandstand to remonstrate with the Club Steward when Brand's nodding smile put him at ease.

"And I'd call the office before you go on Monday to check they have the funds on hand there. It is a goodly amount" Brand said.

The cars weren't hard to find. Only a couple of hundred had made the trip owing to petrol rationing, with the vast majority of racegoers travelling by rail and/or bicycle. They reached Brand's Alvis first. Corbin thought the car's graceful lines suited Brand even if the car's insignia did look like Superman's chest badge.

"So did you guys find some common ground?" Kiki asked, handing Brand a calling card.

"Yes," said Brand, "I've met Corbin's uncle and admire his work immensely."

"Yeah we have many friends in common," said Corbin. "Turns out we just missed meeting one another in Paris at the tail end of the Twenties."

"Let's hope the opportunity presents itself again," said Brand.

"D'accord mon vieux, en Paris" Corbin said ruefully.

7. Near Gazala, North Africa

"Our tank recoveries must improve until we have the upper hand," Rommel said to his Chief of Staff. "And we must continue to keep Tommy guessing as to our true strength and intentions," Rommel continued.

"The diversions and recoveries are both going very well, sir," Westphal said, fearing another of his boss' lunges deep into enemy territory might be in the offing. He'd recently thrust so far into the British lines he'd alighted upon an enemy field hospital, pledging and then delivering medical supplies to his foes. These tactics embellished Rommel's charisma and often threw the British 8th Army into disarray, but they drew few plaudits from the German High Command.

The pressures of the protracted Tobruk siege had also created rifts with Rommel's subordinates who felt his driven style was too hard on the men. More than once Rommel's fat had been pulled from the fire not by his audacity but by his enemy's tactical errors.

Churchill could be as meddlesome as Hitler at times and, whether hiving off supplies for the Greek resistance or badgering wary generals at Tobruk, it could be just as debilitating. Rommel felt the pendulum swinging his way and Hitler's fanaticism for his élan was unabated causing supplies to flow once more.

"For almost eighteen months we've kept the British busy and I believe we're on the verge of neutralizing the southern front," Rommel said.

"Yes sir, those achievements alone should sway Berlin to give you the supplies you need to finish the job," Westphal replied.

Initially at a three Sherman to one Panzer disadvantage, Rommel's tank forces were now at parity, and he had the British armour in a strategic stasis. Rommel enjoyed confounding his enemy and whereas smoke cloaked his ploys in the Ardennes, dust was disguising his numbers in the desert. He was using every motorized vehicle at his disposal to kick up dust and deceive RAF reconnaissance aircraft as to his true strength.

He was poised to swoop down and force the 8th Army into an ignominious retreat Goebbels gleefully dubbed their 'Ghazali Gallop'. The action would lead inexorably to the taking of over thirty thousand prisoners. In recognition of his achievements, and much to the irritation of his rivals, a grateful Hitler made him a Field Marshall, presenting him with a gawdy baton fit for Goering but which Rommel would rarely sport. British generals responded by reminding their troops that, despite all evidence to the contrary, Rommel was neither a superhero nor invincible.

Hitler's well-publicized favoritism was founded in necessity. With the Reich pitched against the world's largest Empire and its largest military, Hitler needed generals capable of achieving much with less. If the Japanese kept their promise to lure the world's largest economy into conflict, the Führer would require many more from the same mould. While the mood was upbeat Westphal took the opportunity to raise a sensitive issue.

"Sir I've received a communiqué complaining that our Jewish POWs are not being segregated and kept on reduced rations,"

Although issued by a more junior Waffen SS officer the signal had the acrid stench of Heydrich and Himmler about it. For several months Rommel had sensed a more virulent attitude towards the "Jewish question" and his distaste for it was growing.

"Signal back that our prisoners are being treated honorably and in accordance with the Geneva Convention," Rommel said.

"Now back to planning our assault on Egypt. Good people are waiting to be freed from the yoke of Limey oppression," said Rommel smiling broadly.

8. The Dorchester Hotel, London

"Hurry up and get your eggs sweet pea, before they get stone cold," Corbin shouted as Kiki came out of the bathroom toweling herself.

"Oh my, someone's gotten out of the bed the right way. Why so jolly?" she said.

"It's right here ma'am," said Corbin waving a telegram that was the answer to his prayers. Kiki knew what it would say. Corbin had been on tenterhooks for days and all London was awash with embarkation rumours and the scent of last chance sex.

Now just weeks after welcoming her weary hero back from Italy she would have to give him up to fate again. The bawdy late night poker games, the tempestuous intimacy and the sweat sodden nightmares would be swapped for a lonely, if comfortable, vigil.

Kiki was wealthy by dint of two assiduous marriages. She'd loved both husbands and the first, a member of the Whitney family, had reciprocated with bequeathed wealth and the second, in line for an Earldom, with a title.

Thanks to his wandering eye she'd been estranged from the Viscount for three years during which Lady Amelia Brown's "torrid affair" with "her dashing, dishy combat photographer" had regularly commanded inches in the British tabloids, accompanied by pictures of Kiki and Corbin arriving at some elegant affair. Before falling in love with Corbin she'd heard all the rumours about his death baiting derring-do in Spain and the full-on parties at the Dorchester.

At first she planned to check out what all the fuss was about and then move on. But the combination of his easy charm and resolute libido had arrested her momentum to the point where she was now making regular hints about third time lucky.

For his part Corbin was in no hurry to tie the knot. Five years her junior his sights were firmly set on his legacy and a keen sense a world at war was the canvas on which it could be writ large. He countered her hints of marital bliss with mention of colleagues recently departed and other fatalistic reminders to carpe diem.

Sure enough the telegram was from the Allied Forces Public Relations Office instructing Corbin to make a will, if not already, register his blood type and stand by for further, imminent instructions. Nevertheless Corbin was not going to allow what might be his last day with Kiki to turn maudlin.

"The weather may be frightful me dear, but we're going to have ourselves a day to remember," he said, looking out over Park Lane to Hyde Park.

Unbeknown to her he'd upped his chances of not returning alive by a decision made a few days ago. He'd been asked, unofficially, if he wanted to be in the first wave of troops for the landing. He wouldn't be permitted to disembark the landing craft, but he would get in close.

There was no shame in following later he was told. Rumor had it commanders were deliberately taking several of their experienced troops out of the first wave so expendable rookies could face the grievous early fire in their stead.

Since being booted from his homeland and spending years adrift, Corbin had vowed to play life with the same abandon that amused his poker playing pals. And, with a callousness he wasn't proud of, he knew later shots of the beach strewn with too many of those dead rookies wouldn't pass the censor. He'd opted for the first wave.

9. Dieppe, Normandy

"Have I not made it crystal clear that this battle will be won or lost at the water's edge, possibly on the ebb tide?" Rommel asked. "If the enemy is allowed to clear the beach they will prevail. They must die here!"

He wasn't given to raising his voice to assert authority but the pounding surf and his growing impatience with tired excuses were sapping his restraint.

"But Field Marshall, we have….," the Lieutenant in charge of this battery began and as quickly halted when he saw Spiedel's eyebrows rise.

Rommel's new chief of staff had heard all the same, lame excuses his boss had endured this morning, and could see no point in this sapling officer reaping the accumulated backlash.

"Sir," the Lieutenant started over, "as you can see the preparations are behind schedule and not to specification," he said, earning an encouraging nod from Spiedel.

"We've encountered some supply difficulties, but we will overcome them sir and be ready to force our enemy back into the Channel," he added.

Rommel sensed he was being handled and with a peremptory salute he repaired to his open topped Mercedes field car where Spiedel joined him.

"You were right to protect his underbelly Hans," Rommel said, "nevertheless this so-called Atlantic Wall is vulnerable and, if not reinforced, the Allies will punch through it with impunity."

"I've received assurances from my sources in Speer's organization that additional girders and scrap turrets are being redirected to us," Spiedel said.

He was referring to the raw material for the innovative defenses Rommel had designed: like the Teller mine topped Hemmbalken intended to decimate invading tanks at the waterline; and the Rommelspargel that would shred incoming gliders as they attempted to land safely. As a 14-year-old Rommel had built a fully-fledged glider with the help of a friend and understood their inherent fragility no matter what their scale.

"While I question his methods, I can only marvel at his ability to deliver," Rommel commented at the mention of Albert Speer.

Having met the reticent architect, Rommel couldn't fathom his acceptance of forced labor and was perturbed by reports of widespread cruelty in his factories in occupied Serbia. Regular Army officers were reportedly becoming as virulent in their Anti-Semitism as the Waffen SS, spurred on since Hitler styled the Eastern Front as a war of annihilation.

To Hitler's immense pleasure, Nazi industrial production had increased exponentially under Speer's leadership despite the punishing impact of Allied bombing. In contrast Rommel's moral compass was straining his relationship with the Führer while burnishing his reputation in less fanatical quarters.

Spiedel opted to postpone some bad news about the havoc the French resistance were reeking on the railways. But this next disappointment couldn't be put off.

"The Führer has endorsed the Kriegsspeil exercise in Rennes and urges all Normandy commanders to attend."

The Kriegsspeil was a war game simulation based on an airborne attack followed by an amphibious assault centered on Normandy. Most of the High Command, including Rommel, valued these sandpit exercises both as a means of gaming strategy and for forging consensus. But their time had come and gone in Rommel's view.

"To what end?" Rommel responded, irritated by the distraction.

"To better analyze the enemy's invasion strategy?" Spiedel offered.

"My God! The time for games is long past!" Rommel exclaimed. "Will it solve the problem of air inferiority; of being outnumbered and outgunned at sea; of the paucity of tried and tested troops and material? It will not!

"Neither will it discern if Patton's command is a real threat or a feint. We must perfect our defenses and be given the autonomy to react to changing circumstances in an instant."

In contrast to many of his peers Rommel wasn't taken in by the massing of Allied forces in East Anglia under Patton's leadership. While respecting his adversary's capabilities he felt it unlikely Eisenhower and Marshall would entrust the most audacious amphibious operation in military history to a cannon with a tendency to backfire. Such a gamble was no more likely than Douglas MacArthur being drafted in from the Pacific theatre. "Dugout Doug" was accumulating successive triumphs where he was, and Marshall knew he would be oil to Eisenhower's water.

And more importantly than all that, Rommel had zero confidence the Führer would empower his generals to act upon any new insights the Kriegsspeil might engender. Hitler had already retained personal control of the Panzer Reserve and moved his fighter aircraft back to defend the Fatherland against merciless Allied bombing.

Both interventions indicating just how little faith the Führer placed in the judgment and loyalty of his front-line generals. And illustrating how easily he could be swayed day to day, hour by hour by the self-serving arguments of the sycophants buzzing around him like flies around ordure.

"Have the Granville paratroop defenses been reinforced with that flak unit from Paris," Rommel asked, groping for some good news.

"Not yet sir," Speidel said sheepishly.

"It's motorized and I ordered its redeployment two days ago. Did they lose their way?" Rommel said.

"No sir, the repositioning was countermanded by Berlin," Speidel replied.

"On whose..... Never mind. You see Speidel we are hamstrung at every turn. Further remonstration with those cronies in Berlin is futile. We must focus our efforts on what we can control including delivery and deployment of those supplies.

"If you receive any inkling the material is being commandeered, I wish to know immediately. I will speak with Speer directly if necessary," Rommel said.

Despite the forecast inclement weather Rommel was keeping a sharp eye on all Allied communications for clues as to their intentions. When a corporal rushed in brandishing an AP news agency flash about imminent Allied landings, Rommel gave equal credence to its content and its unexplained removal from the wire within seconds.

"This is it," he thought, "they're coming."

"Spiedel, get the signal pad. Draft a low priority message to Berlin advising them that I have been taken ill," Rommel said. "I'll be taking a few days to recover while bad weather makes Allied action unlikely. And will visit my family to help speed my recovery."

"Immediately sir," said Spiedel, puzzled beyond imagining.

"No need for haste Spiedel," Rommel replied. "We will leave after lunch tomorrow."

10. Southwark Cathedral, London

During wartime some myths prove impervious to common sense and contrary proof.

The popular press reckoned Hitler had declared certain London landmarks protected, and hence off-limits to Luftwaffe bombers. Some buildings like the imposing Senate House of London University were allegedly earmarked as the Reich's British HQ, others were deemed too significant to destroy.

Airmen knew that was bunkum. It was impossible for bombers to be so accurate night after night, and the expected rocket missiles would have precious little discernment. Nevertheless the myth persisted. Brand wasn't taken in and believed before long St. Paul's would be bombed to smithereens just like Coventry Cathedral had been in 1940.

Before disaster struck, he wanted to do a series of landscape studies of London viewed from the south bank of the Thames. Much as the artist Canaletto had done in oil two centuries prior. And because he'd never have a better reason to attempt the technique, he'd resolved to capture the images as daguerreotypes.

Using daguerreotypes for landscape was never as common as portraiture, yet they produced views of haunting beauty that were almost three-dimensional. Frenchman, Louis Daguerre pioneered the technique in the 1830s and because of their high definition they were dubbed 'mirrors of life'.

Initially they became popular as substitutes for plaster death masks but, as exposure times were reduced, capturing live subjects became feasible if they could be held motionless by hidden neck and derriere supports. Living pets meanwhile remained virtually impossible to capture in sharp definition, frustrating those artists who wished to continue using animals to symbolize human traits in their images. Rabbits for lust, ermine for purity and dogs for either faithfulness or treachery depending on the owner.

These limitations and a noxious developing process which produced only a single non-replicable image meant the technology was readily overtaken by safer innovations that allowed ready reproduction.

Brand's first viewpoint was from the lee of Southwark Cathedral, and he'd arrived in good time to set up and be ready for the late afternoon light. As he ducked under the cloth to frame the inverted image on the frosted glass of the back plane, the panoply of the City of London lay before him. The weather had improved throughout the day and the cloud base had risen significantly giving Wren's massive cupola a steel blue backdrop.

With everything just so, Brand spiked his shooting stick into the turf, took a book from his poacher's bag, and began waiting for the perfect light. A while back Orwell's "Coming Up For Air" had tapped into his conviction that English society stood at a crossroads, and he'd resolved to re-read it. He detected some of his own foibles and predilections in the self-deprecating pessimist, George Bowling. Try as he might though he couldn't concentrate. Couples making their way into the churchyard were interrupting his focus on the novel.

The nearby Borough market was a magnet for local prostitutes and their johns, and twilight was a peak-trading period. The peace of the cathedral grounds and its secluded nooks provided almost enough privacy for a hasty knee-trembler. And with the threat of invasion putting the fear of God into everyone, who cared if you got caught with your trousers around your ankles.

Even though these passers-by had their blood up, there was something about a large camera and tripod that always sparked curiosity. After Brand had seen off half a dozen inane questions, he thought about upping sticks in search of an alternative viewpoint but didn't think he could make the switch in time.

He decided to grin and bear it. From his many assignments in the East End he knew this chirpy nuisance came with the territory. This was the raw heart of Cockney London and close to erstwhile Ripper country, so you became inured to ribald humour and the occasional scream.

But the scream that came from behind a buttress off to his left sent a charge through him. He raced around to see a girl naked from the waist down being penetrated fore and aft by two sailors for whom another tot would be a waste of a rum ration.

He calmly strode over and put his face alongside that of the Drake's Pride on top of this unsavory sandwich.

"I'm betting you two won't be paying this lady any extra for entering her front and back doors?" he ventured.

With that he jutted the spine of his hardback into the young mariner's windpipe sending him out of the girl and onto the grass alongside her. Rising smartly he kicked the lower shipmate full in his left ear spraying blood out onto the turf and down into the miscreant's throat to gurgle there with his groaning.

The girl scampered clear and, both having difficulty speaking, the two mariners sank into a silent movie of their own making. The bleeder from the bottom bunk seemed keen for some more punishment, but his partner was less game and pulled him away.

The hiatus and the Bolo automatic Brand had drawn with menacing calm from his under-jacket holster, convinced the bottom feeder to break off contact. A night in the cells was one thing but going AWOL just before possible embarkation in such circumstances as these could lead to the end of a rope.

They slunk away to lick their wounds leaving the prostitute to recover a semblance of dignity and Brand to return to his camera. The girl caught up with Brand and was about to speak when he pushed two half-crowns into her hand, and with a gentle finger touched her lips before she could give voice to her gratitude.

11. La Roche-Guyon, N. France - 18:00h

The food and wine Spiedel had ordered that evening was as sumptuous as prevailing conditions permitted, but Rommel's mood wasn't lightened by the fayre. He picked over his food and barely sipped the wine. Spiedel was accustomed to the General's Spartan tastes. In the field Rommel opted to eat standard rations and stay attuned to the hardships of his men. And here he preferred to spend most of his time in an underground bunker of the luxurious chateau above.

"I released the signal to Berlin at 17:00hrs, low priority, Herr Field Marshall," said Spiedel. "As yet there has been no response," he added. "My contacts indicate that most of the Normandy command are already en route to Rennes for the Kriegsspiegel.

"Or they've gone elsewhere. The weather forecast continues to indicate low cloud and steady rain making any invasion unlikely."

"And what are the forecast conditions for Southern England and the Channel?" Rommel asked.

"I will check Herr Field Marshall," Spiedel replied.

Rommel checked his wristwatch. Through a brief break in the clouds he glimpsed an almost full moon. "Ideal for the Allies if the storm should abate," he thought.

Spiedel returned. "For the channel and Southern England they call for rising pressure, clearing skies and a sea state of 1 to 2 metres, Herr Field Marshall."

"Let's hope our meteorologists have that wrong," said Rommel. "The longer Monty's men have to click their heels over there, the more anxious they'll be about coming over here."

Rommel knew the accuracy of the Allies' forecasting was superior and was acutely aware of how capricious Northern Atlantic weather could be. Eisenhower's generals would be itching for a green light if the slightest window of opportunity presented itself.

"Perhaps General you would like to get some intelligence about Tommy's morale from a British commando captured a few hours ago?" Spiedel asked.

He knew this was nourishment Rommel would not resist. Rommel nodded his assent with a smile and took the report Spiedel handed over. The British commando was led in and, while clearly not in the pink of health, showed no fear. Instead he seemed bemused by this audience.

Rommel got up close to ask his name and received the customary rank and serial number reply.

"Do you know who I am soldier?" said Rommel.

"I do sir," replied the commando with a tinge of Polish accent hinting he might have grievances to settle.

"May I know what you were doing in the vicinity of the Merville Battery?" Rommel asked.

"I don't know where that is, sir," the commando replied disingenuously. Rommel smiled, sat down, and changed tack.

"Please sit," said Rommel. "Tell me, how is my good friend General Montgomery?"

"Really don't have any special knowledge of the General sir, but I believe him to be in good health," said the commando.

"And looking forward to a trip to Normandy?" said Rommel not expecting a reply. The commando smiled through the silence.

"So how are you Tommies getting along with your GI Joe friends?" Rommel continued.

"We're like peas in a pod sir," said the commando.

Rommel could tell this welcome distraction wasn't going to yield much more value. But it had at least given a measure of the high caliber of troops being sent over in this first wave.

"Do you have questions for me?" Rommel asked. Spiedel could barely believe his ears, even more so when the soldier had the temerity to oblige.

"Yes sir, why has your Army seen fit to annihilate the Jewish people?" the commando asked with an abandon that implied he expected to die once he was handed back to the Gestapo.

"You may leave us Speidel," Rommel said before turning his attention back to the commando.

"I hope you will allow me to answer that question with another? Why do you bring politics into our discussion? We are soldiers you and I, we have no part in such things," Rommel said.

Their dialogue continued for several more minutes before Rommel asked for Speidel to re-enter.

With that he signaled for the commando to be taken away only adding, "Do not worry commando, you will not be punished for your impertinence."

12. The Dorchester Hotel, London - 22:00h

If there was a man to whom Corbin could happily cede the role of alpha male, it was Ernest Hemingway. 'Papa' was an idol of sorts. His narrative could stir hearts and minds while his darker side could chill the soul.

Here in London Hemingway, like Corbin, had been maneuvering for a prime springboard for the invasion, but had found it just as elusive. Anxiety over that and the aftereffects of a recent car accident, the cause of the raw scar on his forehead, had put Hemingway on the verge of a major funk. When Kiki and Corbin had visited him at St. George's hospital earlier, he'd been in no mood for the lighthearted reminiscences they'd tried to distract him with. His mutterings were gloomy, full of foreboding.

But by this evening the black dog appeared to have gotten off his back and he was holding the assembly in his sway: spinning tales, some real, some imagined but all captivating. Wild animals, cuckolded husbands and Hollywood moguls populated a wondrous world described in a mellifluous baritone.

The war had promised Hemingway enormous potential for daring exploits but, so far, his stars hadn't aligned. His insistence on traveling with his growing coterie wasn't helping his cause, and he was becoming afeared about failing to cement his place in history. In this he was not alone.

Martha Gellhorn, Hemingway's estranged third wife, was in London figuring out how to cover the landings, like several other female war correspondents of the day. The Chicago Daily News had assigned Helen Fitzpatrick to Ike's headquarters, initially in Teddington, then Tournieres in France; Lee Miller was scheduled to accompany the 83rd Infantry over to Normandy a few weeks hence for Vogue magazine. Gellhorn planned to steal a march on all her peers, amongst whom she classed Hemingway, by stowing away on a hospital ship and then posing as a stretcher bearer, a ruse she'd used in other theatres of war.

All were invited to this embarkation party at the Dorchester, as was Hemingway's fourth wife to be, another journalist named Mary Welsh. Papa's previous marital transitions had been conducted much like office handovers, but Martha and Mary weren't for sharing dispassionately. Corbin and Kiki were tasked with keeping them either civil or apart.

Martha was fuming about Hemmingway's new contract with Collier's magazine, a prestigious title with which she'd had a happy and lucrative association dating back to the Spanish Civil War. Mary was disappointed her predecessor was present having ensured it was common knowledge she intended to be there.

Kiki was doing her best to maintain order. She wanted to preserve Papa's lighter mood not least because it took the pressure off Corbin to be the life and soul of the party. Corbin was always happy to play second fiddle to Hemingway and, occasionally, reproach the great author when his boorish side got the better of him: a bravery rarely exhibited amongst his entourage. Kiki hoped Corbin's tender attitude towards the fairer sex would never be hardened by exposure to Hemingway's more brusque treatment of the women in his life.

Their friendship was forged amidst the fiery horrors of the Spanish Civil War where Papa's heroic deeds and Corbin's self-deprecating humor had bound them together. Their prior history could be traced back to post WWI Paris where a generation lost to their mother countries took solace in the hedonistic lifestyle of the boulevard cafes and revue bars. Retreating to their cups from anti-Semitism, Prohibition, Bolshevism or whatever else had repelled them from their native lands.

A hush fell on the bar as Hemingway rose unsteadily.

"Here's to the greatest living photographer: may his shutter never jam!" he said raising a toast.

"To the greatest living author: may his nib stay sharp and his wit sharper!" was Corbin's impromptu response and, since most of the assemblage were several sheets to the wind, it passed muster.

Except with Gellhorn who glowered at them both. Ignoring her, Hemingway wrapped Corbin in one of his crushing bearhugs, its force undiminished by numerous physical injuries. Tears welled in most eyes. Churchill, the King and Roosevelt had taken every opportunity to get folks up for the challenge ahead, but now the hour was at hand. Many would not return.

Corbin and Kiki made their excuses at the witching hour so he could get some sleep and be on his way to Portsmouth. Papa had left already to reach the USS Dorothea L. Dix in ample time. His knees, still stiff from the car accident, required him to be transferred to the vessel by Bosun's chair. There would be no such transfer at the distant end. He would not be allowed to disembark with the troops - although he finessed this detail in his dispatches - and would return to Weymouth with the dead and the wounded.

The ride back to Kensington was peaceful, both the weather and Hitler's meddling were keeping the Luftwaffe on base. Hitler had drawn his diminished air assets back to protect the Fatherland, meanwhile urging Goering to fix the technical problems besetting the V-1 "buzz-bomb" and with it rain renewed terror on London, Southampton and Portsmouth.

The V-1, V standing for Vengeance, had moved from drawing board to prototype two years since and still hadn't been launched in anger. Packing almost a ton of explosive Hitler was deeply frustrated by the failure to unleash its destructive power sooner. When its deployment did get underway two weeks later, its ominous silence just before impact would terrorize targeted populations, killing some twenty thousand civilians before the Nazi capitulation. And the V programme delays would become a monotonous feature of the Führer's "if only..." rantings until his suicide and open-air incineration.

"Thanks guv. That's a beauty you're got there, don't let her get away" the old cab driver said as he palmed Corbin's customarily generous tip.

Corbin needed no reminder but, poignant as the risk of losing her might be, he was on the cusp of the defining moment of his career. As if destined, he was about to be part of a military operation that would rewrite the record book and dictate the future course of the war.

Lost in these thoughts he hardly noticed the concierge, but he couldn't ignore Kiki as she goosed his derriere on entering her flat. Her outer garments peeled quicker than a chameleon sheds skin and he turned to see a bustier he'd not seen before and would have remembered. At a time most women would die for a new pair of stockings it seemed Kiki could summon up more silk than the King of Siam. She reached into his jacket to draw out his necktie and, after her fashion, led him down the hallway with a porny catwalk.

Her undulating rear, taut suspenders and the short golden hairs standing erect in the small of her back transfixed his gaze. When dressing she'd decided how she would remind herself to stay feral this evening and not lapse into sentimentality. She could have knotted a hankie but had opted for no knickers instead.

On the eve of her first wedding Kiki's mother had urged her to be a chef in the kitchen and a whore in the bedroom. Over the years, with her customary zeal, Kiki had found ways to conjoin the two ambitions. Corbin had enjoyed many a choice morsel from parts of her anatomy and the kitchen table had been put to a great deal of unorthodox use.

Tonight, bar a few ice cubes, there was to be no exotic fayre - just a straightforward and slow send-off to remember. As he watched her globes sashay into the bedroom, Corbin anticipated a swift end to the preliminaries and a workmanlike performance. Kiki would strike a more Tantric balance between draining his testosterone and his need for rest.

It was nearly an hour into their lovemaking before she permitted Corbin's tumescence to peak like a fine soufflé and then, reluctantly, allowed it to cool.

13. Normandy – 09:00h

Rommel had frustrated Speidel twice already today. First by asking him to ride with him to take notes, only then to say nothing worth noting. And again, when he asked his driver to detour through St. Lô and Caen so he could check on readiness there.

Both towns would be key if invasion came via the Normandy beaches but no more so than four or five other nexus that lay directly on Rommel's route back to Germany. On passing some fields planted with anti-glider defenses Rommel asked if the consignment of captured shells meant to arm the stakes had arrived. Hearing how the bomb-blasted railway network was still delaying the large shipment, he sank back into a moody silence.

It seemed the Field Marshall had something weighty on his mind and sooner or later he might feel inclined to share it. Another thirty minutes of meandering elapsed before Rommel commanded his driver to make another sidetrack into a copse just beyond the village of St. Germain de Montgommery. He asked Speidel to join him as he stretched his legs and, once out of earshot of his driver, Rommel finally came clean.

"Hans you support those who would behead the beast we've created. I do not support that faction as things stand."

Speidel became tense and regretted having ventured his allegiance to the conspirators beyond deniability.

"I don't think you will find someone sufficiently close to the Führer who is willing to die to do the deed," Rommel said. "Your comrades all want to survive and be part of the aftermath, and from that ambition I see only two possible outcomes.

"In one they will fail to form a cohesive command after the assassination and roil the country in civil war. Or, more likely, they will fail to sever the monster's head and, wounded, it will turn to bite them through," Rommel said.

Finding Speidel unable or unwilling to counter this analysis he continued, "Nevertheless change is imperative to prevent many more lives being lost unnecessarily."

Speidel swallowed the lump in his throat and drew in a deep breath as inconspicuously as possible. Finally his boss seemed ready to reassert his independence of spirit. He recalled what Westphal had told him about Rommel's reaction to the Führer's 'defend to the last' order at the second battle of El Alamein. It had opened a deep wound in Rommel's relationship with his leader, even though Hitler had been quick to rescind the order when Rommel had been even quicker to disobey it.

"The enemy has reached out to me personally with a request to parlay and I intend to listen to what they have to say," Rommel said. "It's incredibly risky but I believe we must do everything possible to avoid pointless bloodshed.

"While I can't do this alone, I won't conspire with your cabal until I've heard what the Allies propose."

He paused to gauge Speidel's reaction now all the cards were face up. Speidel knew he would be signing both their death warrants if he bilked now. He was confident of Rommel's unshakeable loyalty to the Fatherland and felt sure he would have racked this matter thoroughly.

"This path is fraught with danger sir, but you can rely on my loyalty," Speidel said to their mutual relief.

"You're right Hans but the potential gain far is worth the risk," Rommel said. "There are many arrangements to make. We must travel to Ouistreham immediately."

14. Portsmouth Naval Yard, England – 21:00h

The blanket of cloud that had stifled the Channel coast for days was unravelling and letting the rising moon's light grin through. The feverish preparations that had energized the wharves for weeks were complete and an uneasy calm had settled on the yard. In a secluded corner a unique Royal Navy submarine, glided up to its dock where a party of renown players awaited her arrival. HMS Graph was the former U-570; captured, repaired and reflagged in 1941 after an elaborate subterfuge had given the Germans every reason to believe she'd been scuttled.

Walter Bedell Smith, Eisenhower's Chief of Staff and Major General Colin Gubbins, Head of the U.K.'s Special Operations Executive, had joined the British Prime Minister and his party for this rendezvous. Ike was in Newbury seeing off the 101st Airborne and welling with tears as the aircraft banked towards the south coast and their destination: Normandy.

Churchill could have delegated the Portsmouth trip too but his fervent desire to read the Desert Fox's intentions firsthand wouldn't permit it. Montgomery may well have wanted to attend had Churchill not excluded him from the arrangements lest the history between these adversaries queered the meeting.

Churchill's bodyguard, Walter Thompson, just wanted the meeting over and to get his boss back to London and abed. The dangers of this excursion were manifold. The clearing weather was favoring the accuracy of a bombardier and extending a sniper's kill zone dramatically. SOE snipers were posted at key vantage points but killing a lucky Axis shooter would be small recompense for the ensuing maelstrom if Churchill was killed.

As Rommel stepped ashore, Thompson thought him smaller than in the newsreels, yet the steely aura was all there, even in civvies. Smith stepped forward to make the perfunctory introductions in the manner decreed by Churchill. To avoid the embarrassment of Nazi salutes no hands were to be extended, nods would do. Churchill's own head barely moved, the ash on his Cuban cigar staying put. Rommel reciprocated by introducing Speidel.

Bedell-Smith motioned Rommel and his chief of staff towards the door of a dank warehouse reeking with the peppery smell of cordite. They sat down at a trestle table and Smith laid out the meeting's primary objective: to see if a trust relationship was remotely possible.

"Sir, I've been instructed by General Eisenhower to assess whether you are acting in good faith?" he said.

This erred from Churchill's more subtle script straightaway, but Smith wasn't inclined to play softball with the Reich's toughest warrior.

"General Smith you are as straightforward as your reputation and I appreciate the candor," Rommel said with a half-smile.

"I've received many Allied invitations to parlay but when your Supreme Commander sent word, I felt compelled to comply despite the risks," he continued. "Rest assured, I would not have taken these risks in some deluded attempt to deceive you."

He was alluding to Deputy Führer Rudolph Hess' farcical defection in May 1941. Since then both sides had been sending regular, furtive invitations to each other's senior personnel in the hope someone sane might take the bait. These entreaties were usually ignored for fear of deception, but every so often one fell on fertile ground, especially those sent in person under Eisenhower's authority.

"I believe we all wish to avoid unnecessary bloodshed and hope we can establish a relationship of trust to that end," Rommel said.

The languid pace with which Churchill barely suppressed a smirk provoked Rommel's next contribution.

"Our armies are poised before a great moment in military history and the die for that engagement is already cast," he said. "I don't expect you to divulge anything about your imminent invasion plans. Just as I will betray nothing of our defenses."

Rommel's use of the word, 'betray' made Speidel uneasy but his poker face was performing better than the Prime Minister's this night.

"Nevertheless, both sides are also on the cusp of unleashing potent new weaponry that will transform modern warfare," Rommel said. "It is in everyone's interest that the power of these weapons is never brought to bear," he added.

Churchill was bridling at how Rommel was taking control of the meeting and by his assumption that Axis intelligence was on a par with the Allies.

"If the Field Marshall is referring to the flying bomb, he can rest easy," Churchill said slipping into his adversarial, Parliamentary style. "We have been expecting them for some time and neither the RAF nor the British people will be cowered by them."

Before Smith could wade in and referee Rommel replied. "No Prime Minister I refer to the V2 which flies at ballistic speed and will outpace even your new Meteor jet."

Smith doubted Churchill had intended to catch this trophy with his sprat but the tit for tat seemed to be working so he let it ride.

"You see Prime Minister your ULTRA decrypts have not given you a complete monopoly on good intelligence," Rommel said.

Every funny bone in Gubbins' body wanted to react to that thrust. He banked on both sides accumulating roughly the same amount of good information. The trick was in bringing it all together efficiently and interpreting it well. Churchill was less nuanced than Gubbins and much less amused now. His face had set into the same scowl the photographer Yousuf Karsh had captured a few years before. Contrary to his expressed intention to be parsimonious with intel Rommel ploughed on like a Panzer.

"Whether conventional, nuclear or chemical, the new rocket's payload will be fearful. It will eclipse your Manhattan warhead," Rommel said.

This literal bombshell had its desired effect, and a frisson went through the assembly, everyone trying so very hard not to yield a tell. Rommel might be bluffing but no one dared assume the Germans couldn't build the world's first atomic weapon and use it to crown their advances in rocketry. And both sides had ample experience with chemical warfare. They were glimpsing Armageddon.

"Now I too may be living up to my reputation General Smith and have thrust a little too far, too quickly," Rommel said. "Our trust must be mutual, and my further openness carries conditions," he added.

"No doubt and agreed," said Smith inviting Rommel to continue.

"Left unchecked the Russian army will beat a path to the English Channel and merely replace one tyranny with another," Rommel said. "Meantime exploiting your air superiority you may try to bomb the Third Reich into oblivion.

"That will only make the Russian advance easier while prolonging the present conflict and its tragic death toll," said Rommel.

Churchill had held his peace long enough. "What's left of Europe's Jewry will gladly take their chances with Mr. Stalin rather than Herr Himmler!"

Churchill saw he'd nicked his enemy's Achilles' heel: the regime Rommel had championed had become a vicious, criminal killing machine. It was left to Smith to act as a peacemaker, not a role he was known for.

"Field Marshall, it's clear to me you have traveled here at great personal peril and in good faith," he said. "I'll be reporting to the Supreme Commander immediately and feel sure he will want to keep this channel open," Smith added.

Now the German Enigma code machine was a sieve, devising a structure to let Speidel and Smith communicate undetected wouldn't be difficult. Smith handed a paper outlining a proposed structure to Speidel who scanned the contents quickly and gestured his approval to Rommel.

After another round of nodding to conclude the meeting, Smith made to escort Rommel and Speidel back to the waiting sub. All the spooks present would've been happier to see just those three go back to the quayside, but Churchill had other ideas and strode after them. Before he followed his boss, Thompson motioned Gubbins to check out a photographer he'd spotted on the other side of the basin.

Only a few hours after being ferried to the Samuel Chase Corbin could appreciate why the GIs were so aggrieved with their recent treatment. For two days they'd contended with the close confinement of the overcrowded ship and the rough sea state at anchor off Portland Bill.

Hardy stomachs were digesting some of the best food they'd had since crossing the Atlantic. Others were losing what might be their last square meal with no disrespect to a galley crew ordered to cook up a feast to remember. Despite the best efforts of the maintenance detail the ship had become awash with human detritus from backed up heads. That combined with the diesel fumes from the ship's gensets had even seasoned innards roiling.

Pending the go signal The Chase had put into Portsmouth for maintenance where she was sluiced out with a local disinfectant called Jeyes Fluid that was just as pungent and disagreeable as the filth it addressed. Although all were now anxious for Ike to pull the trigger and get them over there, most of the men aboard were glad to be back in port for a spell.

Rumours of a recent foul up off the Devon coast had everyone leery of languishing in coastal waters. A communication breakdown had turned several fully laden troop carriers off the Dorset coast into target practice for three German fast boats that had chanced upon them. Hundreds of Allied troops had been lost in the course of nothing more than a training exercise.

Below decks there were only so many words men not given to writing could commit to a last letter, be it to a sweetheart, a child or an unborn. With those committed to paper most marines were making or losing a fortune at cards or craps, while others were with the padre praying.

Corbin played poker for an hour but was enjoying neither the disinfected atmosphere nor the pathetic abandon with which most hands were being played out. He played aggressively himself, but it seemed many of these guys were already resigned to penury or death. Conversation was unsettling: complete strangers felt at liberty to divulge intimate details of their lives as if talking to their confessor.

Back up on deck Corbin located the officer of the watch and asked if he could step down to the quayside to test the timing mechanisms of his cameras.

"The slightest movement can skew the results, so I need to be on solid ground," he lied.

The officer knew one end of a camera from another and when he was being sold a pup, but he admired Corbin's chutzpah and let him disembark on condition he stayed within hailing range.

On the dock Corbin laid his kit out on a packing case forward of the gantry and took a moment to fill his lungs first with fresher air, and then some cigarette smoke. Conscious of being watched by the ship's sentry, Corbin drew a few drags and then started an elaborate show with his cameras.

He had no intention of wasting precious film in this charade but had forgotten one of his Contax II cameras was already loaded from a previous assignment. He set the shutter release delay for three seconds and adjusted the aperture and shutter for a long exposure.

With exaggerated kinetics worthy of a French mime artist, he pushed the shutter release button while keeping time with his chronograph. The sentry seemed content with these theatrics, so Corbin reset the Contax for a five second, then a ten second delay. He repeated the charade over and over, throwing in some malarkey with a flexible wire release he kept in his bag but never used.

Unsurprisingly all four cameras worked perfectly, Corbin being a stickler for keeping his kit well maintained. Nevertheless he hoped to be able to string this jape out for a while longer and stay shoreside. Just then the officer of the watch reappeared over the gunnels and ordered Corbin back aboard.

"If you're not back aboard pronto buddy you'll be thumbing another ride," he said as Corbin gathered up his kit and scrambled aboard.

As he skedaddled he thought he heard a rifle shot above the roar of the ship's engines as the crew of the Samuel Chase got her ready to be underway.

———————————————

As the nets were lowered to give clear water to the HMS Graph, a serving U-Boat, U-491, had slipped in behind her. The U-491's captain was keen to discover why a fellow commander would be risking his boat to sail up the Solent and, without means to communicate undetected, he felt obliged to follow underwater and lend support if necessary.

The skipper had her raised to periscope depth very carefully and began surveying the scene. Astonished but equally sure the portly figure on the dock was Britain's Prime Minister, he came away from the conning tower and asked the two SS officers aboard to join him in his quarters on the double.

"Herr Kastner, in view of what I have just seen I wish to vary your orders," the skipper said to the smaller of the two men.

"Please continue Captain," Kastner said. "Albeit you have no authority to alter our orders."

"Understood but hear me out," the Captain said. "The British Prime Minister is in a warehouse on the wharf ahead of us. I can raise the boat sufficiently for you to exit through the tower and paddle to shore. You will have a clear shot at Churchill when he exits. However we will clear the area after you disembark so you will not be able to reboard."

His original orders had been to offload the SS agents off Portland Bill so they could report on enemy strength in the vicinity of Weymouth. To his mind this unforeseen opportunity presented compelling reason to adapt those orders if they could be relied upon to comply.

However the SS were a law unto themselves and these two, the one foxy, the other ursine, were particularly incalcitrant. Even if they agreed it would be a delicate maneuver, but his Chief could control an ascent like none other and the Captain was confident detection could be avoided. The risk was worth the prize on offer.

After a moment's thought and without conferring, Kastner assented to the proposal. The Chief began bringing the craft up to a level where the conning tower hatch could just be raised. Trager was tasked with raising the hatch once the Chief adjusted the negative pressure within the boat to make the lift feasible.

As Smith bade Rommel and Speidel farewell, Churchill came up behind them and asked Smith and Speidel to give them a moment.

"Field Marshall, I do appreciate that a soldier has a duty to serve, no matter the character of his political masters.

"That said I hope we can agree that the criminal acts of your masters have gone beyond all human tolerance," Churchill said.

"Prime Minister, the legitimacy of my country's Government will be judged in the proper forum sooner, if we can cooperate," Rommel said. "I sincerely hope my hazardous visit has created a basis for cooperation."

From the warehouse door Gubbins had his binoculars trained on the photographer fiddling with his equipment on the dock across the basin. The fellow was giving the rendezvous no attention, engrossed in some Chaplin-like buffoonery. Gubbins thought Thompson might have been over-reacting given the fool's theatrics and the absence of a long lens on his camera. But Churchill and Rommel cut recognizable figures and a photograph of this congress, however blurry, could be propaganda dynamite.

When the photographer abruptly grabbed his gear and started rushing back on-board the transport ship, Gubbins was galvanized into action. He immediately ordered a young agent in his retinue to give chase and seize the film.

The SS agents were pawing their inflatable dinghy to shore and the Chief was easing the boat back down in a few minutes. They unwrapped a G43 sniper rifle from its prophylactic and polythene sheathing and settled down. From their vantage point they could see the guarded warehouse where the meeting was taking place and Corbin's antics on the opposite side of the basin. They zeroed in on the warehouse.

As the meeting party emerged Kastner was mortified to recognize another familiar face through his spotting scope.

"Concentrate on Churchill, Trager" he told his comrade, too late to prevent the shock of discovery impacting the shooter's aim.

Having narrowly missed Churchill with his first shot, Trager was composing himself for a second when a pistol shot came back in their general direction. Pistol potshots didn't pose a mortal threat but return fire would betray their position to opposing snipers. They abandoned the rifle, slipped back down into the dinghy and made their escape.

No sooner had Gubbins issued the order to intercept the frenetic photographer than a shot rang out and a bullet ricocheted off the wall beside him. A chip of masonry sliced his cheek as he crouched and saw Speidel bundling Rommel aboard the sub.

Thompson was darting after Churchill who had drawn his Colt 45 and was striding off in the direction of the shot's origin. Thompson caught him in a flying tackle and Churchill rotated into it, saving his head from injury.

Churchill's long-suffering bodyguard was very glad of it. The PM's pug would be the focus of reels of news coverage over the coming days. To have him visibly cut and bruised would stir up all sorts of distracting press speculation, to say nothing of Lady Clementine's displeasure.

As he scoured the scene for the sniper's whereabouts, Churchill peered down over his prostate girth to address his bodyguard.

"Thompson we must take a careful look at your job description," he said. "I don't recall any requirement to abuse me like a sack of potatoes."

On receiving his orders from Gubbins the young British agent had commandeered a Harley Davidson from the VIP convoy and raced off. After speeding past Dock 2 and Nelson's flagship he came to a checkpoint and was challenged for the password of the day.

"Look, I don't know what's so precious back there but I'm under orders from Supreme Command to reach that American vessel before she leaves port," he said. "So, be a good chap and lift this barrier pronto?"

"Not without the password sonny. Now turn that bike around and stick your orders where the sun don't shine," the MP Sergeant replied.

The Sergeant looked like he'd been round the block a few times and wouldn't be for changing, so the agent ostensibly did as he was told, just slowly. As he did, he scanned about and saw some cases propping up a plank to the right of the checkpoint. He rode back past HMS Victory and out of the Sergeant's sight. Then he turned and gunned the engine. He was doing over thirty when he hit the plank, enough to send him and the bike sailing over the barrier. He'd made another forty yards when automatic fire began fizzing past his head, just as he cut left and headed towards the American vessel's dock.

As he neared the ship he could see there was already 10 feet between the vessel's stern and the dock and there was nothing to ramp from this time. He stopped and shouted at the top of his lungs to the sailors coiling the stern lines, but the ship's engines drowned him out.

Returning to the checkpoint and likely arrest he saw General Gubbins had followed the sound of gunfire and was setting the MPs straight.

"Quite a stunt laddie, but judging by your face, you didn't get there in time?" Gubbins asked the agent.

"Afraid not sir," the agent confirmed.

"What's your name son?" Gubbins asked. "Duke, sir, Alastair Duke" he said.

"Well Duke, we're under strict orders not to delay passage of the invasion vessels, so I won't be asking her to put back in," said Gubbins.

"I'm going to have to find you a swift passage to Omaha my boy."

Part Five – 6th June 1944

15. Hayling Island, England - 00:30h

The two SS agents had been rowing down the Solent for almost three hours when they opted to make landfall and scuttle the inflatable. By hugging the coast they'd eluded the heavy flow of vessels exiting Portsmouth Harbour and some immense concrete structures under tow. Kastner had never seen their like and was glad their skeletal crews and the tugs pulling them were consumed by the challenges of moving such ungainly megaliths.

Now on dry land they jogged north planning to steal a vehicle and get on a main road to their required destination: London. They'd cleaned the daub off their faces as best they could and were in civilian, albeit damp clothes but concocting a good cover story was going to be tricky.

"So Trager what should we say we're doing if asked?" Kastner quizzed his colleague as they approached the outskirts of a village.

"Not sure, sir," said the bear.

"Then best you leave the talking to me, agreed?" Kastner said and Trager nodded. "From now on we speak only English and, in your case, only when absolutely necessary."

Up the road they spotted a dark green Austin 7 that was about as basic as a car could be, but adequate if Trager could squeeze himself into it. Kastner cut and cleaned a twig from a nearby tree to gauge the gas tank. Reputedly petrol was as scarce in England as in Germany so taking a car with an empty tank would be counter-productive. Finding the tank almost full Kastner popped the primitive door lock with his prized Hitler youth knife and then cross-wired the ignition.

Everything was going well up to the bridge that separated Hayley's Island from the mainland and was guarded by a platoon of the Home Guard. The Guard was a reserve force of grocers, butchers and bank managers who volunteered to defend the homeland while most full-time troops were abroad. They'd originally been dubbed the Local Defense Volunteers but when those initials were parodied as Look, Duck, Vanish, Churchill had insisted on a renaming.

Kastner and Trager didn't have time to scout for an alternative crossing and, even if they had, they wouldn't have found one. They'd have to talk or blast their way through if challenged. Much of Kastner's boyhood had been spent with English relatives and though he hadn't enjoyed their company, they'd left him with an excellent command of English.

As an old soldier with a shotgun flagged him down Kastner came to a steady halt and pulled down the driver's window.

"Yes corporal, how can I help you?" he said.

"I'd like to see your papers sir and to know why you're out after curfew," said the silver-topped, crochety Great War veteran.

"Here are our papers and I'm taking my friend here to the ENT clinic at Guy's Hospital in London. He's got bad case of quinzies threatening to block his windpipe," Kastner said.

Most of this dialogue was going right over Trager's head as he kept his collar up, his mouth shut and the safety on his pistol on fire.

"Are you sure you need to go all that way sir?" the corporal said. "We have some very good doctors here on the south coast."

"No doubt," said Kastner, "but my friend is a Wagnerian baritone of some repute, and this affliction could ruin his career."

Invoking Wagner really was tempting fate, but Kastner enjoyed living on the edge.

"Very well sir, but if you don't mind me asking what brings you down to the island in the first place?" the corporal asked handing back the forged papers.

"We came in the hope the sea air might do the Maestro some good, but it hasn't proved to be the case," said Kastner.

"Well Hampshire doesn't suit everybody sir, just most people."

With that the corporal smiled and raised the barrier to let them pass. He was the local butcher and as he reentered the guard post he recounted what Kastner had said for the village GP and the innkeeper.

"That's funny," said the doctor. "I don't think Guy's owes much of its reputation to its ENT clinic."

16. Mid English Channel - 04:15h

The best ride Gubbins could secure for Duke amidst the frenzy of the embarkation was a tank landing craft bound for Juno Beach. She was jam packed with amphibious Sherman tanks and their crews, but room was found for one more soul.

It was a ponderous voyage of several hours even at the vessel's twelve knot top speed but, with his happy knack of being able to sleep on a log, Duke spent most of it in Dreamland. From Arromanches, Duke's objective was to head west towards Port en Bessin and Omaha Beach.

"The Gold landings are scheduled an hour later than Omaha to take account of the tide," Gubbins had told him. "So your chances of evading capture and reaching Omaha in time are slim my boy. But of such deeds are heroes made."

"Thank you sir, I'll do my best," Duke said.

"I know you will lad," Gubbins said. "Give this authorization to the Beachmaster on your return and ask him to get you aboard something faster."

Duke woke to the sound of bombardment, alongside men wound like springs and eager to get stuck in. The stocky soldier next to him had an incongruous whiff, strong enough even Duke could smell it.

"If I didn't know better, I'd swear you've been playing with plasticine," Duke said. The soldier gave him a knowing smile and explained.

"That beauty over there is my Sherman and after three days of bunging her every orifice with plasticine she's as waterproof as a duck's behind," the soldier said.

"Are you sure?" Duke said with a laugh.

"Well mate if you find yourself sheltering behind her on the beach in the morning, reckon you'll have your answer," the soldier said offering Duke a cigarette.

"What's your name soldier?" Duke asked. "Jones, Jim Jones and what's your name Mr. Spook?" the soldier replied. Duke looked at him askance.

"Well, they generally reserve these rides for men in uniform. You're in mufti and not carrying a camera so I'm guessing you're SOE," Jones explained.

"You may be right," Duke said, "But it's all for one and one for all today."

"I'd drink to that, but I never drink and drive a tank," Jones said with a broad grin.

A few hours later Jones and his fellow tankers were driving up the beach, giving welcome cover to the flesh and blood infantry that surrounded them. Many tanks, even those fitted with inflatable skirts, never reached the shoreline – but Jones had, testament to his caulking skills.

17. Off Le Havre, English Channel – 04:30h

HMS Graph made decent progress once she cleared the shipping lanes pouring traffic out of the Hampshire ports. The captain had taken advantage of all opportunities to surface run, but congestion and regular radar scanning had forced him below on several occasions. He'd also become aware of a persistent signature astern which his hydrophone operator was convinced belonged to another U-Boat.

On reboarding Rommel and Speidel had been shepherded by a fluent German speaking officer to the Captain's quarters and afforded the privacy the curtain door could provide. There was every reason to suspect microphones had been secreted in the cramped space, so they passed written messages to one another in between the successive dive maneuvers. The return journey was taking longer than the trip over and, once the euphoria of the Portsmouth meeting had worn off, they settled back into an anxiety stirred up by the risk of discovery and the prospect of the battle ahead.

The Graph's progress slowed further when the skipper was forced to skirt around the armada mustering off the Normandy coast. However placing the rendezvous point ten nautical miles off Dieppe rather than Le Havre was paying dividends.

The skipper had his boat brought up to periscope depth at the prearranged location and began searching for the E-Boat that would take the Field Marshall and his A-d-C ashore. He conned the fast boat approaching the coordinates at pace and had the Graph surfaced to make the rendezvous. The booming of a massive artillery barrage could be heard to the west and the remaining clouds overland were being lit red.

Speidel was vexed by the curiosity of the fast boat's thirty-five man crew and was very relieved to see the Graph's makeshift Kreigsmarine emblems had survived the passage. The disguised Royal Navy Lieutenant who'd welcomed them now bade them farewell in bellowed but perfect German, barely audible above the thundering noise of bombardment and the E-Boat's idling engines.

"It has been an honor Herr Field Marshall," he said as Rommel clambered into the inflatable sent over by the fast boat. "I hope we have an opportunity to serve you again."

"Thank you, Lieutenant. Good hunting," Rommel said with similar gusto.

The E-Boat's skipper wasn't altogether taken in by the subterfuge, but he wasn't willing to give rein to his suspicions either. This was Rommel after all and whatever he was doing must have been blessed by the High Command. He'd take the precaution of adding a cryptic note to his log, even though he'd been told not to, and leave it at that. For now he wanted to be back on the hunt having spent valuable time circling while waiting for the sub to make contact.

His E-Boat made decent headway on a sea state that was slowly improving from the churning soup of recent days. In twenty minutes she was moored and disembarking Rommel and Speidel on the Dieppe quayside. From there Rommel made off eastwards towards his home in Heerlingen and Speidel sped to their headquarters in La Roche-Guyon where two uninvited SS officers were waiting to greet him. Speidel suppressed his fear this could be his comeuppance and returned their salute.

"Good morning Herr Major General, with the compliments of Herr Reichsminister Goebbels" the senior SS officer said, handing him a communiqué.

Hoping his voice would stay steady and distract attention from the slight tremor in his hands, Speidel read its content aloud.

"The Reichsminister regrets the Field Marshall was not at home for a photography session commemorating Frau Rommel's 50th birthday celebrations.

"We wish you a speedy recovery and a prompt return to duty," Speidel said.

Their job done, the SS officers saluted and turned on their clicked heels. By sending officers from his own chain of command Goebbels was signaling his misgivings about Rommel's behavior. The sickness story was wearing thin. Rommel had been on sick leave before El Alamein and Goebbels attributed the German defeat, in no small measure, to Rommel's unscheduled absence.

However when the Reichsminister raked over his misgivings at a movie-screening that evening, Hitler had flown into a disbelieving rage and stormed off into his private quarters. For ensuing hours his generals sought permission to deploy the Panzer Reserve, but Hitler remained resolutely incommunicado. Unbeknown to Rommel his actions had provoked one of the most telling tactical prevarications of the war.

Goebbels' menace wasn't lost on Speidel. Having roused his caustic curiosity their actions would be under a microscope from now on. With luck the Allied action would act as a stupendous and irresistible diversion, but Goebbels was a difficult dog to shake off once he'd sunk his teeth in.

Out in the English Channel Commander Dahlmer and the crew of U-491 had been tracking HMS Graph until a heavy concentration of Allied shipping made the pursuit impossible. Whenever the Graph broke surface and they themselves weren't being swamped by radar signals, they had tried to establish contact but had been unable to do so.

Breaking off their pursuit they tried without success to find a safe route into Le Havre and, when that proved non-viable, they sailed west. Repeatedly bombarded by sonar from enemy vessels, the commander considered deploying anti-sonar chaff as a precaution, but it proved unnecessary. The Allied ships seemingly had no interest in engagement.

For his part the sheer weight of numbers led the captain to believe any attack on the enemy vessels would be a short-lived triumph followed swiftly by certain destruction. The Allied ships might have bigger fish to fry, but they would make short shrift of a lone, meddlesome U-Boat if taunted.

Unwilling to risk surfacing until close to the Cotentin peninsula, it would be three more hours before Dahlmer would put into Cherbourg, file his report and send a signal to Berlin which Kastner had asked him to convey.

18. Soho, London - 06:00h

Driving the Austin Baby 7 had reaffirmed Kastner's respect for German engineering. What little suspension the vehicle possessed wasn't intended to carry the likes of Trager, and the car had traveled at a tilt all the way from Hampshire. Somehow the wheel bearings had held out and they had made it to outer London.

The road to London was dark and deserted. Most people were observing the curfew and any animals game enough to traverse the King's highway had long since found their way to the tables of families desperate for a little extra protein. With only pitch darkness ahead and sleep an unaffordable luxury, there was every reason to swap stories while brushing the rust off Trager's English.

Trager had been a devout member of the Hitler Youth since 1931. Always tall for his age, he had personified the ideal of Aryan superiority in his adolescence, but as he filled out and carried 135 kilograms of mostly muscle on his six-foot five frame, he stretched the credibility of the specious legend.

Kastner came in at the opposite end of the scale. His stature was more akin to that of his overall commander, Heinrich Himmler and, like him, he'd become inured to straining his neck to make eye contact with the statuesque soldiers he surrounded himself with. Men like Reinhard Heydrich, whom Himmler had fostered and Kastner had idolized even before his assassination in 1942 at the hands of Czech SOE agents.

They deftly negotiated another couple of checkpoints on their journey, Kastner changing his story each time for the joy of it. Trager, ever practical, had preserved the polythene sheet from the sniper rifle which came in handy for pilfering fuel to keep the Austin 7 trundling along.

On reaching Shepherd's Bush they grabbed some bread and dripping and weak tea at a makeshift café amidst the dust and rubble of an abandoned bombsite. Kastner reveled in the sight and dusty smell of the devastation the Luftwaffe had wrought and lamented Goering's inability to perpetuate the mayhem. It had been months since London had felt the airmailed terror German cities were experiencing nightly.

Kastner got them out of there before they aroused too much unwelcome interest and, having time to spare, they abandoned the Austin, which was running on fumes again by then, and began strolling towards their pre-assigned location. They walked through Kensington and onto Piccadilly towards an area Kastner had wanted to visit, ever since being forbidden to do so during a school trip in the early Thirties.

Soho's brothels and strip clubs were a reminder that London was, before all else, a port city just like Kastner's native Hamburg. Mariners sought out the same shore distractions the world over, and those that could afford to get out of the East End found them "up West". Soho's gawdy neon lighting had been switched off, but trade continued in venues like the Windmill Theatre, renown for never letting the war put it out of business. It being almost six in the morning the theatre was temporarily closed for cleaning but a couple of working girls were hanging around hoping for one last trick before dawn.

Kastner claimed never to have paid for sex in his life but not even his dwindling circle of friends believed him. He looked every inch like someone who would need some form of inducement to coax another soul into congress of any kind. The officer in him remembered the mission but the boy in him, the greater part, was in the mood for more mischief. More so when he saw Trager was uncommonly distracted by the come-hither being put out by the tall girl propping up the frame of the stage door.

"Good morning ladies, as you can see my friend here is interested in what you may have to soothe a weary traveler," Kastner said.

"Ooh ladies is it," said the shorter girl interposing herself between Trager and the taller girl as he approached to get a closer look. She was unwisely over-compensating for a dread that was enveloping her. It had been a long unprofitable night and they were skint, but she was already regretting this encounter.

"Well wouldn't you say so," Kastner said, with an edge Trager was coming to recognize as the introit to someone else getting hurt. Trager couldn't tell why these girls had set Kastner off but when his colleague led his hand into the taller girl's crotch, he realized his oversight.

As his paw recoiled from the genitals hanging there, Trager stepped back and Kastner put the small girl's Adam's apple into a vice-like grip. From experience, Trager was sure Kastner would finish this strangulation despite there being no military merit to the act, if left to his own devices.

He laid his hand on Kastner's shoulder gently to relay these forebodings, and Kastner acknowledged the gesture. Once in the process of killing Kastner the assassin remained uncommonly calm of body and receptive of mind.

"Well it seems you two are packing more than my friend is prepared to pay for, so why don't you take your trade somewhere else?" Kastner said.

Kastner released his grip and both girls beat a retreat, the shorter one spewing some Anglo-Saxon expletives Kastner hadn't heard in quite a while.

"Which goes to show my friend, never judge a book by its cover," Kastner said. "Now, if our U-Boat Captain has done as I asked our sleeper agent will have been activated, so let's get to the rendezvous point."

19. Omaha Beach, Normandy - 06:15h

The landing craft that had looked so strong and purposeful from a ways off, felt vulnerable and awkward to Corbin now. Making their ponderous progress against the surf the scent of disinfectant and excreta bestowed on them by the mother ship abided. It was enriched with the odor of seaweed and fresh blood as the front ramp dropped to rob the human cargo of their last vestige of protection. They were on their own and there was nothing left to do but run, leap and charge.

The men at the front found to their cost that the landing craft had not been taken far enough into the beach. Some jumped and, in full battle gear, found themselves sinking down several feet, hissing lead following them through the swell. Those who hesitated were raked where they stood by murderous fire from a machine gun nest on the cliff above them.

The LST skipper, realizing his error, gunned the engines and drove the craft forward until the lowered ramp thudded into the sand, halving two infantrymen and sending those still standing careering towards another rain of fire.

Corbin was furthest aft, and his adrenalin peaked as he waited for the vessel to stop and a path to open up. He scrambled forward over stricken bodies and propelled himself into a flying leap that won him an early footing on the sand.

He sprinted as best he could to the shelter of a structure he had targeted while waiting for his turn and panted some breath back into his lungs. He was trembling uncontrollably and thought twice about unpacking a camera from the plastic bag he'd held high on disembarking.

He was too near the water's crashing edge and made a dart up the beach only to be forced down into the sand by the searing hot metal missing him by whiskers. He lay prostrate for a while and tried to gather his thoughts amid the maelstrom.

His shovel found nothing but hard shingle just below the sand, so he dug deeper into his agitated mind for a fresh game plan. The situation looked hopeless, but he hadn't come all this way to play dead. After two minutes that felt like twenty he girded himself for a charge towards a disabled tank off to his right.

Just as Corbin flexed to rise he was knocked pancake flat by the legless upper body of an infantryman freshly scythed by an artillery shell. He turned his head to see the GI's face muscles go through their last contortions not a foot away. His once vital body weighed brutishly heavy; he was fair skinned and clean-shaven, athletic and young. A bat of his blackened eyelids beckoned Corbin forward to catch his last word. Deafened by the blast Corbin didn't hear the word on most dying lips that morning, he only felt the breath "Mother" made on his neck.

Conscious he could be no further help to the youngster's shattered bone and flesh, Corbin screamed and launched himself towards the tank. In its shelter he unpacked his Contax and, trying to focus on action not death, shot the few scenes of progress being made within range of his lens. In short order he exposed 36-frames, shooting each scene at least twice to compensate for the unsteadiness he felt in his hands and to bracket his shots by half a stop.

He switched cameras and went on shooting not just what would pass the censor's chinagraph pencil, but also a record of the macabre sacrifice of the fallen. His work wouldn't be solely some gung-ho celebration of the heroics of armed conflict. That wouldn't justify the voyeurism the work's creation entailed. The misery and filth had to be shown too if it was to serve as a new challenge to stop committing the same bloody, perverted mistake.

With all four cameras used up Corbin faced a decision point: reload fresh film and move to another vantage point – both actions fraught with risk of failure - or get the hell off the beach and meet his deadline. Reloading a Contax required the back of camera body to be removed completely and clean, dry hands to get the film onto the sprockets. Neither was realistic in his current location and state of agitation, so he started looking for an escape route.

He would ponder for the rest of his life whether fear or pragmatism sent him back towards the water. Whichever it was, once he'd set his sights on an LST ferrying the wounded back to the Samuel Chase, his legs found new vigor to speed him away from the cruel fire.

20. Jig Section, Gold Beach, Normandy – 07:25h

Trying to get clear of the landing zone at first opportunity Duke broke right and exited the edge of the enemy's field of fire. The countryside above the beach wasn't plain sailing either but it was evident the enemy was still in shocked disarray. He rigged a razor wire trap between two trees on opposite sides of the coast road and waited for a motorcycle courier or jeep driver to come speeding unknowingly towards a grizzly decapitation. He kept the wire down as a few speeding trucks whizzed by, then a cyclist came up the rise to his left, but at a pace at which the wire would have no lethal effect.

The bike was a tandem and its solo rider was a purposeful but overtaxed girl who grew comelier as the labored crank of her pedals edged her closer. Duke's first inclination was to break cover and go to her aid, but he held the chivalry in check and observed her closely first.

She was very easy on the eye. The stripes of her Breton dress accentuated athletic thighs while its V-neck drew attention to her ample cleavage. Complete with braids of onions and garlic in the bike's wicker panier she was a Calvados honey trap. But atop all the stereotypes was a face of exquisite beauty and an expression of sheer exhilaration. Duke found her elation commendable given the volume of heavy munitions flying overhead.

He broke cover and waved her down. Almost at a halt any way she came to an ungainly stop as inertia caused the tandem's unwieldy weight to steal her balance. As if to spring the trap she'd baited, she fell into his arms. Duke was confident of being able to deal with her moves, but wary of accomplices she might have on hand. Once satisfied the immediate danger of ambush had passed, he unhanded the girl and asked her name in perfect French.

"Gabrielle, monsieur. Et comment appellez-vous?" she said.

Duke had no qualms about continuing in French, it being one of the languages he commanded with native fluency. However, amidst the mother of all bombardments, he felt more comfortable bellowing in English.

"I am a British agent on an urgent mission. I must get to Port-en-Bessin immediately," he told her.

Gabrielle let out a whoop of delight and gave Duke a kiss on the lips which would, in other circumstances, have prompted spirited reciprocation. Her wearing Arpège, his mother's favourite perfume, dampened his urge to return the gesture. She smiled, released her grip on his head and smoothed down her dress.

"Forgive me mon ami, we've been waiting for this dawn for so many tear-stained nights. Welcome to France and please know I am at your service," Gabrielle said.

"No need to apologize," Duke said. "But perhaps we can continue chatting as we take a ride to Port-en-Bessin?"

"Of course. My pleasure," Gabrielle said and made to take the back seat.

"No, I think you should be up front," Duke said. "Better if you steer."

Gabrielle was accustomed to using her attractive physique to distract the enemy and made the switch readily. Five miles of spirited pedaling followed, ballistic projectiles winging relentlessly overhead. Duke marveled at the audacity of the ships directing so much explosive force in the same direction as the invading troops. Gabrielle seemed oblivious to it all, consumed by the anticipation of liberation.

As they approached Omaha Beach and looked down on the fierce fighting, Duke was initially encouraged to see that they were in good time. His relief turned to sorrow as he viewed the carnage through his field glasses and began to realize why time had only seemed to be on their side.

The Americans were pinned down by the batteries on the cliffs above the beach and successive attempts to progress were met with brutal reply. It was several minutes before he spied someone matching the description Gubbins had given him and, in that time, Duke and Gabrielle witnessed sights they would take to their graves.

The photographer was darting from behind the cover of various structures, intermittently shooting pictures of troops wading, weaving, cowering, and succumbing. Duke began devising a route to his position, but it looked hopeless. It seemed smarter to wait for the defensive fire to abate and the American troops to make headway off the beach.

That was until he saw Corbin making his way back towards the water and an LST that was ferrying wounded to a transport vessel lying offshore. Duke felt duty bound to try a suicidal interception but, after several tastes of lethal German fire, he bailed and headed back to Gabrielle. Two other members of the resistance had joined her, and their Peugeot truck bearing ambulance markings was in a nearby copse. Gabrielle entrusted Duke to them.

"Goodbye British Agent. Perhaps Paris next time?" she said as she brushed his cheek.

Duke kissed her hand and said, "Mademoiselle, it's my fervent hope we will meet again in the City of Light. Bonne chance!"

He knew the chances of further contact were infinitesimal, but stranger things had happened, and a woman possessed of such unquenchable brio would be worth seeking out.

The resistance soldiers sped Duke back to the British sector dodging careering Nazi convoys en route and then bade him safe passage back to England. Duke could only hope that Corbin would be returning to Portsmouth whence he came and that he would finally intercept him there.

21. Omaha Beach, Normandy - 08:45h

Aboard the LST Corbin was about to start unloading the film
rolls and getting them ready for dispatch when a medic
demanded his help. He compressed a neck wound until the
recipient yielded to it, and then began labelling an arm and a leg
so they would not be separated from the soldiers to whom they
belonged. Why exactly he wasn't sure but felt no inclination to
argue. The medic then demanded he go to the back of the vessel
and retrieve a batch of saline drips.

No sooner had Corbin retired aft than a bewildering cloud of
white stuff showered him like snow on a December day. A
German shell had ripped through the superstructure not four feet
from where he'd been standing a moment ago, and the kapok
was what remained of the medic's flak jacket.

He slumped down in shock and asked himself again why he'd
gotten into this line of work. The ruptured LST limped back to
the leeside of the Samuel Chase and the morbid task of unloading
the dead and wounded began. Back on deck Corbin sought
permission to make for the bridge and the ship's captain.

"Skipper, would you be willing to take a film pouch back to
Portsmouth where a courier from my bureau will collect it?"
Corbin asked.

The skipper was in no mood to play Pony Express or make
promises. "Son, strictly speaking you weren't supposed to go
ashore. Much as I admire your desire to get back into the game, I
won't break the rules twice and, no, I can't guarantee delivery of
your films.

"If you want to be sure your pictures get back to England, best you carry them yourself." The captain waited a moment for that to sink in and then ordered his vessel underway. Corbin's mind knew this was the better course, but his heart was still with those brave men he'd left behind on the beach.

Before his pity could drag his mind back there wholesale, he found a nook and began checking his kit. Adrenalin still had his heart pumping hard and his hands trembling, but from somewhere he summoned up the professionalism to discharge his cameras.

Normally Corbin would label his films with copious detail to let photo-editors get to the good stuff as a deadline loomed. They loved him for it. But these were abnormal times, and he was only halfway through labelling when Morpheus gathered him in.

22. Belgravia, London - 13:00h

Brand had spent the morning in his darkroom and was getting ready for an afternoon magazine assignment. After a close shave he was cleaning the golden cuttings from his Rolls razor when the intercom buzzed. He was intrigued when the concierge announced a telegram from his family in Switzerland. He'd had a letter from his father only a week ago so he assumed this could only be bad news about his mother's wellbeing. Brand's anxiety turned to agitation when he realized the telegram wasn't truly from his family at all.

His 'father' recounted a visit from a Mr. Schroeder who'd asked to be remembered to Brand and suggested a rendezvous in London during an immediate visit. Brand had come to dread this message and now, so late in the war, it presented like a bad joke. But there could be no mistaking its purpose and how seriously the sender intended it be taken.

For centuries the Schroeders had earned a reputation as tall, immensely powerful men capable of lifting very heavy weights. They toured the vineyards and breweries of Germany at harvest time to stack the laden barrels into the cellars. A literal translation of their name was Strong Man - Brand's SS code name. This then was his long-awaited activation and soon enough he'd know his objectives. He was instructed to proceed with all haste to the predestined rendezvous point and await contact.

As Brand dressed in the pre-designated garb he tried to get his mind into gear, primed for the duty he was bound to honor. For months Brand had assumed the war would be over before he was called back into active service, and it took some time and self-discipline to get used to the changed circumstances and be on his way. As he stepped out onto the street he hoped with his whole being this mission would justify his late in the day resurrection.

23. Trafalgar Square, London - 15:00h

After their Soho shenanigans and a greasy spoon breakfast for Trager, Kastner and his colleague had passed impatient but uneventful hours waiting for their rendezvous. They'd been rooted to their posts at the north and south-east corners of Trafalgar Square waiting for a tall, athletic man wearing a brown fedora and a red, white and blue badge on the left lapel of his dark blue suit.

The badge signified the wearer as a contributor to the Spitfire Fund by which the British Government was collecting public donations to subsidize the construction of Spitfire fighters. Brand enjoyed the irony of making this symbol of British resistance his signifier, more so because his handlers in Berlin hadn't recognized its symbolism.

Kastner and Trager were to ask the wearer the way to Cricklewood and, only if he said he knew of three good ways, were they to assume their contact was successful. Brand's agitation hadn't subsided and when he saw Trager approaching his mood darkened further.

After all these years an agent who carried himself like a drayman and spoke English gleaned from a tourist phrasebook was activating him? Was his stock in Berlin so low or had so many good men been lost on the Eastern Front that the service was reduced to agents of such common bearing? Whichever, it didn't bode well for the strategic importance of this mission.

"I know of three ways," Brand said as Kastner came scooting down from the adjacent corner of the Square. Trager had been under strict instructions not to engage with the contact on sighting but skipping lunch had gotten the better of his patience earning him a disdainful glower from Kastner.

Brand could see Kastner was cut from a different skein of cloth but found the pattern just as vulgar. Very likely plucked from the obscure ranks of a provincial police force, his darker tendencies would have been given a long leash within Himmler's SS.

He was of medium height and scrawny but, what he lacked in physique, he made up for with an assured persona and an English accent that was as good as Brand's own. They walked over to the steps of St Martin-in-the-Fields and Kastner gave Brand a full briefing.

"So you see, not only is this breach of security potentially of the gravest propaganda value, but your own professional expertise is extremely relevant," Kastner concluded.

Brand saw no point in disclosing his personal connection to Corbin and doubted the trailing threads these two dunderheads had left dangling could be gathered back up into a successful outcome, even with the advantage of prior connection. Neither was he inclined to share the other implication of his activation with an underling like Kastner.

"How did you get here Kastner?" Brand asked, and on being told continued, "It would have been better had you disposed of the vehicle properly. Best you leave it where it is now. You can just as well walk east along the Strand to Fleet Street."

Kastner wasn't accustomed to taking criticism from outside his line of command. However, the Strong Man had a reputation for calm ruthlessness he'd long held in high esteem. His exploits during the interwar years were part of SS folklore but, since '39, he'd disappeared into deep cover.

Allegedly he had a mission to assassinate Roosevelt, Churchill or Stalin or all three depending on who was telling the story. When Kastner was assigned the Strong Man as the contingency contact for his inaugural overseas mission he'd radiated with pride.

He was unaware that the fraught relationship between Goebbels and Himmler had since resulted in a devaluation of Brand's stock in Berlin. Brand was Goebbels' creature and Himmler resented how the illustrious exploits of this Swiss import had, for a while, outshone his favourite henchman, Heydrich.

Goebbels had been extolling Brand's talent since 1931 when he'd presented him with first prize in a short film competition at their shared alma mater, Heidelberg University. With a Master's degree from England's oldest university under his belt, Brand had opted to strengthen his Germanic roots with a doctorate at Germany's oldest university. Having become captivated by the work of Ferdinand de Saussure whilst at Oxford, he'd chosen the study of semiology as his research field to the delight of his Heidelberg tutors who were overjoyed to have such a talented academic applying himself to the work of the celebrated Swiss philosopher.

The short film competition had been a welcome distraction from the rigors of doctoral research and had given Brand an opportunity to experiment with some Saussurian theories about the interaction of language and signs. It had also, inadvertently, given his career another dimension.

Goebbels sensed much promise in the handsome prize winner who came up to the stage that day and hoped to recruit him into propaganda duties in Berlin once his doctorate was defended. Only Brand's long family tradition of military service prevented that outcome, but Goebbels had stayed in contact and tracked his acolyte's successes.

The resentment Himmler harbored had been rekindled after Heydrich's assassination. Hitler placed the highest orders of valor on Heydrich's funeral pillow but his private accusation that Heydrich's "stupidity" was the cause of his demise had infuriated Himmler. Riding in open cars with insufficient escort was asking for trouble, but even Himmler thought his Führer could have left that demeaning observation unspoken.

Himmler bided his time with typical patience and when Goebbels had needed support to ward off Martin Bormann's latest machinations, Himmler grasped his opportunity to cauterize the wound. In the horse-trading that followed Goebbels sacrificed Brand's bright future to gain Himmler's support. Brand was exiled to Britain along with several other sleeper agents to lay low. If and when he was activated it would be to assassinate King George VI or some other high value target.

"Go to this address and post watch for the photographer described here or a Press Agency courier he may be using to deliver his films to the Bureau Chief," Brand instructed Kastner, handing him a scribbled note.

"When you have the films, you are to meet me at this address," Brand said exchanging an engraved calling card. "Meantime Trager and I will deal with your stolen vehicle and attend to some other business.

"Do whatever's reasonable to recover those films Kastner, but, please, no more loose ends."

24. Portsmouth Naval Yard, England - 15:00h

"Damn, I thought you'd croaked," the medic said as Corbin was startled by a few slaps on the cheek.

"You need to shake a leg, or you'll be on your way back to France pretty damn quick," the corpsman added and strode off to supervise the taking on of fresh medical supplies.

Corbin rubbed his eyes to focus on the unmistakable and welcome broadside of Nelson's HMS Victory across the basin. As he joined the line to go ashore the air was thick with rumours about how the invasion was going. The jungle drums said the British and Canadians were making good progress towards their Day 1 objectives and not taking heavy casualties. Whereas the US forces were still pinned down on Omaha and facing a homicidal hail of fire from the Point du Hoc.

Scuttlebutt about some of the overnight parachute and glider landings behind German lines varied from disheartening to bizarre. Missed landing zones and over-ambitious loading of aircraft had taken the bite out of many airborne offensives. Rommel's defenses were taking their toll, but the Allies' errors were helping him just as he'd hoped.

"Sounds like we're in the middle of another grand Fubar," said a cynical private whose head was swathed in gauze.

"Yeah, 'cept this one's recognizable. It's got Dieppe written all over it," chimed in another wounded GI being borne on the next stretcher.

"Berlin by Christmas my ass," the bandaged cynic replied.

"Hey! You two, I didn't just loose this leg over there so I could come back here and listen to your crap!" snapped a Ranger Sergeant, brandishing a limb shod with a brown boot matching the one he was still wearing.

"I was at Dieppe, and it felt a whole lot different to what we've done today," he added. "Now, pipe down before I have these orderlies bring me over there so I can give you two a good shellacking with the three limbs I've got left."

Applause and cheers rang around the deck as the two privates resumed the horizontal and followed the sergeant's advice.

25. La Roche-Guyon, N. France - 15:00h

Spiedel had left two messages with Rommel's wife asking him to return his call the instant he arrived home. He'd tried several more times but the few undamaged lines to Germany were jammed.

All morning he'd been receiving discouraging reports of Allied success and he wanted to relay these and the disquieting message from Goebbels to his commander. He was very glad to hear Rommel's voice on the other end of the line eventually.

Both men were guarded in their conversation and by its conclusion no eavesdropper would have been any the wiser about recent assignations.

But Rommel now knew beyond doubt he'd aroused the suspicions of perhaps the most paranoid member of Hitler's inner circle. He asked Spiedel to let Goebbels' staff know of his improved health and that he was returning to Normandy with all haste.

It was a limp response unlikely to dispel the doubts he had spawned, but his chosen path was now irreversible, and his mind needed to clear down and get back onto the battlefield. He bade farewell to Lucie and the children, more uncertain than ever whether he would see them alive ever again.

26. Portsmouth Naval Yard, England, 15:15h

Unloading the Samuel Chase onto friendly shores wasn't as perilous as Omaha Beach but the slow unloading process and the chaotic dockside were testing Corbin's nerves just the same. He was anxious to get his exposed film into the courier's pouch and en route to the bureau chief's office in London.

At all costs the prints needed to reach New York within two days to make the next edition. But that was insufficient reason to barge ahead of wounded countrymen, most of whom would take no further part in the war, even if they survived. On finally clearing the dock Corbin looked around for the bureau's courier but, seeing no tell-tale armband, he headed to a nearby checkpoint.

"Private, can I use your phone please?" he asked the callow youth standing guard.

"I'll need a good reason, sir," the private replied, his neck reddening within a collar three sizes too big for it. Corbin presumed this reply meant there was a working phone in the guard post, so he persevered.

"I've taken pictures over there in Normandy that are vitally important to the war effort, and they have to get to London pronto.

"A courier should have been here to pick them up, so I need to find out from London what's happened to him," Corbin explained.

"Young fella in civvies tried to get in here about an hour ago and we sent him packing. Can't get in here without a pass.

"If he's hung around you might find him outside the main East Gate," he volunteered.

"Well can I make that call to my boss and double check?" Corbin asked.

"Sorry sir, phone's not working," the private said.

Corbin throttled the temptation to demand why that gem of intel had remained a secret till now and asked directions to the East Gate through gritted teeth. The gate was almost a mile away and, with only Shank's pony available, Corbin began legging it. With full kit his run soon subsided into a trot then a fast walk.

The short Burberry trench coat he'd bought in Regent Street two days ago now seemed so superfluous that he started looking for someone in greater need of it. But then it came in handy. Using the inside out coat like a plaid matador's cape, he flagged down a pretty ATS girl driving a Willy's jeep in the opposite direction.

"My dear I'm sure a lady as pretty as you must know of a young man who can make good use of this trench coat. Please accept it with my compliments," Corbin said, relieved to see the smile break out on the young woman's face.

"You're that American photographer aren't you? How come you're walking this way, the war's other there?" she said, before realizing the stains on his fatigues were of other people's blood.

"That's a very long story but if you have time to run me up to the East Gate, I'd be very happy to share it with you," Corbin said.

She didn't really have time but neither did she run into characters as attractive as Corbin every day. She made time. Corbin was well into his telling of the morning's events when they reached the perimeter gate.

To his enormous relief, Corbin saw a young chap wearing the bureau's armband and marking time beside an Enfield motorcycle the other side of the barrier.

"Thank goodness you made it sir," the courier said.

"When those pictures are published, you'll see how lucky I've truly been kid," Corbin replied as he handed over the bag to the lad. "God's speed buddy," Corbin said.

"And to you sir," the courier said as he sped off towards the A3.

Corbin tried once more to make a call up to London but got even shorter shrift from the guards at this gate.

"No sir, no way. Now make up your mind whether you're coming or going 'cos you can't loiter here," said an MP whose patience had been tested by the PA courier and was left in no mood for further persuasion.

Corbin figured he'd stay on base for the time being until he'd had a chance to report in. He turned back and started walking only to be delighted to find his ATS 'chauffeur' had hung around.

"Oh, I couldn't leave you all alone in this foreign land," she said.

"You have no idea how at home that makes me feel Miss…?"

"It's LeStrange, Samantha LeStrange, Sam for short," she said with a warm smile. Pretty without makeup or any airs and graces, she was what Stanley Holloway would call an English rose.

"So, you were behind that tank turret?" Sam said, easing Corbin back into his storytelling. Tired as he was Corbin was diving into some superfluous detail about Contax cameras when Sam slapped on the brakes like a boat anchor.

Standing dead ahead was a muscular man in his mid- twenties, legs firmly planted, and arms extended to level a Mauser automatic at Corbin's forehead. There wasn't an ounce of doubt behind that forehead that this guy would be as happy to shoot as ask questions, so he raised his hands. Sam wasn't following suit.

"You'll do well to follow your passenger's good example Miss," the man said.

Duke's threatening demeanor reflected the rigors of the return sailing and his repeated failure to corral his target. The rain had stopped but the sea state remained challenging and the going had been hard in the swell. Rather than risk Corbin eluding him again amongst the congestion disembarking the troop carrier, he had gone to the nearby sentry post to await him there. Only to find Corbin had already been and gone.

On learning of Corbin's East Gate objective, he set off in pursuit on foot. At his unburdened pace he'd expected to have caught up by now and was weighing his options when the Jeep approached.

He elected not to alert Corbin to Gubbins' suspicions, imagining the newsman would be even more reluctant to relinquish the films if he knew of their potential propaganda value. He expected Corbin to be reluctant nevertheless, but he was in no mood for protracted negotiation.

"Get out of the Jeep sir and hand over your films," Duke said.

"Hand over my films? Why in God's name would I do that?" Corbin said.

"Two very persuasive reasons sir: I just asked you nicely and I'm holding the gun," Duke replied.

"I'm a photographer pal not the village idiot so neither had escaped my attention. But you're going to have to give me a much better justification," Corbin said. Duke closed his eyes momentarily in exasperated disbelief.

"Sir, we have reason to believe that you have taken pictures of a top-secret nature and they must be handed over," Duke said.

"I wasn't the only photographer taking pictures over there this morning, are you confiscating their film too? And anyway, who's 'we'," Corbin retorted.

"We, sir, are the Supreme High Command and the pictures were taken last night here in HMS Nelson," Duke said.

Sam could feel her ATS career going down the drain of history with the gunman's last revelation. She admired Corbin's sang-froid at gunpoint so why, oh why had she taken pity on a chap so evidently capable of taking care of himself?

"I didn't take any pictures last night," Corbin snapped back, "I was holed up on a troop carrier from mid-afternoon to the get go," he added. Then he realized.

"Oh I get it. You must be talking about the camera testing I did on the dock. I didn't take any shots, or at least, I don't think I did," Corbin added.

"Well, given the uncertainty, we're going to need proof and we can only get that by reviewing all of your films. Last time of asking, please, hand them over. Once the sensitive pictures have been excised you can process whatever remains as normal."

"Well, I'm sorry pal but the films are already well on their way to our bureau chief in London," Corbin said. "If you want to stand any chance of catching up with them best you stop harassing us and get after them."

"Well since we've become such firm pals let's do just that," Duke said using the pistol's barrel to direct them back into the Jeep.

"Now look here," said Sam summoning up courage from she knew not where. "I'm already in over my wellies with this palaver. You chaps do as you please, but I was due back at my boss' beck and call half an hour ago."

"Miss you can either help me complete my mission or the next officer you play your face to will be convening your court martial," Duke said.

As Sam drove off from the East Gate, Corbin tossed the bundled Burberry towards the short-tempered guard and shouted,

"Cheerio, old chap and thanks for all your help!"

27. Knightsbridge, London - 17:30h

Although Brand's mother tongue had lain mostly dormant in recent years, it was infinitely better than Trager's English, so they spoke German. Kastner had continued to insist on Trager speaking in English till now and he took full advantage of the regained freedom on their way to pick up Brand's car. By the time they were parking outside Kiki's flat, Brand knew more about Trager's background than he thought imaginable.

In another time this amiable giant would have lived out an unremarkable agrarian life in Bavaria with only the annual Oktoberfest to add spice. Adolescence in the Hitler-Jugend had set him on an altogether different trajectory in the service of his Führer. His father had been a member of the regular army in WWI and had been disappointed when his son was recruited by the SS. The civilian roots of the Schutzstaffel and its early exploits in Bavaria reflected a different understanding of patriotic service than Trager Senior had dutifully pledged to his Kaiser.

Brand had already called Kiki to ask if he could drop off some prints Corbin had expressed an interest in at a recent get together. Although she couldn't see the big hurry given Corbin's likely extended absence, she didn't want to seem unfriendly and told Brand to bring them round.

"We're collecting a trunk of personal effects from number 15, we're expected," Brand told the concierge who called up to announce Kiki's visitors. Kiki was even more puzzled to hear Brand wasn't alone but thought little of it.

When she saw the stranger was as tall as Brand and much broader, her anxiety mounted. Brand's measured familiarity and the mammoth's smile calmed her somewhat. She offered them cocktails that were refused and apologized for not preparing any food as her housekeeper had left for the day.

"She'll be celebrating the beginning of the end," Brand said paraphrasing Churchill. With that Brand stealthily closed the distance between himself and Kiki and, spinning her round, cupped her mouth with his right hand and restrained her arms with his left.

In what Brand was happy to see was a syncopated action, Trager doused a handkerchief with the chloroform Brand had given him and held it to Kiki's nose. Sadly for Trager he didn't take the precaution of approaching her side on and Kiki's right knee connected with his gonads before the drug could sedate her.

Not to embarrass Trager further, Brand kept a smile off his face and asked the man mountain to go find Kiki's steamer trunk. He couldn't be sure Kiki possessed one, but it would give Trager some privacy to check if fatherhood was still an option in his future. And it allowed Brand to gaze on Kiki's form for a while, undistracted.

Kidnapping Kiki was less bootstrap, more overkill but now he'd been flushed out of cover Brand had decided to bid six spades. If caught in England, he'd be hanged. If brought to account in a beleaguered Germany, he'd probably be shot. A Lady of the Realm might prove useful collateral in ensuing negotiations and would certainly help lure Corbin in, if necessary. And besides, from the moment he'd first seen her, he'd wanted a chance to photograph this remarkable woman.

Trager came back into the room with a large trunk, and they placed Kiki, gagged and bound, inside having slit half a dozen inconspicuous air holes into it. Brand sent Trager down to the car with the trunk and followed a short distance behind so he could either placate or neutralize the concierge as required. He need not have worried: Trager was able to carry the trunk with such ease that the concierge would never have imagined its content.

"Mind how you go," the concierge said as they exited the building.

28. 85 Fleet St., London - 18:15h

After waiting across the street for a couple of hours Kastner decided to get closer to the drop point. With fabricated assurance he strode into the Press Association headquarters as though he belonged. As a former journalism major he was curious to explore a building he'd heard so much about. As well as the PA, 85 Fleet Street housed bureaus and representative offices of all the world's major press and picture agencies.

It was the nerve centre of Fleet Street and the famous English newspapers - The Times, The Telegraph, The Express - all traded nearby. They tapped into number 85 for raw material from around the globe that their own staff networks couldn't provide.

Kastner was delighted to see an attractive young woman manning the reception desk.

"Good Evening Miss," Kastner said, deliberately ignoring the band on her third finger left hand. "I'm visiting my old friend Mr. Coley on the third floor, alright if I go straight up, I'm in rather a hurry?" he added as he signed in as a Mr. Bentley.

Before entering he'd waited until a taxi full of visitors drew up outside and gotten into the building just in front of them.

"Do you have an appointment sir?" the girl asked as the other visitors crowded her desk and Kastner made way for them.

"No, but Frank will be very happy to see me, rest assured" Kastner said as he began climbing the stairs.

The men at the desk were journalists here to pick up a Reuters sub editor and then continue a lunch that had begun at the Wig and Pen Club six hours earlier.

"Cam on darlin'," the pack leader said. "Let's not shilly-shally, get Smithers down here pronto and we'll be on our way quicker than you can say Jack Robinson."

The girl was well-educated and well brought up and resented being patronized on account of her mild Cockney accent. Judging by the fumes, these scribblers had been macerating their livers for hours, and her best bet was to comply and be rid of them.

Kastner continued to find the directions Brand had given him deadly accurate and had no trouble locating Coley's bureau. As he walked down the main corridor, he could see into a newsroom crowded to untidiness with furniture, typewriters and reams of paper and, happily, very few people.

A man fitting Coley's description was pacing a glass-paneled office in the far corner. Kastner walked back towards the top of the stairs, snuck into an adjacent closet, and waited with the door ajar. He didn't have long to wait before a motorcycle courier bounded up the last flight of stairs and made to turn towards the newsroom. Kastner exited the closet in a brown cow-gown he'd found hanging there and, with a cigarette between his lips and an accentuated limp in his gait, asked the young man for a light.

"You look like you've been riding hard my lad while I've been pushing a broom all day" Kastner said.

"Not half sir, I've been riding like the clappers from Portsmouth," the courier said.

"Oh really, what's all the hurry then?" Kastner said.

"In here's the first pictures from the landing beaches, a scoop if ever there were one," the teenager said.

With that the pimply, perspiring youth condemned himself to a short life that ended in a cloud of cigarette smoke at the tip of Kastner's favourite blade. Kastner released the grip that had suppressed the boy's last cry and dragged his body into the closet.

He searched the pannier bag the lad had been carrying and found four films with the undeveloped stickers still wound tight around them. Together with a note from Corbin to Coley saying which films had the best shots.

As Kastner left unhindered, Mr. Smithers was still nowhere to be found and the beleaguered receptionist was suffering yet more tomfoolery from his blotto pals.

29. Belgravia, London - 19:15h

Kastner was impressed by the location and luxury of Brand's apartment building. His teenage stay in England had been suburban and mundane. He clung to the hope that the Third Reich would last a thousand years and that he'd plunder comparable trappings for himself and his descendants. A successful mission with the Strong Man would certainly help his cause.

Tales of the riches plundered in conquered countries were rife within the officer cadre. Senior SS officers were purloining immense personal wealth and securing a comfortable future for themselves in the new order. There was a compelling incentive to gain high rank and with it a share in the sequestered pie.

Kastner handed the films over to Brand.

"No problems?" Brand asked.

"None. The courier needed some persuasion to surrender the films, but my response went undetected," Kastner reassured him.

"You killed him?" Brand asked.

Kastner nodded with a smile.

"If that's your idea of leaving no loose ends Kastner I'll have to be more specific in future," Brand said. "I'm going to get these films developed. We'll be leaving as soon as I'm done."

Brand hurried to his darkroom and began developing the films in the order suggested in Corbin's spidery editorial note. By the time he had two developed films hanging in the drying cabinet there were still no images of Churchill or Rommel to support Kastner's story.

He was nurturing a suspicion Kastner had inflated his narrative for some reason. Perhaps he had seen something significant last night, but a treacherous act by Rommel seemed far-fetched and just as likely an SS ruse to discredit the Field-Marshall.

With no ready way of knowing for sure and with Berlin willing to draw him out of cover to pursue the matter, Brand decided to persevere. He was about to begin work on the last film when he heard a loud crash and rushed out to find the source.

Ostensibly Kastner had entered Brand's bedroom just to observe the creature who had done such damage to his humungous colleague's privates. Once inside though he was unable to resist the opportunity to mess with a partially bound, groggy woman. He might have guessed from Trager's discomfort that Kiki was unlikely to take this unwelcome approach lying down.

Sure enough, Kiki rounded on Kastner like a dervish, kicking and hissing as she wrenched against her wrist bindings. In a deluded attempt to calm her down Kastner had drawn his knife and was feinting it at her when Brand entered.

Brand grabbed Kastner at the plexus under his right arm releasing the knife and then delivered a blow to the back of his neck that rendered him unconscious.

In truth he'd wanted to give Kastner a slap on hearing of the courier's unnecessary demise, so this opportunity to dole out some punishment was welcome. However he anticipated a reaction from Trager and turned to deal with it. It didn't materialize. Trager had followed Brand so far then stopped, filling the bedroom doorway as he watched him cope with Kastner.

"If you have any issues with my treatment of your colleague Trager, we should address them now," Brand said.

"I have none," said Trager. "Kastner's cruelty will be the death of him someday. What do we do now?"

"I'm going to take some pictures of this woman with your help, then you will deliver them to Fleet Street," Brand said.

Brand would have liked to have taken some artistic pictures of this beautiful woman, but she was in no mood and there was no time for art, just artifice. Retrieving a new instant camera he'd been asked to critique by an American friend, he set about his work.

While Trager popped out for a copy of the evening paper, Brand posed Kiki as best her humour would allow and took a test picture. The colour representation of this new-fangled camera left something to be desired, but the likeness was good enough.

It was only when Trager returned and asked if he could cook some supper that Brand remembered the drying cabinet and he darted back to the darkroom. The protracted heat had melted the emulsion off the carrier of two of Corbin's films. The other looked like a good printer might be able to extract a dozen images and Brand, in empathy and shame, was almost of a mind to do the work.

But he had enough on his to-do list already and they needed to be getting out of town. He cut the negatives and put them into sleeves before adding them to the envelope with a shot of Kiki holding the newspaper and a short note to Corbin and Coley demanding any other film from the eve of D-Day.

He gave the envelope and a set of false license plates for the Austin to Trager and sent him on his way.

30. 85, Fleet St, London 19:20h

Before the war Duke had been destined for a career in journalism and had worked two internships on Fleet Street while at Oxford. He was a gifted linguist and part of a new breed of scribbler that didn't believe the world best viewed through the prism of a pint pot. As a gopher he'd endured plenty the like of Smither's pals and, ordinarily, wouldn't have given them the time of day. But enough time had been lost already.

"Excuse me gentlemen, Miss can you direct to Mr. Coley's office please, it's very urgent," Duke said as Corbin rushed in behind him.

The leader of the pack was already angry that after adjourning to a nearby bar for another hour, Smithers still wasn't downstairs. He didn't take lightly to having his harassment of the receptionist interrupted.

"Ooh, gentlemen are we now, well how's about you get to the back of the queue sonny?" he said.

Before he could turn to revel in the cackling of his mates, the drunk's left cheek hit the receptionist's desk hard. Simultaneously his writing hand took an excruciating journey up to the nape of his neck and the cackling stopped. The journalist was in great pain made unendurable by none of his buddies lifting a finger to help him.

"Now Miss, Mr. Coley's office please?" Duke repeated, unperturbed by the pathetic wriggling of his prey.

The receptionist thought this was one instance when she could forego the formality of a sign in and gave Duke his directions before calling up to Coley. Duke whispered some advice to the whimpering journalist before releasing him and bounded off towards the stairs with Corbin in hot pursuit.

Sam was no longer part of Duke's impromptu team. At a Home Guard checkpoint near Liss all three had been detained on the orders of Admiral Sir John LeStrange, Sam's uncle. Having pulled strings to get her onto his staff as a driver, the Admiral had been furious when Sam had gone AWOL that morning of all mornings. And the Admiral's adjutant had been in no mood to comprehend or validate Duke's explanation.

While Duke was placating the adjutant, Corbin took the opportunity to call Coley and hear that the courier had not yet delivered the films. This seemed odd but, as he and Duke were demonstrating, there were ample ways to squander precious time when the South Coast was on full alert.

Once the Admiral and Gubbins had parlayed, Duke was found a motorcycle and sidecar and wished Sam no hard feelings before she set off back to Portsmouth and a keelhauling from her uncle.

Not since his boyhood had Corbin ridden in a sidecar and he couldn't recall traveling in any vehicle as fast. Glancing up at Duke every time a seemingly certain crash was narrowly avoided, he was reminded of what he'd read and heard of the exploits of the Arabian adventurer, T. E. Lawrence. Although much taller, Duke's swept blonde hair, patrician nose and tanned skin all exuded the same air of come what may.

Coley met them halfway up the third flight and rushed them back into his office. Corbin introduced Duke and gave Coley a sketch of salient events. Coley's mild irritation at now having to deal with the spooks as well as the official censor was heavily outweighed by his relief at seeing Corbin in good shape. The unfiltered reports coming back from Omaha Beach were harrowing and he'd doubted he'd ever see Corbin again. Although he was his most capricious shooter, Corbin was also the most fun and his work was par excellence.

"Which still leaves us with your missing films and a looming New York deadline," Coley said.

He'd gone as far as dress rehearsing the journey Corbin's prints would have to take from his darkroom to New York and was acutely aware of how little slack was available in the timescale.

"I don't think we're going to make it, especially now we have to keep Mr. Duke's shadowy friends happy," Coley said.

"Don't worry on that account Mr. Coley," Duke said. "I'll do everything I can to rush the remaining pictures through all channels once we've extracted those of interest to my boss."

"Thank you but unless my dispatch rider shows up soon it'll all be for naught,' Coley said. "He must have crashed. Is there anything your people can do to track him down?"

Although he didn't fancy his chances, Duke was placing a call to try when an ear-splitting scream came from the corridor. A rotund cleaning lady in a floral turban and matching apron was running down its length as best she could and screaming like a banshee. Coley caught up with her and met an air of cheap scent and even cheaper gin as she waved frantically back towards the closet at the top of the stairs, unable to wheeze any commentary.

Duke followed her gesticulations back to the closet, the murdered courier and his empty knapsack. Corbin confirmed this was the same fellow he'd handed his films to in Portsmouth and that a note to Coley was also missing.

All three men had seen their share of horror, but the double S carved on the boy's forehead gave them pause. Not only were the letters perfectly proportioned, but they were also incised into the flesh with a V-shape, the cuttings scraped off whatever tool had been used onto the boy's leather jacket. The psychopathic carver had clearly taken time and pleasure leaving his mark on this poor boy.

"Who in hell could have done that?" Corbin asked no one in particular.

"I don't know," Duke said, as he gently closed the boy's eyelids. "But you've rightly identified the bastard's origin."

Downstairs the receptionist was now sitting in the shadow of one of the biggest men she'd ever laid eyes on. He said the envelope was for Mr. Coley and before she could get anyone in Coley's office to answer, the giant had walked away, bowlegged.

31. Belgravia, London - 20.20h

Trager's nether regions were more comfortable walking than sitting and he was glad to squeeze out of the Austin after parking it where Brand had instructed. Nevertheless he gave Kiki credit for standing up for herself. When he arrived back at Brand's flat, he found her sitting bound and gagged next to two bags in the hallway. Kastner explained.

"He wants to get out of London and closer to an escape route through Eire. We'll be leaving soon." Kastner saw Trager's puzzlement and added, "Southern Ireland." Trager's puzzlement was with the direction rather than the destination, but he made nothing of the accustomed condescension.

They draped a coat over Kiki's shoulders and trooped over the road to the Alvis where Brand handed the keys to Trager. It was a snug fit but compared to the Austin this car was a pleasure to drive despite its heavy payload. Brand sat in the back behind Kastner and when they were out on the open road removed Kiki's gag and the scarf covering it. It was several minutes and a few dagger-like stares before she took advantage of the freedom to speak.

"Where are you taking me?" she said with a slow, measured timbre she hoped would mask her fear. She doubted Brand or the huge German were given to cruelty, but this other Nazi was demonstrably different. He did smell like the enemy, and she saw in his furtive eyes that he wouldn't hesitate to pick up where Brand's intervention had forced him to leave off.

"We'll be spending a day or two in the country," Brand said. "As soon as Corbin and his friends let us have something they don't really need, you'll be free to go."

"If, whatever it is, is such a trifle why are you going to all this trouble to get it?" Kiki asked.

"Because war makes us all do strange things," Brand replied.

"You know how many friends we have, many in high places, so good luck getting away it," Kiki said.

Brand was content to wave this off with a nod of his head and a slow blink. The journey to Bath would be a long one and there was no point making the atmosphere any more disagreeable than it already was. Kastner had other ideas. Swiveling in his seat towards Kiki he exclaimed a warning at a volume which was both unnecessary and unwelcome in the confined space.

"Be quiet bitch! We won't hesitate to kill you and your high and mighty friends if they get in our way!"

Brand reached forward and patted Kastner's right shoulder lightly in a gesture that could pass as encouraging but was really meant as a painful reminder. Kastner tried to freeze his reflexive flinch, but Brand and Kiki sensed it and were glad the incident at the flat had left its dent in his perverted psyche. Brand knew Kastner would be looking for an early opportunity to regain some respect and would be dangerous until then, and likely beyond.

He'd heard how the Eastern Front had depleted the SS allowing twisted characters like Kastner to rise up. Self-promoting, avaricious and mindless in professed obedience to their Führer, they were unpredictable and loathe to take orders from superiors not in a position to aid their advancement.

Now Kastner's respect for Brand's storied reputation was wearing thin, he'd require careful handling and regular reminders of his own frailty.

32. 85 Fleet Street, 20:00h

The receptionist had been eager to get home before dark and leave all the madness behind her. A police interview, the ambulancemen requiring access to the service elevator and fending off numerous journalists had made her tarry. Then the night watchman who relieved her was just as eager to hear all the gossip about the dead courier.

It was another half an hour before he had gotten round to taking Brand's envelope up to Coley's office. The City of London police were still interviewing Duke and Coley and Corbin, dead beat, was snoozing. The watchman nudged Corbin and he roused with a start.

The "URGENT" signs that had made so little impact on the receptionist and the watchman gnawed at Corbin as he tore the envelope open. As he stared at Kiki's defiant expression in the Polaroids it was as if his innards had been drawn.

He dashed across the newsroom to where Duke, Coley and a police inspector were finishing up, skimming the enclosed note as he went. In his haste he didn't review the exposed negatives included in the envelope or register the name of the note's author.

Only when the police inspector read the note aloud did it dawn on Corbin his fellow smudger was conjuring up this torment.

"What the hell do we do now?" Corbin pleaded.

Part Six – 7th June 1944

33. The Royal Crescent, Bath - 01:15h

"Take the next left then second right," Brand instructed Trager.

Trager had exceeded the speed limit only when prudent, driving very steadily despite his lack of rest so that even Kiki, in her riled state, was able to grab some sleep. Brand was tempted to do likewise but, mindful of the danger of Kastner catching him unawares, he stayed en garde. A small torch and a clutch of Daily Telegraph crosswords had helped.

"Pull up just here Trager," Brand said. As Kastner got out of the car, he deliberately left his seat down rather than help Brand. Trager attempted to help Kiki exit, but she would have none of it, retaining what dignity she could with her hands bound and her gag, scarf and drape restored.

As Kastner cast his eyes around the majestic shallow arc of the Royal Crescent his dwindling respect for Brand was morphing into a green, caustic envy. The Crescent was one of the most elegant streets in Europe and Kastner held a mental picture of it from being forced to read illustrated editions of Jane Austen in secondary school.

As bright moonlight bounced off its myriad Ionic pillars the mental picture was surpassed. The setting was marred somewhat by the exigency of vegetable allotments and beanpoles where once a graceful green sward had swept the eye away. But the Crescent and the nearby Circus retained their magnificence.

Brand was happy to find the buildings in good shape. Heritage optimists who hoped Bath was off-limits to the Luftwaffe had been given a rude awakening during the Baedeker Raids in April 1942. Numbers 2 and 17 had taken the brunt and his damage at the western end of the terrace had been limited to broken glazing and damaged roof slates, since repaired.

They hurried Kiki into the house and, before turning on the lights, Brand checked that the blackout curtains were drawn tight. The city's denizens were still paranoid about the risk of more bombing and the last thing Brand needed was a visit from some officious air raid warden.

"I suggest we all get some rest," Brand said. "They'll be some canned meat and soda crackers in the kitchen if you're hungry," he added.

Trager was ravenous and needed no further invitation. In ten minutes he reappeared with a tray loaded with the best the charlady had been able to buy with Brand's ration book. Meantime Kastner had skulked off to the basement to sleep and Brand had released Kiki and made her as comfortable as she chose to be.

She picked at the plate Trager passed her now Kastner was mercifully out of sight. She appreciated the need to keep her strength up ready for any opportunity to escape.

Their hunger sated, Brand directed Trager to a bedroom on the first floor and Kiki to one on the second. Confident Trager wouldn't misbehave, he would sleep on a day bed in the ground-floor hallway with the safety off his trusty Bolo automatic.

From there he could guard the stairs and monitor the street from the hall window once the house lights were off and the blackout curtains could be opened. And from the vantage point of a higher position over Kastner, he could finally relax a little.

34. The A40 near Reading, England – 08:30h

If the motorcycle ride up to London had its hairy moments, the drive down to Bath had Corbin's every hackle raised. Duke had swapped the bike for one of his uncle's cars in Mayfair. On hearing the Bentley's thunderous engine echo around the mews, Corbin anticipated more butt clenching miles. The four seater had been supercharged and its 240 horsepower propelled the long bonnet into the road ahead like a missile.

"Don't fret old chap," Duke said. "We'll be there in no time. This beauty can pass anything but a petrol pump."

Conscious of the Bentley's prodigious thirst Duke had loaded up the back seat with jerry cans of gas his uncle had hoarded in the garage. With the top down the inevitable fumes were not a problem. Whenever he felt Duke could afford to be distracted Corbin shared his insights into Brand's work and character.

"He's a walking contradiction. There's no mistaking the silver spoon in his mouth but he works very hard to disguise it," Corbin said. He's also gifted so heaven knows why he was attracted to service for the Nazis."

The tone was disparaging but Duke sensed that had more to do with Kiki's abduction. Corbin evidently respected Brand's insouciance and admired his work.

Brand had done a decent enough job covering his tracks but not everything was as watertight as Duke had expected. His colleagues had a growing file on Brand, but they'd never been able to gather enough evidence to step into him. There's was always just enough plausibility to encourage moving on to easier prey, of which there was plenty.

The fact he'd left the Bath connection discoverable disquieted Duke. It could be a red herring, but it was the best lead they had, and the alternative of clicking their heels in London appealed to neither Corbin's temperament nor his own. Duke's colleagues back in the SOE's Baker Street HQ had promised to keep digging and he'd pledged to call in regularly for updates.

Given Kiki's notoriety and Duke's lack of success, Gubbins had offered other agents to join the mission even though resources were stretched wafer thin. Duke had declined in deference to the Landings telling Gubbins and Corbin it was better to keep some resources in reserve should Bath prove to be a false trail. It was a cogent line and gained Duke the latitude he needed to try and redeem himself.

Corbin would take all the help he could get, feeling guilty for having put Kiki in Brand's sights. But he couldn't argue with Duke's reasoning and hoped to God this chase would lead to Brand and some sweet revenge.

35. La Roche-Guyon - 09:25h

Speidel had hoped to have seen the last of Goebbels' messengers, but they were back. From their expressions it looked as if they were enjoying their work.

"We must see the Field Marshal at once," the senior officer said.

"You're aware that we are quite busy?" Speidel replied sarcastically.

It was enough to set them off and they bundled past Speidel and into Rommel's office before Speidel could draw his pistol. Rommel looked up from his desk calmly and motioned Speidel to holster his weapon.

"Herr Field Marshall you are to stand by for a call from the Berchesgarten at 09:30 hours," the SS officer said.

"Of course," Rommel replied. He'd been expecting Goebbel's call and had been rehearsing solid rebuttals since hearing about the Reichsminister's misgivings. Sending his henchmen again was heavy-handed but typical of Goebbels' attention to detail and a reminder of a self-importance only ever subordinated in obsequious service to his master.

The difficulty they'd had rousing the Führer for permission to unleash the Panzer Reserve had lulled Rommel into not expecting Hitler to be on the call. But Rommel was unaware of Dahlmer's signal. The U-Boat commander had included mention of sighting Rommel in his report to U-Boat headquarters.

Ordinarily Commanders' signals were reviewed by Kriegsmarine High Command before on-send to Berlin. This was no ordinary day, and the unverified Rommel sighting was included in dispatches to Berlin before Admiral Dönitz had it recanted as an error. The Admiral wanted to question Rommel himself before making such an accusation. Goebbels had seen the withdrawn report and had no such reticence.

Rommel was unsettled by the spiteful voice that addressed him.

"History is littered with the treachery of generals but your deeds will be truly infamous," Hitler said.

Rommel had no desire to conduct his defense over the phone and had no illusion it would have any impact now Goebbels had cut him adrift.

"Lucie and the children are under surveillance and if you wish to see them whole again you will do exactly as Reichsminister Goebbels tells you," Hitler continued.

Rommel had rehearsed a stoic reaction to this anticipated threat to his family. But hearing his wife's name spoken with such vehemence by the Führer himself unnerved him, as much as it amused Goebbels' goons who were under orders to observe him throughout the call and report on his demeanor.

Before he could regain his composure Hitler, incandescent with rage, slammed his receiver down, leaving Goebbels to continue the lopsided conversation.

"You will become a channel of misinformation to your new friend Mr. Churchill," Goebbels hissed.

"For now, you will carry out your duty to the Fatherland upon your honor as a soldier of the Reich," he continued.

"But you will be closely monitored. If we detect any further treachery the next sight you have of your children will be of their severed heads on pikestaffs."

36. The Royal Crescent, Bath – 09:50h

After their exertions Brand wasn't surprised when Kiki and Trager slept in soundly. Wary of Kastner's behavior he'd been checking on him regularly through the night and the problem child had not left the basement. With little down there to form the basis of mischief, Brand had taken advantage of the respite to snatch some sleep and do some travel planning. He was inclined to stick with his plan to head west.

In common with other geopolitical schisms, the Reich had been probing how to exploit the IRA's conflict with the British government for years. In the thirties introits to IRA leadership had focused on how best to aid a secession and a reunification of Ireland in concert with Operation Sea Lion – the invasion of mainland Britain. A combined Ireland would retain its independence much like Spain, Hitler's envoys had maintained.

Brand's assassination mission had been part of those outreach operations. The shortlist of targets had included the King, Montgomery and Lord Mountbatten, but Churchill had abiding appeal to an organisation that had been wanting to kidnap or kill him since a plot in 1922 – the circumstances of which had brought Walter Thompson into Churchill's entourage as a personal detective.

Back then Brand had mixed feelings about the choice of Churchill. He shared Hitler's begrudging respect for the showman, but he'd never expected him to become PM and he felt the King and his Queen might prove to be much more significant to British morale. Their refusal to be evacuated to Canada; their defiant, post air raid appearances in the East End; and the King's distracting travels to Malta and North Africa had borne Brand out to an extent.

Nevertheless Brand had accepted the IRA's preference and seemed to make promising progress at first. But infighting within Sinn Fein led to regular command changes making it very difficult to maintain a course of action. Then when Goering's Luftwaffe lost the Battle of Britain and Hitler backburnered a British invasion, the Nazis' Eire ambitions were scaled back to merely encouraging the country's continued neutral stance.

Brand had been left with a network of contacts in Eire many of whom, he felt sure, would be interested in exploiting the embarrassment value of Corbin's photographs, and resurrecting plans to kill Churchill. First, he had to get across South Wales and secure a ferry passage to the Irish Republic.

Nazi political intrigue had also targeted the Principality during the Thirties reaching out to Plaid Cymru's leadership. They proved less responsive to plotting Churchill's demise despite his military suppression of the Tonypandy Riots. Except for twenty odd party members who asserted national allegiance to Wales as grounds for conscientious objection, Plaid Cymru remained in step with Westminster and the seeds of Nazi collaboration fell on unaccommodating Welsh slate.

By following the A40 Brand's party would stay well north of Cardiff, Swansea and other industrial centres. Luftwaffe attacks had tailed off considerably but there was little point in taking the risk. A route through the Brecon Mountains would be scenic by day and unimpeded by night, providing they avoided military training exercises.

The Alvis was running magnificently, and he'd had Trager transfer a reserve of hoarded gasoline to the trunk after the giant had fed and watered himself. Next, he needed to check his emergency exit, just in case of need. In the basement he found Kastner cleaning a 45-caliber version of the popular Walther handgun. Brand wondered how Kastner had gotten hold of this experimental version of the P-38, especially one with the uncommon Walnut grips but he suppressed his avid curiosity until he might use the topic to distract the deviant.

After pleasantries of a sort, Brand purported to be retrieving supplies for the journey and went into the next room to check the escape route. Behind a sliding shelf unit, he found it pretty much how the excavators had left it in 1938. They'd never had cause to build an air-raid shelter quite that long and narrow before, especially for a single-family residence, but Brand had assured them it was intended to serve the neighbourhood not just himself.

All seemed in order, so he repositioned the concealment, collected a carton of canned pilchards from its shelves, and retraced to where Kastner was no longer. He dashed upstairs to find Trager engaging with Kastner in the kitchen. Brand had a sense Trager was developing a pronounced protective instinct towards Kiki and suspected she had been Kastner's objective until Trager had waylaid him.

"The propaganda and military value of that film is eroding by the hour," said Kastner. "I hope you have a plan to get them, if not us, back to Germany where they can be exploited?"

Brand wasn't sure Kastner was reading the tea leaves correctly. Even if incriminating images were on the fourth film, it was unlikely even Goebbels could spin Rommel's treachery into a patriotic narrative. Despite his setbacks in Africa and his largely unheralded work on the Atlantic Wall, Rommel was still a hero of the Reich and any discredit on him would reflect just as badly on the whole regime. And after Hess' defection it would be very difficult to frame the venture as an elaborate deception.

Alternatively portraying the meeting as a desperate Allied attempt to sue for peace would fly in the face of daily saturation bombing of the Fatherland and informal reports from Normandy of Allied successes. The true value of the films now lay in how a third party like the IRA could use them.

"Of course," Brand replied. "We'll be setting off as soon as we've all breakfasted."

Kastner sneered at this bourgeoise affectation, viewing it as pandering to Kiki's frailty and another sign of Brand not being a true Arian.

"The British authorities will by now be in hot pursuit, and I doubt you've covered your tracks that well, given all the trappings of your ostentatious lifestyle," Kastner needled.

"A hot pursuit enlivened by your unnecessary killing last night," Brand said.

"An important aspect of our mission was successfully accomplished," Kastner replied.

Although tempted, Brand realized continued argument would only consume more time and, with a long journey ahead, there was little point getting this unstable character het up again.

"Very well Kastner, you are correct, we should be making tracks," Brand said. "Trager, please go and rouse the Lady and ask her to get ready quickly. We can pack her some food for the journey."

Brand really did think Kastner was right about one thing. Whoever Corbin had enlisted to help rescue his titled girlfriend would be able to draw on Scotland Yard and, perhaps, the SOE to help track them down. There was nothing at his London flat to link him to the Bath property and there were few beyond The Crescent who knew of Brand's ownership. But it wouldn't take a smart investigator more than a few phone calls to pick the trail up again.

Trager came back downstairs in what was, for him, a state of some perturbation.

"She's locked the door and isn't answering," he reported.

"Are you sure?" asked Kastner.

Brand didn't wait for any answer to that particularly dumb question. He grabbed the master key ring from the hall table and raced up to the second floor with Trager in close formation. He doubted Kiki had tried to leave via the casement window. It was over 30 feet down to the ground with five and seven feet separating the window from the two drainpipes. But he couldn't be sure how desperate a fretful night might have made her.

Kiki continued unresponsive to the knock, so he unlocked the door and stepped in, wary of her exact whereabouts and intentions. Trager remained courteously at the threshold once more until Brand signaled whether he wanted him to enter.

The room was in total darkness but the light from the doorway revealed Kiki on the bed face up under a sheer silk sheet which barely disguised her nudity. She'd made use of an eye shield and earbuds from the dresser and, judging by the bottle on the bedside table, had taken one or more tranquilizer pills. Her mouth was closed and her breathing shallow. Brand checked her pulse at her neck finding it steady at sixty-five. His touch was enough to rouse her, and she reared up with a start baring her torso.

By now Kastner had caught up and had barged past Trager. Brand quickly raised the sheet to cover Kiki, thwarting Kastner's boyish gawping while Kiki uncovered her eyes and ears.

"We have to be on our way," Brand informed her. "Please get dressed immediately."

Despite the sedative Kiki gathered her composure instantly and glared at him with a refreshed vehemence.

"What choice do I have?" she hissed back.

Before Kastner could get her day off to another belligerent start Brand ushered him out of the room without responding.

37. London Road, Bath – 10:05h

Duke was pleased with how far the Bentley had progressed on two tanks of petrol, but it was time for another top up and a call back to HQ for an update. He left Corbin to deal with the refueling and headed over to the telephone box. Happy to find the box in good order he pressed the A Button to deposit his coins and place his call.

His colleague shared Brand's address and added a warning. A lackadaisical report from a checkpoint in Reading indicated Brand and Lady Brown were travelling with two additional males. Their descriptions suggested both could be dangerous but neither more so than Brand who, according to trusted sources, was well-educated, a crack shot and skilled in martial arts.

His colleague urged him to seek out the help of the Bath Constabulary and offered to contact them on his behalf. Duke accepted the offer but said he couldn't guarantee he'd be able to wait on them. Time was of the essence and if they were still in Bath they needed to intercept them before the trail went cold again.

Duke signed off, pushed the B button to retrieve his precious change and headed back over to Corbin to share the new intel and lay out a plan.

"You can wait for the Bobbies if you like but I'm heading there tout de suite!" Corbin said.

In his last evaluation Duke had been criticized for occasional impetuosity and had been urged to temper that tendency. Although he was mindful of this being an excellent opportunity to do just that, he also agreed with Corbin's assessment of the flight risk. They forged on.

38. The Royal Crescent, Bath – 10:20h

Duke had, he thought, parked well away from Brand's property but it was a quiet morning on the Terrace, and he'd underestimated Brand's acute hearing and his passion for automobiles. Brand had been awaiting Kiki's descent in the drawing room having dispatched Trager to refuel and load the Alvis. On hearing the discernable whine of a Bentley supercharger enter the Terrace he strolled over to the window and conned Corbin and his travelling companion, who looked for all the world like a fellow secret agent.

Duke and Corbin made their way over to Brand's property via the Ha Ha, a ditch which separated the upper and lower lawns unaware they had already been spotted. By the time they got to the front door Brand had collected Kiki and followed the others downstairs and into the shelter.

With his pistol unholstered Duke rang the doorbell just as a Black Maria drew up and offloaded three burly West Country constables, their sergeant and, to Duke's amazement, a woman police constable. Still hearing no answer they shouldered the door.

The door jamb splintered the peace of the Crescent as three eighths of the Bath Rugby Club's scrum charged into Brand's hallway and fanned out, truncheons at the ready. After five minutes of frantic searching of the above ground storeys, Duke led them over to the cellar door.

The light switch didn't shed any light, and rather than investigate why, Duke borrowed the WPC's flashlight and led the way down the stairs. The air was musty, with overtones of machine oil and what the WPC thought might be Chanel No5, though she didn't dare share her intuition. There was no sign of Brand, Kiki or anyone else.

Behind the shelving unit masking the shelter, strict silence was being maintained. Once Kiki had been gagged again as a precaution, it was lights out. Brand had wanted to sit Trager down to create more airspace but the seldom used springs of the bunk beds couldn't be entrusted with his bulk. So, bar Kiki, they all stood at the far end of the shelter, uncomfortably close, conscious of each other's breathing.

Kiki became aware of that evil smell again, just as she had at Newmarket. This time there was no doubt from whom it emanated. Her face being no more than six inches from Kastner's scrawny backside made it as attributable as it was nauseating. She turned to face away, creaking a spring as she did so, and prompting Brand to draw his pistol.

The sound carried faintly into the cellar beyond prompting Duke to call for absolute silence. After a minute that seemed like an eternity, it was dismissed as something old houses give off from time to time and the search party withdrew to the ground floor.

From his schooldays Duke knew old houses also habitually featured hiding places and he had a nagging suspicion one had been overlooked in their search. He asked the sergeant to keep a sentry posted at the property for a least a day after their departure just in case some fugitives came out of the woodwork. Then he went to report into base and source any further leads.

On handing the flashlight back to the WPC Duke congratulated her on her service. She had become something of a local celebrity when recruited alongside some three hundred other women into the twenty thousand strong English Police Force. As serving police officers began volunteering for military service en masse, various backfill measures were deemed necessary, even female recruitment. Most WPCs were consigned to administrative duties hence Duke's surprise at seeing one being sent out on a call.

"You must be highly regarded to be sent out on a shout," he said. Duke hadn't intended his words to be so patronizing but, no sooner had he given them breath, he rued them.

The WPC was inured to bias, overt and explicit. It wasn't by chance her flashlight had been the one he 'borrowed', but rather his conditioning. And his 'compliment' was no more offensive than she received daily at the station, or at home for that matter. Her father had been dead set against her joining the Force.

"Yes, I'm really lucky," she replied. "We have a chimpanzee trained to make the tea back at the nick. Leaves me free to venture out with the boys once in a blue moon" she added with a melodic Gloucestershire burr.

Corbin let out a guffaw despite the frustration of the futile search and the marking time. He wasn't a stranger to the odd chauvinistic gaffe himself, but he'd thought Duke's flirting monumentally ham-fisted. She was emboldened to continue.

"I don't suppose you caught that whiff of fresh perfume in the cellar? Chanel No5 I think."

At the mention of Kiki's favourite undergarment Corbin bolted for the cellar door and hardly touched the stairs as he made his descent. The rest piled in after him and the search resumed with renewed purpose. After a few more everlasting minutes the hidden door was discovered and opened to reveal no-one.

No sooner had the search party evacuated the cellar earlier, Brand had ushered his three companions through a second concealed door at the far end of the shelter and up into the garage of his mews house behind the main property. Trager had pushed the Alvis out into Marlborough Gardens and north a piece before joining them aboard and starting the engine. By the time Duke realized his oversight they'd put three miles between the Alvis and the Crescent.

Duke got back onto London to ask for fresh alerts to be broadcast and the Police Sergeant followed suit. Duke knew Brand would be keeping to B roads, at least until he'd broadened the necessary search area, so the chances of a checkpoint catching him out were slim. Duke could either wait for a tip off or get back out on the road. But which way?

"This Bath trip had either been in the hope of holing up for a while or a waypoint en route to somewhere else," Duke reasoned with Corbin. "With well over a hundred overlooking windows this Crescent is a lousy hideout and Lord knows the four of them leave a lasting impression."

"Brand knew his goose was cooked as soon as he hooked up with those Nazi goons so he must be trying to get back to Germany somehow," Corbin replied.

"He's heading for the Free State"," Duke said, using the sobriquet applied to Eire and its neutral wartime status.

It was a hunch both of them thought warranted their continuing westward, while the general cordon remained cast over all possible escape routes. And since the shortest ferry crossing embarked from Fishguard they would proceed there. Duke conferred with the Police Sergeant who agreed with the logic.

"I was hoping you could help me with getting my petrol cans refilled?" Duke asked.

"I'll contact the depot and tell them to expect you. Vera can show you where it is," the Sergeant said. "In fact, Vera can tag along for the pursuit if you think she might be of assistance," he volunteered. "A police liaison kind of the thing?"

Vera and the Sergeant didn't see eye to eye. He was old school and the recruitment of women into the Force was a travesty in his opinion. He'd begrudgingly made her welcome, but he'd drawn a line when she nagged him about going out on patrol. Then when she'd gone way over his head to complain about discrimination, he'd lost all patience with the initiative. Brought to account he'd covered his tracks.

"Of course sir, as you wish, I'll get Vera involved in operational duty," he told the Assistant Chief Constable. Adding to himself, "In spades!"

Duke sensed there was a hidden agenda at play, but he needed that fuel, and an extra set of smart eyes and ears wouldn't come amiss. She might even allow Duke to hedge his destination bet providing she could drive and take orders.

"Oh, don't you worry about that sir!" the Sergeant assured him. "The constable's a first class driver and she always respects the chain of command, don't you Vera?" he asked rhetorically.

The travelling trio gathered up some food and drink for their journey and bade the Sergeant and his men farewell.

39. La Roche-Guyon – 11:00h

If Rommel ever could fully confide in Speidel, he could no longer. Their common upbringing in Swabia was no longer a happy coincidence but a curse which Goebbels would exploit to bolster Hitler's paranoia of disloyalty amongst his generals.

"The Reichsminister wanted to ensure we understood the importance of routing all public relations announcements through his office," Rommel said disingenuously.

Speidel had listened in to the Berlin call surreptitiously and knew he was being lied to. He didn't blame his commander; he could easily empathize with his dilemma. If he continued to conspire his family would be executed. If he kowtowed to Hitler, he would perpetuate a regime he no longer believed in and be complicit in the loss of countless additional lives.

Speidel had to find a way to console his boss and bring him back into the fold with the conspirators. Hitler's vehemence was testament to the sway Rommel had over public sentiment. If Rommel agreed to lead Germany back to peace the people would follow him once Hitler and his cronies were dethroned.

Rommel would benefit from a few days of distracting work and dispiriting casualty reports before the matter could be broached again. Both would be in ample supply if Speidel bided his time and his collaborators in Berlin remained patient.

"Have no concerns about that sir," Speidel reassured him. "We will keep all communiques factual and brief and leave it to the Ministry for Public Enlightenment and Propaganda to be frank with the German people."

The allusion to Goebbels' frequent assertion of transparency was ill-judged and not lost on Rommel. He squared on his assistant.

"This is not the time for sarcasm Speidel! Or treachery!" he shouted, striding over to the wall map and leaving his chief of staff in no doubt that the path back into the fold would be a rocky one.

"I wish to review the latest reports from the front immediately. And an accurate disposition of our Panzer Reserves. Dismissed!" Rommel said with a sweeping gesture.

40. West towards Fishguard – 12:00h

Brand kept Trager on B roads that would lead eventually to the A40 and the Brecon Beacons. It was a twisty, roundabout route, but it avoided the Aust Ferry across the River Severn which would, he felt sure, be on alert after their close shave in Bath. Now they were indubitably being pursued, Brand wasn't sure an A Road could be safely taken at any point but there were plenty of time-consuming alternatives. And the further they got from the last point of contact, the less notice the Checkpoint Charlies would be taking of the broadcast alerts.

Duke and Corbin were another matter. Although he'd outfoxed them back at the Crescent, he didn't take either of them for fools. They might well surmise his escape route was via Eire. Their problem would be choosing whether he was headed due west to Fishguard or north-west to Holyhead, or even north to Liverpool. If they were sighted heading towards Gloucester that would confound them further.

Once he'd made his mind up Brand knew fretting served little purpose and these miles were a good opportunity to relax, providing Kiki and Kastner kept their claws in. They'd returned to their previous seating positions so he could keep the protagonists apart and Trager seemed game to drive to the Irish Sea and back again if needs be.

Small wonder - the Alvis was proving to be an excellent touring car. The longer wheelbase Brand had selected made for a smooth ride even over rough back roads and the 4.3 litre engine was humming despite its heavy burden.

Due south of Brand's Alvis the Bentley was barreling along the A4 having crossed the Severn at Aust. While they refueled at the Gloucester Constabulary depot Duke had called HQ and then his Aunt Gertrude to see if she might be able to help him.

First Lieutenant Gertrude Allen was an 'Attagirl', a pilot in the Air Transport Auxiliary stationed at RAF Cosford in Shropshire. Having been taught to fly by her father in the Twenties she was a shoo in for the Auxiliary when they cast around for female pilots to deliver Spitfires, Lancasters and two dozen other aircraft types from manufacturing plants and repair factories to the forward bases. The RAF was mustering every available male pilot from the Commonwealth and beyond. The Attagirls freed up scores of those pilots for combat duty.

"Hello my darling nephew. What sort of trouble are you in?" she said, intimating his poor record for keeping in touch. Aunt Gertie knew full well his job didn't afford him much opportunity for familial duty, but she was an inveterate tease.

"My dear Aunt Gertie, I'm so sorry," he said. "Please know my absence has only deepened my affection for you."

"No doubt, what can I do for you?" she said. Duke was her favourite relative by a country mile and she herself wasn't the world's best at keeping up with other family members.

"I need a ride from RAF Rhoose to RAF Brawdy please," he asked, naming the air force stations nearest Cardiff and Fishguard. "Today," he added gingerly. He didn't dare add that he might need an onward flight to RAF Holyhead.

"Oh, is that all?" said Aunt Gertie. "Well, I was just sitting here waiting on your call, so I'll get straight onto that for you. Any particular aircraft you'd prefer?"

"Anything fast Auntie – it is for King and Country – from the very top" he pleaded.

Gertie was about to deliver a repaired Bristol Beaufighter to the East Coast of Scotland, and she didn't anticipate any insoluble objection to her submitting a roundabout flight plan which kept her well away from harm.

"You can help me deliver a Beaufighter if you wish?" she offered. "It's not as sleek as a Spitfire and not as fast as you drive Uncle David's Bentleys, but that's the best I can do at short notice."

All joking aside the Beau, powered by its two Hercules radial engines, could achieve a 320mph groundspeed, when not firing its guns.

"I'm about four hours out of Rhoose – I'll see you there! Got to go," he said and rang off before she could change her mind.

Duke believed this aerial option was a good contingency if he'd guessed wrong and Brand was indeed heading northwest to Holyhead. While WPC Wright and Corbin brought up the rear in the Bentley, he could fly ahead and reach Fishguard or Holyhead ahead of Brand and his cabal.

Duke anticipated difficulty getting Corbin onside with this plan. He'd want to get to Lady Brown by the quickest possible means. So Duke kept it to himself until they were approaching RAF Rhoose, and Corbin, having never ventured further west than Newbury racecourse, remained oblivious to the ruse.

———————————

Brand had been savoring the relative calm of the journey until they approached Gloucester. Before giving his next instructions he took the precaution of drugging the snoozing Kiki lightly once more. It was an unfortunate necessity he would have much rather foregone. He then pinned up her blonde hair and put a brunette wig from his prop collection on her, securing it with her scarf.

With two miles to go before reaching the city he proposed to Kastner and Trager that they cross the pedestrian Over Bridge leaving him and the 'sleeping' Kiki to cross the river by road. They would regroup a mile further on from the Over Bridge.

Even this plan had its risks, not least the conspicuous car, but that had to be balanced against stealing a viable alternative and transferring four jerry cans into it in broad daylight. Not to mention Brand's reluctance to abandon a car he was growing very fond of. Predictably Kastner didn't like the plan. While he'd enjoyed witnessing Kiki's repeated subjugation, he sensed Brand was jettisoning Trager and himself in the hope of improving his own chances of escape. Brand indulged Kastner's objections for another mile before stomping on them.

"Given your performance thus far Kastner I can see why you'd think I'd jump at a chance to ditch you." he said. "Fact remains the four of us trying to cross a major road bridge together in this vehicle is a recipe for certain failure.

"Besides which, I'd be very sorry to forego the camaraderie of Trager here. Stay close to him and you'll be fine."

As Trager brought the Alvis to a measured halt within sight of the footbridge, Kastner capitulated to the logic in Brand's candor and begrudgingly acquiesced in his own inimitable fashion.

"Be in no doubt Brand, if this is a double-cross we'll hunt you down and kill you," he said, flattering himself Brand would find that in any way threatening.

As Brand drove past Kastner and Trager he couldn't help noting their resemblance to "Dick und Doof" as Laurel and Hardy were known in Germany. To get the thought out of mind before reaching the road bridge, he reminded himself Stan had never killed anyone as far as anyone knew, and Ollie carried about as much fat as Trager sported muscle.

"Destination please sir?" the checkpoint sentry asked Brand.

"We're attending my mother-in-law's funeral in Shropshire," Brand fabricated. "You'll have to excuse my wife. She's desperately upset about her mother's sudden death and has taken a tranquilizer to get some sleep before the service."

"I'm sorry for your loss sir. Where's the funeral exactly?" the sentry asked.

"Church Stretton, St. Laurence's," Brand replied.

He'd chosen Church Stretton as a cover story because it was on a route to Holyhead, and he'd gotten the church name from the 1939 Baedeker guide to Great Britain. The same guide the Luftwaffe had used to target Bath.

It wasn't the only precaution he'd taken. Before leaving London, he'd put false license plates on the Alvis and substituted its Red Triangle badges for a pair from a totaled Rover 12 he'd plundered at a breaker's yard in Acton. It wouldn't fool anyone who knew anything about cars but, there again, the average sentry wouldn't. If a cognoscenti did challenge the discrepancy, he could claim to be disguising his ostentation for shame in this time of austerity.

"Righto sir. I wish you and the missus a safe onward journey," the sentry said with a nod to his colleague to lift the barrier.

Kastner and Trager had an even easier time of it. The 5th Glos. Battalion of the Home Guard didn't have the manpower to man the Over Bridge post night and day, so the daytime shift had been cancelled. Not only was the daytime deemed less risky but the grocers, butchers and other tradespeople who comprised the Guard had to keep their businesses running.

As a result, Kastner and Trager strolled across Thomas Telford's bridge unchallenged causing Kastner's suspicious cogs to whirr yet again.

"You see Trager, we're being betrayed," he said, distrusting as ever.

"I don't think so but what do you propose," Trager said, ever practical.

"Let's continue walking out of the town centre and take stock," Kastner proposed.

Less than half a mile further on Trager heard the now familiar note of the Alvis' exhaust approaching. Taking back the keys from Brand he set about transferring Kiki to the back seat. In no time they were heading west once more towards Brecon.

41. RAF Rhoose, near Cardiff — 15:05h

As he bombed down the A4226 with the airfield in sight Duke was buzzed by an aircraft flying ultra-low. The surprise distraction punctuated the argument Duke and Corbin were having after Duke had revealed the reason for their diversion to the airfield. Predictably Corbin was opposed to the new tactics and when he saw the heavy fighter overhead wanted to know why such an aircraft couldn't carry four.

"Three would be just fine too," Vera interjected. Although she had deep respect for the RAF and their flying machines, she'd never flown, and this lark had already blessed her with sufficient new experiences.

Aunt Gertie had been tracking the Bentley's progress since just east of Newport and had been making time wasting circuits till now. She couldn't resist getting her nephew's attention as she made her approach into Rhoose.

The tower wasn't fazed by her antics. First Lieutenant Allen had a reputation for the dramatic; a carryover from her pre-war experience as an acrobatic pilot. She'd radioed ahead to notify Rhoose about her joining party and Duke and Co had no trouble gaining access to the installation. Aunt Gertie was well-liked and admired. She was rated to fly everything from Moths to Lancasters and respected as a pilot unafraid to fly into harm's way if the need arose.

During the Battle of Britain Gertrude had flown more replacements to the forward airbases than any other female pilot and had her fair share of scrapes. Once adjacent a dogfight the Luftwaffe pilots didn't know or care whether you were on combat duty. On more than one occasion, Gertrude had to evade a stray 109 or 190 that had lost contact with its formation, but she'd yet to encounter one she couldn't shake off. Aunt Gertie brought the Beau to a stop on the apron and exited as gracefully as the aircraft's canopy permitted.

"Hello, my darling boy," she said with an affectionate hug which Vera found endearing. "These must be your new playmates?"

Corbin was still fuming and impervious to Aunt Gertie's jovial familiarity.

"Indeed they are, Aunt Gertie. Thrown together to pursue a mission of the highest importance." Duke said.

"You can tell me all about it when we're airborne," Aunt Gertie replied. "I have to be in Scotland before nightfall so let's get a move on!"

"Pardon me Skipper…" Corbin interjected. "How many souls can this bird carry?

"Two ordinarily," Gertrude replied continuing to stride back towards the Beau, the three trailing behind her like ducklings behind a hen.

"So, it's possible to carry more? Four maybe?" Corbin pleaded.

"Yes, in extreme discomfort. Two of you would have to make like sardines below the navigator position. But since this aircraft has been reequipped for reconnaissance, it's possible," Gertrude said.

"You see Duke!" Corbin said triumphantly. "No need to split up. With your connections I'm sure we can requisition another vehicle at the far end."

Vera could see where this alpha banter was heading and was having none of it.

"As long as you blokes are happy to be the sardines," she said. "Otherwise, I'll happily drive the Bentley back to Bath and my liaison duties will be over!"

By now Gertrude had completed her walkaround inspection and was impatiently waiting to show her passengers how to occupy the navigator's position and the space below. She loved the Beau almost as much as the Spitfire, but she was an awkward bird to get in and out of.

"Let's be having you," she urged. "One, two or three? All the same to me!"

Duke was rapidly processing his options, conscious if he didn't go along with Corbin's modification there'd be more squabbling, and Aunt Gertie might just be done with the lot of them. If that was the outcome of this tangent, Brand would have gained over an hour on them whether he was headed to Fishguard or Holyhead. And, on balance, he thought the benefits of having WPC Wright string along outweighed the risks of her driving a powerful, expensive car into the night unaccompanied.

"Lead on Vera," he conceded. "You get the navigator's chair."

While Aunt Gertie helped Vera wriggle up into the dorsal bubble and get strapped in, Duke parked up the Bentley and ran back to discover just how cozy this mercifully short flight to Brawdy was going to be. Very, it turned out.

42. Thirty Miles from Fishguard – 16:40h

The bucolic backdrop of their journey seemed to have a calming effect on all the Alvis' occupants, even Kastner.

"You must find these mountains reminiscent of your Swiss childhood, Herr Brand," he enquired.

By now Brand expected nothing to come from Kastner's mouth unattended by an ulterior motive. Although beautiful the Welsh Mountains didn't aspire to rival the Swiss Alps so Brand presumed this was an attempt to dig into his true allegiances. He parried with a quixotic response to put Kastner off track.

"There was a time when meadow, grove, and stream, did seem appareled in celestial light," Brand said, paraphrasing Wordsworth.

"It is not now as it hath been of yore; The things which I have seen I now can see no more." Kiki countered, now fully revived from a slumber so lightly induced she'd taken it for natural.

Brand's admiration for Corbin's taste in partners was growing apace although he still thought the combat photographer had been lucky in love, as in so many aspects of his professional life. For sure Lady Amelia was a fascinating woman and, in different circumstances, he might have put aside his pragmatic celibacy.

"Ah you're both Romanticists, no surprise there" said Kastner.

On the contrary, Brand felt the surprises were coming thick and fast. It was one thing for a Lady of the Realm to quote from the "Imitations", altogether another for a middle ranking SS officer to recognize its origins. Perhaps there was hope for Germany yet. That frail hope was punctured by Kastner's next line of questioning.

"Tell me, do you share a love of Schubert too?

Kastner loathed Schubert and had been disappointed when his oeuvre wasn't classed as degenerate by the Nazi regime alongside the work of Schoenberg and Mahler and the visual art of Klee, Picasso, Chagall and others.

Brand was of a mind to a debate the comparative merits of Aryan endorsed art. How, for instance, the Gleichschaltung or coordination policy had put Wagner on a pedestal despite the composer's alleged Jewish heritage, and the extra-marital affair thought to have led to his fatal heart attack. Personal weaknesses the Führer abhorred. Kiki stole his thunder by taking a different tack.

"I love Schubert especially his Adagio," she said, citing a work she felt sure would never make it into Kastner's record collection. "If only he could have a lived a normal span and given us so much more…" she mused.

Kastner was getting reaccustomed to British sardonicism. He looked over the lip of this foxhole and walked away from it. He turned to ask a question of Trager.

"My colleague, would you like me to relieve you of the driving duty?"

Trager had tuned out the conversation until his name was mentioned and, while puzzled by Kastner's generosity of spirit, he had no need of it. He hadn't enjoyed driving a vehicle more since his days as a tanker in North Africa. His immense size could be a problem for the rest of the crew but his driving acumen, as adept in reverse as going forward, had proved invaluable in close combat. Trager would have happily served out the war as a tanker, but the SS had redirected his above average intelligence and phenomenal strength to more demanding duties. Since when he'd done precious little driving.

"Thank you sir, I'll be happy to continue on to the objective," Trager replied.

"Bravo Trager!" Brand interrupted. "We're close to the port now. Thanks for getting us here so smoothly. Please take the next right."

As they came over the crest of a hill, they got a view of the harbor and the ferry. She was at the dockside getting ready for the evening sailing in just over two hours' time. There was only a small queue of vehicles waiting to get aboard and Brand didn't anticipate that changing much on a wartime Wednesday night.

"We'll park up here for a while before descending into the town," Brand said.

Kiki saw that as a prelude to another dose of chloroform and offered this argument as a prevention.

"If you forego the pleasure of drugging me again Brand, I promise not to betray your mission," she said. "It's doomed to failure anyway, so there's no sense in me being a heroine."

Brand wasn't sure he trusted her and Kastner certainly didn't. They neither accepted nor declined her offer for the time being.

43. Approaching RAF Brawdy – 16:45h

Aunt Gertie's piloting had been as benign as the prevailing weather and Vera was reveling in the thrills of her first, albeit short, flight. The same couldn't be said for the pair packed nose to tail below Vera. The nosegay of moldy webbing, machine oil and kerosene fumes was nauseating, even for accustomed air travelers like Duke and Corbin. Both were determined not to add to the stench by barfing and were much relieved when Vera relayed Aunt Gertie's instruction to prepare for landing.

"I've been prepared since takeoff," Corbin quipped trying to keep his mind off his miserable predicament. The high point of his trip had been discovering a near full bottle of Benzedrine in a cleft near to where his left hand had been hanging on for dear life. The American military distributed over seventy million Benzedrine pills through the course of the war. Even straightlaced Monty had doled out a hundred thousand amphetamine tablets before the Desert Rats' victory at the second battle of El Alamein.

No sooner had Corbin trousered the bottle of speed for future use than a loud crack came from the rear of the aircraft and the Beau entered a disconcerting plunge. Having steadied the aircraft and radioed in a distress call Gertrude gave Vera the news they were diverting for an emergency landing at RAF Manorbier. Some of that, notably the unusual name of the alternative base near Tenby, was garbled in the relay but the bruised sardines got the gist of it.

"Just when I thought things couldn't get peachier," Corbin said.

"Aunt Gertie won't let us come to any harm," Duke shouted back to Vera. "She's one of the best pilots in this war!"

Having asked for a confirmation Duke was more concerned with Manorbier being twenty miles further from Fishguard than Brawdy.

Even if Gertrude had been able to hear her nephew's endorsement, she wouldn't have had the bandwidth to bathe in it. The Beau was handling like a flying coffin, and she was going to need every ounce of her nouse to prevent it planting itself. The problem appeared to be with the rear control surfaces, though she had no way of confirming that with a neophyte in the navigator's seat.

RD867 was cleared for immediate landing at Manorbier, and Gertrude made a B-line for the airfield. She'd asked for as much runway as possible because without nose up or down control she'd be relying on extra speed to maintain pitch.

Gertrude and Vera were both fortunate not to be sitting alongside one another. Vera because she would not have known how to help, and Gertrude because she didn't need a potentially hysterical passenger next to her. Gertrude needn't have worried. Vera was staying commendably calm.

"If there's anything I can do from back here...," she trailed off. "Otherwise, I'll just keep quiet."

Gertrude revisited her earlier assumption. She seemed like a bright girl.

"If you could look back at the horizontal tail surfaces and tell me what you see that'd be a help. I'll try moving them up and down..... Anything?" Gertrude said.

"Nothing," Vera reported.

"And now tell me if you see any part of those tail surfaces moving," Gertrude instructed.

"Yes, the far edges are moving up and down slightly," Vera told her.

"Righto, thanks ever so my dear," Gertrude said.

Gertrude welcomed this reassurance as she lined up for the Manorbier strip. It being late afternoon there'd likely be an offshore breeze, hopefully not too fresh. Gertrude looked over and saw the windsock was pointing limply out to sea which was heartening.

Even if she said it herself, the landing was nigh on perfect. The tail wheel had met the turf with more force than usual, understandably in the circumstances, and her passengers certainly had no inkling of how hairy things had been for a while up there. At least not until the ground crew outside the Bellman hanger gave Gertrude a rousing round of applause. Duke wasted no time busting open the escape hatch and falling to the ground unceremoniously on top of Corbin.

"Thanks a million for the evacuation warning!" Corbin said as he checked his head for permanent damage where Duke's boot had connected.

"Sorry old chap, needs must," Duke said. Having gathered himself he rushed over to the control tower and asked for a secure line to London.

For once the line to Baker Street was crystal clear as Duke waited to report in. On hearing a click Duke assumed the line was lost and was about to replace the receiver and start over when a voice commanded, "Update me with extreme economy laddie."

Duke knew immediately it was Major General Gubbins. He straightened in his seat and launched in, being careful to stick to the facts.

"Tidy kettle of fish," Gubbins responded. "You see Lady Amelia is related to the Honorable Dorothy Paget who, in turn, has the ear of the Prime Minister," he added. "Which also explains why I'm talking to you, perishing eejit that you are, instead of focusing on the War in France. You remember the war? It's been in all the papers," Gubbins said in a crescendo of sarcasm.

"The Fleet Street murder was unfortunate. Getting outfoxed in Bath was an embarrassment to the Service. But I'm going to give you one last chance to redeem yourself for no better reason than the Landings have curtailed my other options," Gubbins said.

"Reports from a freshly demoted corporal in Gloucester suggest Brand and Lady Amelia are en route to Liverpool or Holyhead by way of Shropshire," Strong said. But that's conjecture, may be a false trail."

"Yes sir, I think…." Duke said before being rudely cut off.

"Shut up and listen! Brand appears to have ditched his two accomplices though there are reports of two men matching their descriptions being in Gloucester at the same time.

"I think your hunch about Fishguard has merit, but we need to cover the bet," he continued. "I'm going to put Flight Lieutenant Allen and her aircraft at your disposal for the time being. Don't balls it up again my boy!" he said.

With another click the line really did go dead and Duke registered the accumulated dry heat around his collar. The medics at training school had told him he had anhidrosis, an inability to sweat and hyposmia, a poor sense of smell, before threatening to disenroll him. He survived, thanks to the overwhelming demand for agents, and copped ridicule for the remainder of his training. But at times like these his afflictions cloaked his inadequacies.

While the engineers were confirming Gertrude's suspicions that both elevator cables had sheared off, for the want of two tuppenny grommets it turned out, she was called over to the station commander's office.

Group Captain Noteworthy presented a caricature of self-possessed manhood draped in a shroud of pipe smoke. Titivated moustache, manicured nails and, standing to greet Gertrude as his master studiously failed to do, a young, spritely Dalmatian.

"Sit down, Jaffa!" Noteworthy commanded.

He sat at a desk which almost filled the available space, over-compensating for the leadership and flying shortcomings that had become apparent during his previous role as a Wing Commander. Even his disobedient dog had been left intact to project as much machismo as possible.

Now commanding this far-flung outpost, putting up unmanned drones for target practice, he was a far cry from the bemedaled service record of his father. But respect for his illustrious forbear had propelled him up the slippery pole, accumulating grease with rank.

"Quite a piece of flying…," he paused to look up with feigned surprise at her insignia before returning to his Daily Express, "…Flight Lieutenant."

"Thank you, sir. The engineers say they can have me ready for flight in thirty minutes, so I'll soon be out of your hair and en route to Scotland," Gertrude told him.

"Change of plan I'm afraid old girl," he said. 'You're to refuel and seek direction from an Agent Duke as to your next destination.

"All this has been cleared with Ponsonby up at Cosford, and if, as seems likely, you hop over to Eire, landing rights will be negotiated ere you arrive," he assured her, looking well pleased with his little play on words.

Bemused more by the prospect of taking orders from her nephew than the threadbare "old girl" expression, she nodded, saluted, and left Noteworthy to his pipe and unfulfilled dreams.

On exiting Noteworthy's office the flight engineers bolstered Gertrude's faith in the Beau's airworthiness. After first restoring some faith in mankind.

"Take no notice of him, Lieutenant. Complete tosser," the Sergeant said, conscious almost everyone leaving Noteworthy's office needed some reassurance the war was worth fighting.

"Yeah, couldn't fly his way out of a brown paper bag," a private chimed in.

Although sorely tempted Gertrude didn't encourage their banter. As elusive as equality would prove to be with men like Noteworthy in authority, he held a rank deserving of respect. The Sergeant sensed her awkwardness and changed the subject.

"Your bird is A-1 now Lieutenant, have no worries about that," he said with a salute.

The engineers were well aware of Gertrude's reputation and felt honored to help her get back aloft. They'd swarmed the aircraft and given it a thorough going over while replacing the cables. They'd also installed a device of Gertrude's design at the navigator position. Gertrude was very grateful. Previous misadventures in rapidly repaired aircraft had sensitized her to the risk of turnaround time trumping thoroughness.

"I'm so sorry for getting you into this Aunt Gertie," Duke said on sensing her displeasure.

"Not to worry, Agent Duke," she said. "Flight Lieutenant Allen reporting for duty. Where to next sir?" Duke took no pleasure in this role reversal. He was, however, fighting for his career and felt sure she'd come around eventually.

"We've run out of time to head them off in Fishguard, but we need to get some photos of them boarding, if indeed they do," he said. "If he hasn't swapped vehicles that Alvis of Brand's won't be hard to spot.

If we get a positive sighting we'll fly on ahead to Rosslare. If not, we'll head up to Holyhead, same pack drill except we then proceed to Dublin, not Rosslare. Any questions?" he said.

"Does anyone need one or two of Monty's little helpers?" Corbin said before boarding.

"I have my own," Gertrude replied while Duke pocketed half a dozen. Vera had no idea what Corbin had on offer and didn't want to get into an enforcement of the 1925 Dangerous Drugs Act, as amended, so she made to tie her shoelaces until the bottle was back in Corbin's pocket.

While down there Vera began belatedly twigging the implication of one aspect of Duke's marching orders. Unless she could recognize the distinguishing features of an Alvis seen from the air, and she couldn't, she'd have to concede the navigator's position to Duke. Her turn to be a sardine. She thought about trying to bail again but, in all honesty, she was having too much fun.

After one or two awkward squirms between WPC Wright and Corbin, Vera signaled via Duke that they were ready for take-off.

"No need to shout anymore," said Duke. "See that pipe to your right? That's our new speaking tube. Just tug on my trouser leg to get my attention," he instructed. "Good old Aunt Gertie," thought Duke. "She really thinks of everything."

Once aloft the Beau appeared back to rights, and Gertrude soon had them closing on Fishguard in much better shape than their previous flight. She began circling the harbor so they could get some snaps of the vessel and its boarding payload. During three more circuits they were able to shoot pictures of Brand's Alvis driving aboard the ferry and the vessel casting off and making way.

By the second go round it was obvious to Brand they'd been spotted. And, as if to dispel the last scintilla of doubt on high, Kastner was kind enough to stand and give the circling aircraft a Nazi salute.

44. Aboard the Rosslare Ferry – 18:45h

Brand was thinking through his options as he looked over the churning wake from the ferry's aft deck. Kastner was machinating too and flitting around Brand like an irritating gnat.

"Your plan was critically flawed Brand and now we're sailing towards either certain apprehension or annihilation," Kastner shouted above the roar of the engines.

Brand took a good look round to ensure they were not being overheard. He shepherded Kastner into the lee of the stern superstructure for some respite from the din.

"My dear Kastner, if you can't summon the willpower to help solve this conundrum, may I suggest you stay silent while I do?" Brand asked.

"I say we dispose of the girl and take our individual chances when we dock," Kastner offered. "That way at least one of us may get through and complete our mission."

"And the undeveloped roll of film?" Brand asked.

"You decide who carries it," Kastner replied. "If we evade capture, we can get the evidence back to Berlin. If the carrier gets caught, they destroy the film," Kastner said. Whoever escapes can report the Field Marshall's treachery to Berlin with or without the photographic evidence and let them assess the veracity of the report."

Brand had to admit this was a better plan than he'd expected from Kastner, and he needed to review his counterarguments before responding. He still had no intention of imparting the true extent of his mission to this firebrand.

"Where's Trager and Her Ladyship," Brand asked, vying for processing time.

"At the rear of the passenger lounge, keeping out of sight," Kastner replied. "But I think you knew that Brand. Why aren't you pointing out the weaknesses in my plan? Could it be there aren't any?"

"I know you want that to be true, Kastner. But no plan is without its inherent weaknesses," Brand said. "And that's why we need a stronger one."

"I'm all ears," Kastner said with a sneer.

45. Above St. George's Channel – 19:00h

Like his Aunt Gertrude before him, Duke had taken some flying
lessons from his great uncle, but they'd paused when he went up
to Oxford and then came the war. Along the way he'd learnt how
to calculate range and con landmarks to set a course. Thanks to a
generous top up at Manorbier the Beau could stay airborne for
fifteen hundred nautical miles, enough to run between Fishguard
and Rosslare twenty times if necessary.

Corbin and WPC Wright had assumed, with good reason, that
this flight would be a straight hop over to Eire once the ferry had
left Fishguard with their quarry aboard. Duke had allowed that
assumption to persist after agreeing with Gertrude that they
would track the ferry's progress in case Brand and company took
to a lifeboat as they neared the Republic.

It seemed unlikely but the Irish Sea was forecast to be 2-3 feet
and they had Quinbus Flestrin on the team to do the rowing.
Moreover the captain of the neutral vessel would do nothing to
hinder them. Despite Gubbins' pleading, the ferry company had
ordered its Master to surveil but not apprehend this dangerous
party for fear of putting Irish citizens in harm's way.

Thus the sardines had unknowingly embarked on a possible five-
hour flight characterized by sweeping arcs and punctuated by
regular calls up to Duke to ask, and eventually implore, whether
they were there yet.

Oddly Corbin wasn't the one complaining, and the reason lay in
his little bottle of pills. What Corbin had taken to be straight
Benzedrine was, in fact, a compound also comprising
Scopolamine. The latter to suppress air sickness tempered with
the former to boost alertness. Clearly Corbin in his drained state
was more susceptible to the sleep-inducing ingredient and twenty
minutes after takeoff he was out for the count.

Initially Vera had rejoiced in her bedfellow's inactivity – those twenty minutes had featured more of the dreaded fidgeting she'd observed between the boys out of Rhoose. She regretted not taking whatever it was he was on.

But, as the flight wore on, she began taking Corbin's radial artery pulse and gave Duke a warning to be wary of those pills. The last thing Vera wanted was to lose contact with Gertrude while surrounded by two comatose men in the back of this tin can.

Fortunately, Duke hadn't felt the need for any more speed. His adrenaline was doing a fine job all on its own.

As darkness fell the ferry, which was making good headway on the surface below them, became fully illuminated and unmistakable under a clear summer sky. As promised, Gertrude had received her clearance to land, and she had given her current ETA.

The Irish authorities directed Gertrude to coordinates which Duke was certain would put the Beau in the drink. Smelling a rat, Gertrude went on the radio to Dublin again.

"Repeat please Dublin," she asked. "Those coordinates appear to be off dry land."

"Roger RD867, those are the coordinates of former Naval Air Station Wexford, and, no, we are not expecting you to sprout pontoons. Please approach with caution and you will con flares marking out a grass runway due west of those coordinates. Go ahead," the controller said.

NAS Wexford had been a US Navy seaplane station in WWI conducting anti-submarine warfare to protect the shipping lanes from America to Bristol and Liverpool. While the Curtiss seaplanes based there used the sheltered waters of Wexford Harbor to come and go, a grass runway had been created to allow conventional aircraft to fly in spares and supplies. The runway had survived the destruction of the ensuing civil war in a serviceable state and the enthusiasm of local amateur glider pilots had prevented its return to arable use.

"Roger, Dublin," Gertrude replied still suspicious it was she who was being rogered. "And the onward transport?" she enquired.

"An armed detachment of the Garda will be standing by to take you to Rosslare Harbor, approximately 15 miles due south," Dublin assured her. "Afraid that's as close as we can get you. Go ahead"

"We're very grateful Dublin, that is all," Gertrude signed off.

46. The Irish Sea

Brand had taken Kastner indoors to take him into his confidence.

"We are going to commandeer this ship and signal Berlin to activate 'Operation Strong Capture'," Brand said. "Unavoidably the communication will have to be unencrypted but by the time any Allied Forces can react, it will be too late.

"We will be collected by U-Boat and taken to a safe haven, likely St Nazaire, a submarine base in Northern France," he continued.

Kastner fumed at the implication he didn't know about the heavily fortified pens on the Loire estuary. Especially after all the unsuccessful attention Churchill had given to their destruction. But hearing more of the plan was more important than correcting the aspersion.

"Go on," Kastner said.

"We will sedate Lady Brown once more, if necessary, to ensure her compliance and facilitate her discrete placement in the captain's quarters. But otherwise the plan is straightforward and, in these conditions, easily executed. It will be for the U-Boat commander to decide whether he sinks the ferry after we disembark."

Brand thought the sinking of a neutral vessel unnecessary and unlikely but everything was possible and he knew the spice would appeal to Kastner's unedifying side.

"Why don't we just toss her overboard now," Kastner asked.

"Because she's a valuable bargaining chip either for us, if we get boxed into a corner, or for the Reich as we repel the invading forces in Normandy," Brand said. "Surely you can see that?"

Kastner shrugged and continued his objections.

"And what about the aircraft that's been tracking us since we left Wales?" he asked. "Don't you think the U-Boat will be in mortal danger from an attack by a Torbeau?"

Owing to the sleeve valves on its radial engines the Beaufighter was nicknamed "Whispering Death" by some adversaries, but its continued surveillance hadn't escaped Brand or Kastner. However Kastner had mistaken Gertrude's aircraft for the torpedo version of the Beaufighter.

"Oh Kastner, is that the best they're teaching you fellows at the SS Junker schools these days?" Brand taunted. "The Beaufighter carries its heavy munitions, be they torpedoes or bombs, outboard."

"The one above us has neither and has, I suspect, been re-equipped for reconnaissance missions otherwise it wouldn't be capable of carrying three occupants," Brand added.

"Three?" Kastner asked.

"While you were pulling your little stunt with that Nazi salute, I observed a female pilot and the agent accompanying Corbin in the navigator seat," Brand said. "There is zero chance my photographer friend has given up the chase for his beloved Lady, and he will have found a way to squeeze onboard somehow.

"If he has it will be because this Beaufighter has had its Hispano inboard cannons removed leaving only its wing mounted Browning machine guns to bother us during the transfer," Brand said, driving home the advantage of superior intelligence gathering and deduction.

"And if I'm wrong, I doubt that Attagirl pilot has any experience firing such weaponry, especially when a deck mounted Flak gun is firing back at her."

Kastner was silenced by the sheer magnitude of Brand's knowledge base and a natural inferiority which, try as it might, his flawed self-worth could not suppress.

"If there are no further objections let's collect Trager and set about hijacking this ship," Brand said. "I'd like you to take Lady Brown down to the cabin and then go to the radio room."

Kiki had been regaling Trager with stories about her Austrian relatives and winters spent skiing in the resorts around Mount Piz Buin. As a teenager Trager was a champion skier and very familiar with the resorts his interlocutor remembered so fondly.

"Now tell me, Hans," she asked, "Where on earth did your father find a set of skis strong enough to carry you down a mountain?"

"Oh, I wasn't as bulky back then, so it wasn't so difficult. Though I did have a habit of breaking the bindings," he said smiling. "Luckily my equipment was provided by the team I competed for, so my parents didn't have to foot the bill."

Kiki could picture the type of team picking up the tab. She'd seen ever larger parties of Hitler Youth on the slopes during her visits in the thirties. Her relatives weren't enamored of Herr Schicklgruber's Lebensraum concept but became resigned to the prospect of this maniacal son of Austria absorbing his homeland into his adopted Fatherland at the first opportunity.

Overall these amicable reminiscences confirmed Kiki's impression that Trager was of a wholly different ilk to Kastner and befriending him could only work to her advantage. If she could locate the streak of decency Brand kept well-hidden she would have evened up her odds of escape considerably.

Kastner wasn't pleased to see the fraternization going on and told Trager as much with a Hochdeutsch phrase Kiki couldn't understand.

"I'd like you to accompany me topside please Trager," Brand said. "Lady Brown, you will go with Herr Kastner to your cabin below please," he told Kiki. Brand had reserved two cabins for the crossing for convenience and in case Kiki needed to be constrained.

"Herr Kastner you know what to do after escorting Lady Brown," Brand added.

Kiki didn't like the idea of being escorted by Kastner one bit and Brand wasn't keen on the option either, but he wanted Trager's intimidating bulk with him when he entered the bridge. If control was achieved with minimal kerfuffle and no gunfire, the ship's company would comply with their captain's orders, however disagreeable they might find them.

Sailing at night through U-Boat infested waters apparently held little peril for this vessel's crew. The cloak of neutrality had lulled them into lax onboard security and the would-be hijackers had no difficulty finding their way to the bridge, and the open portside entrance.

"I'm sorry sir, the bridge is off-limits to passengers," a young cadet said as he barred their passage. His sallow complexion blanched on seeing Brand's Bolo pointing between his dilating pupils. Following the flick of its barrel the boy moved aside allowing Brand clear sight of the captain.

"Hands up gentlemen," Brand ordered. "Captain Rudge, my colleague and I are commandeering your vessel," he explained.

"Really now, you and whose army," Rudge replied belligerently.

"The Fuhrer's," Brand said. "Other members of my team are strategically positioned around the vessel and will not hesitate to kill any member of your crew who resists," Brand continued while Trager moved steadily forward ready to pounce if required.

"It's a hackneyed phrase Captain but resistance really is futile in this instance," Brand said motioning the skipper to move back from the control console he'd been inching towards.

"Your compliance will spare your vessel and the lives of your passengers and crew. In little more than an hour we will disembark, and you'll be free to proceed to Rosslare. For now, please order all stop, extinguish all deck lights and broadcast this announcement over the tannoy," Brand said as Trager handed over a handwritten note.

Captain Rudge was a WWI survivor of two sinkings who respected the boundary between personal bravery and the responsibility of command. Having lost countless comrades in the first show he was loathe to imperil yet more. If these raiders were getting off his boat in the middle of the Irish Sea they'd likely be stepping onto a U-Boat which could just as easily blow them out of the water, neutral flag notwithstanding.

"Passengers and crew, this is your Captain speaking," Rudge began. "You will have noticed we've stopped. This is owing to a minor technical issue up here on the bridge. Repairs are being made and we expect to be back underway very soon. I will keep you informed of our progress mindful that some of you will be trying to get some rest. Thank you."

By now Brand was expecting a call to the bridge from Kastner confirming his control of the radio room. Masking his irritation he waited a few minutes before going alongside Trager to whisper a minor change of plan in German. All the time watching carefully for any sign he was being understood by their four detainees.

Leaving Trager to maintain control of the Bridge, Brand made his way to the radio room to find no sign of Kastner or anyone else. Assuming Kastner's exuberance had gotten the better of him yet again, Brand dealt with the pressing matter of signaling Berlin using his Schroeder call sign. Tense moments passed before the opening line of a Goethe poem came back in Morse code.

"Des Menschen Seele Gleicht dem Wasser," the operator replied.

"Seele des Menschen, Wie gleichst du dem Wasser!" Brand responded.

Brand felt his heart beating irregularly and inhaled deeply to calm himself. After all these years the unearthing of this rescue plan was fraught with possible failure. Would it still be on record? Would the distant operator have ready access to it? To hear it coming to life, even down to the specified frequencies for continuing the dialogue, was a marvel.

"Your request is acknowledged Herr Schroeder," the operator confirmed. "What are your coordinates?"

Brand complied having transposed them with a simple pre-arranged cipher that wouldn't fox a decent cryptographer for long but would buy valuable minutes.

Kastner's continued absence was nettling Brand. He signed off with Berlin after receiving an ETA for the sub and left a note for Kastner in case they missed one another. He then returned to the bridge. Kastner wasn't there either, but Trager remained in full control of the situation. Brand gave the Captain some more calm reassurances having becalmed his own metabolism.

But his indulgence of Kastner's contradictions was depleting rapidly. Smart yet impulsive, part cultured, part philistine, Kastner had desperate need of a mentor who could draw out his potential. Brand hadn't been given the job and he didn't want it. What he would insist upon would be for Kastner to start behaving as ordered for the rest of this mission.

With Trager coping marvelously Brand decided to go and track down his loose cannon. On a forward stairway between decks they reunited, Kastner looking disheveled and out of sorts.

"Another time, another place Kastner, I would have you court martialed," Brand said.

"The radio operator wanted to be a hero," Kastner claimed. "It took longer than I would have liked to accede to his wishes."

"Not unlike the courier in London. Seems everyone wants to be a hero near you. Where is he?" Brand asked.

"In Davy Jones' locker," Kastner replied.

"Make that your last mistake of this mission Kastner," Brand said. "Or you'll be joining him."

Up above Gertrude and Duke lost contact with the ferry when the vessel came to halt midway through its voyage and doused its lights. Stopping so far offshore was unexpected and, for a while, Duke worried the vessel could have taken a sharp change of course to head for an alternative port – Dublin perhaps or even France if the vessel had taken on enough fuel for the return trip.

Gertrude circled back round and started a succession of slow semi-circles down the line of their previous track to cover off the risk of a course change. After ten minutes of this steady banking Vera was struggling with her tight confinement but, on balance, was very pleased with how she was coping with this inhospitable environment. Corbin remained dead to the world but exhibiting a pulse.

"Vessel at 10 o' clock Skipper," Duke reported with relief in his voice and Gertrude turned gently to confirm the sighting. With the ferry back in view they resumed circling, trying to pick up a clue as to what was going on. There didn't appear to be any sign of distress on deck and no Mayday call had gone out. Gertrude decided to cut through the mystery and hail the ship on 500kc, the international distress channel. She checked they weren't in the half hourly silent period and began broadcasting.

"Merchant Vessel, this is aircraft RD867 circling above your position. You appear to have lost power, what is your status, and do you require assistance? Answer."

Brand opted to ignore the initial message and wrote down a response for the Captain to convey in response to the inevitable repeat.

"Roger RD867, this is TSS Andrew. Please switch to Frequency 480 and stand by. Acknowledge."

"TSS Andrew this is RD867. Wilco. Switching to 480." Duke responded.

Brand took his time switching channels, every second being valuable in this cat and mouse game. He then had the Captain continue the charade.

"RD 867 this is TSS Andrew. Minor technical problems caused us to stop. Repairs going well. Expect to be underway imminently. No cause for concern. That is all."

"Roger TSS Andrew," Duke persisted. "We are on U-Boat patrol in this area and will remain in contact until you are underway. Acknowledge."

No further communication ensued.

Gertie had deliberately signaled whoever was commanding the vessel that she wasn't buying it. She relayed the gist of the exchanges to Duke adding:

"It seems like Brand and his gang have taken control of the vessel somehow."

"Agreed, the skipper would have mentioned his neutral status otherwise. Of course there's another reason Brand might not be worried about a submarine attack," Duke said.

"He's hailed his next ride," Gertrude replied.

Oberleutnant zur See Heinz Dahlmer had been ordered to take U-491 to Brand's coordinates full speed. He was patrolling adjacent the Bristol Channel when he received his new orders and at surface speed confirmed he could rendezvous in approximately one hour.

Under cover of darkness the sleek, black form of a surfaced submarine wasn't that easy to pick out amongst the waves. And, with its FuMB aerial providing radar detection alarms, a well drilled crew could be back below in moments. Providing the Royal Navy hadn't found yet another way to outfox their detection equipment.

U-491 wasn't the closest U-Boat to the Strong Man's position. However, ever since Dahlmer's Portsmouth report had leaked temporarily, Karl Dönitz, Grand Admiral of the Kriegsmarine, had ensured all further signals connected to Field Marshall Rommel's alleged excursion were routed immediately for his eyes only. Having retained direct control of the U-Boats on becoming Commander in Chief of the Navy he was perfectly placed to handle this delicate situation.

Dönitz had been happy to hear Dahlmer's boat was in the area and able to respond in good time. He reasoned it was worth adding an extra fifteen minutes to the rendezvous time to keep all this hearsay ringfenced. Dahlmer was less pleased with the prospect of giving up his quarters to his incoming passengers and downright displeased to hear Kastner was coming back on board. He already had an ornery SS liaison officer aboard which was more than ample for one boat.

But it now seemed his Portsmouth report was being taken seriously at a senior level, and the prospect of Reich's most illustrious Field Marshall being brought to account for his actions more than offset the inconveniences. With the matter on the desk of Grand Admiral Dönitz he could put his full attention back onto protecting his boat and his men and he could best do that by getting these unwelcome passengers to where they wanted to go promptly.

Brand remembered something he should have done earlier.

"Herr Trager, please go to the radio room and disable the transmitter using the lock they use when the vessel is in port. You should find the lock in a draw below the set. Make sure the lock cannot be removed and report back immediately," Brand ordered.

"I have signals experience, send me," Kastner volunteered.

Kastner's uncharacteristic helpfulness convinced Brand to keep him close until the submarine arrived. He told Trager to get on with it. Once the German exchanges had ended Captain Rudge piped up.

"If you're waiting for another vessel to rendezvous, you should be aware of the strong currents in this area," he said. "We're beyond anchor depth and I reckon we've already drifted more than a nautical mile from the location where we cut engines."

"Thank you Captain, what do you recommend?" Brand said.

"We should power up and return to the original waypoint."

"Make it so but keep the lights out," Brand said. "And be in no doubt, if you take this vessel further from our rendezvous point, it will not go well for you and your crew."

Rudge nodded and issued the necessary commands. He wanted these Nazis off his boat. Brand couldn't be sure of the Captain's motivation and was leery of putting the vessel back under power. But it would beguile their observers for a while and make the U-Boat's job easier. As the engines roared back into life, Trager returned to the bridge.

"This man was in the radio room and refused to disable the apparatus until I insisted," Trager said pushing the radio operator ahead of him.

"Herr Hauptscharführer Trager please take over here. Herr Obersturmführer Kastner, please come with me," Brand said signaling his problem child to lead the way.

"Would you like to revise your earlier report Kastner?" Brand said as they descended the stairs to the overnight cabins.

Kastner didn't reply and Brand could see the foot of the stairs might appeal as a good venue for his long overdue retaliation. Kastner's right hand was out of sight and having weighed his options, Brand knocked his would-be adversary unconscious with a chop to the Vagus nerve just below his left ear.

It was a cheap shot but deliberately non-lethal and carrying Kastner's prone body the ten paces to their cabin was less likely to draw attention than a gunfight or a stabbing in a narrow gangway. He unlocked the cabin to find Kiki unconscious too. Alive, barely, she was bleeding from a cut on her bottom lip and her neck showed evidence of strangulation. Blood under her right-hand fingernails indicated she'd put up a fight. He checked her shallow pulse and lifted her legs onto the bunk to make her more comfortable. There were no obvious signs of sexual assault. Her panties were pulled up and there was no bruising or bleeding south of the hem of her silk camisole.

He turned his attention back to Kastner. Lifting his head by the scalp and peeling back the roll collar of his sweater Brand saw the reciprocal damage on her assailant's neck. He balled a face cloth, rammed it into Kastner's mouth and held it in place with the gag Kiki had been wearing until recently. He then bound Kastner's wrists and ankles with strips of bedsheet and gave him a generous dose of Chloroform for good measure. He moved the trussed troublemaker to the adjoining cabin and locked both its doors after collecting two pistols, ammunition and a knife from about Kastner's person.

Brand dampened another face cloth and began mopping the blood from around Kiki's mouth. She was coming round, and he knelt at her side so he wouldn't be looming over her when she came to her senses. Despite this precaution Kiki recoiled into the head of the bunk on coming to and recalling her recent ordeal.

"Please be calm, Lady Brown," Brand said. "I apologize for Kastner's actions and assure you it was never my intention you should be harmed in this way."

"Bullshit! You set that deviant on me, and you already knew full well what he was capable of!" Kiki retorted.

"Kastner disobeyed a direct order by entering your cabin and, when we reach Germany, he will be court martialed," Brand said.

"More BS," Kiki said. "When he gets home, if he ever does, you'll pin a medal on him! Your regime is rotten to its core as the whole of Jewry knows full well!"

"I understand why you'd believe that," Brand said. "If even half of what's rumored about SS activities in the East is true, you have reason. But let me assure you there are still high-ranking German officers who abhor such behavior, and they will prevail."

"Spare me Brand," she said. "If the Third Reich ever had a moral compass it was screwed before it left the Bierkeller. And you and all your fellow officers will atone for its atrocities. No firing squads for you monsters – you'll all hang and, if they sell tickets, I'll buy front row!"

"You are a remarkable woman, Lady Brown, but in this you're mistaken," Brand insisted. "Right will prevail, and in short order. I must leave you for now. Kastner is incapacitated next door and the connecting door is locked. I will send Trager back here in a while to check on your well-being. I take it you have no aversion to his ministrations?" Brand said.

"No, he seems genuine enough… for a Nazi," Kiki said.

Duke spotted the vessel coming about and making headway shortly after the Captain had set his new course.

"He's back underway," he told Gertrude. "Please try and reach him again."

Her calls went unanswered.

"No answer, what's he up to," she said on the intercom.

"Well he won't get to Rosslare that way. On his current course he's heading to France."

As Brand exited the cabin he was approached by an old lady.

"Is everything alright in there, young man?" she enquired.

"Yes ma'am. Why do you ask?" Brand said.

"There were some goings on in that cabin earlier and we just wanted to know everyone was alright. I knocked but couldn't get a reply," she said.

"Oh that was my widowed sister I'm afraid, nightmares" Brand explained. "She's had the worst time with the bombing and we're just bringing her over to our country estate for some rest and recuperation. I'm so sorry you were inconvenienced."

"My, my. Must have been awful for the poor lass. You know....," she attempted to continue before Brand cut her off.

"I do hope you can excuse me Ma'am, but I'm just going to get a mug of Horlicks from the galley for her."

"Oh my husband and I would have a cup every night before bed in the Punjab. It'll do her the world of good, though I don't think it's been as creamy since Mr. Horlick died. He was English you know, lived to a ripe old age" she said to Brand's back as he ascended the stairs.

Brand was glad the old biddy's curiosity had interrupted Kastner's misdoings. And once more he boggled at this officer's lack of self-control. His repeated inability to control his urges had moved him into the discard end of the hand Brand was holding.

Back on the bridge all was calm. Trager gave Brand a reassuring nod and, as he walked past the binnacle hosting the ship's compass, the heading appeared consistent with the Captain's promise to get them back to their rendezvous point.

"Captain please make an announcement to say the repairs have gone well but we need to stop again briefly to make some minor adjustments. I can dictate something if you wish," Brand volunteered.

"No thank you. I think I've got the hang of it," the Captain said with an insincere smile.

That done the ship's engines were once again all stopped, and Brand picked up a pair of binoculars – Zeiss he was bemused to see – and started scanning the bible black surface for a periscope. His ride was late.

———————————

Dahlmer had been forced to take his boat down to one hundred metres to evade the attention of a British frigate steaming towards Pembroke Dock. The crew had donned their felt slippers as the boat went into silent running. All crew without a battle station took to their cots.

He thanked his lucky stars he'd been in sufficient depth to make the dive and waited for the frigate to start raking its search apparatus over them. On it came passing over several times giving off sounds that ranged from the chirping of a crazed chickadee to the screech of a runaway trolley car. The hydrophone operator took it all in his stride, calmly whispering the frigate's position to the executive officers.

Eventually Dahlmer had to put out a Bold decoy before making a run for it. It created an underwater curtain of chemicals which confounded the enemy's search apparatus by giving off a sound signature similar to a sub, allowing the actual boat to speed away to safety. All this evasion had delayed their progress by almost an hour.

"Take her up to periscope depth," he ordered as they closed on the coordinates. He scanned the horizon.

"Merchant vessel Port 10. Two thousand metres, not moving. Surface," he said.

"Mystery solved. He *is* rendezvousing with a U-Boat," Duke said.

"Okay I'll take her up a few thousand feet in case they get saucy with that deck gun," Gertrude said.

"Copy that," Duke said and relayed the news to Vera.

"I'm going to report the U-Boat sighting in the hope there are some fighting ships in the vicinity," Gertrude said.

"Good idea but is there nothing we can do to prevent his escape Aunt Gertie? We can't let him get away scot-free!"

"Impede maybe, prevent unlikely," she said. "Although I'm not supposed to, I could try using those wing guns to make life uncomfortable for them, but they'll be shooting back at us," she continued. "Are you up for that?"

"Too bloody right," he said.

"No need to swear Alastair," Gertrude reproved him. "Your mother, God rest her soul, brought you up better."

"You know there just may be a way to tip the scales without risking civilian casualties," Duke said.

"I'm all ears nephew dearest," Gertrude said. "Killing a Lady of the Realm would not embellish my service record."

Dahlmer had gone aloft with his gunners leaving his XO in the control room. Minimum hands on deck meant less time to get below. In drills each man was allotted exactly 1.5 seconds to descend the tower and relied on someone being below to catch him should he fall.

When Dahlmer saw the joining party he was dismayed. He'd expected three and was aggrieved to see a woman was amongst them and that the whale size agent was still part of the equation. A U-Boat's efficiency in cutting through water, especially underwater, was in large part dictated by the distribution of weight within her skin. Each man had a designated station during dives to govern how the boat would behave. Positioning the big fellow was going to be problematic again.

He put that aside for now and set about getting a better fix on the circling aircraft and then scanning the horizon for enemy ships through the powerful bridge binoculars. A solo air attack could be repelled but the odds would change dramatically if additional planes or surface vessels entered the fray. The RAF's anti-submarine tactics had improved over time. They now preferred to attack in concerted strength calling in naval vessels to provide surface gunnery and depth mining. It was an homage of sorts to the U-Boat 'Wolfpack' tactics.

Dahlmer's eyesight was revered by the crew as one of the boat's best defenses. He scoured the horizon and saw nothing, but these waters were rife with anti-submarine vessels and at twenty knots they could quickly close into firing range before they became visible. All the hunter needed was an accurate spotter and this lone fighter aircraft was doing that job admirably.

Over on the ferry Trager had collected Kiki from her cabin. She'd been able to make it up onto the deck but wasn't up for much else. Trager enlisted the help of a deck hand to deploy the smallest lifeboat. Without orders from the bridge the sailor had been reluctant until Trager got within slapping distance.

When Brand could see them up on deck and readying the lifeboat he asked Captain Rudge to accompany him to the cabin deck after first reminding the bridge officers that any monkey business would result in their Captain losing his life.

Brand bound and gagged Captain Rudge before locking him in Kiki's cabin and going next door to collect his other captive. SS Obersturmführer Kastner was still under the influence of the narcotic and Brand didn't have time or the inclination to wait on a gentle rousing. He filled a jug with water and doused Kastner with it. This further humiliation left the recipient steaming with rage. Brand waited for the thrashing to stop and then laid down the terms of his release.

"Herr Kastner, by your intemperance you have jeopardized the success of a mission of vital importance to the Third Reich," Brand said.

Kastner was straining to speak but Brand left the gag in place and continued.

"On our return to Germany you will be court marshalled. Your best chance of sparing your family the shame of your death will be to assist me in the successful continuation of this mission.

"I'm going to remove your bindings now and I wish to hear whether you intend to cooperate or not. If not, I will kill you here and now. Please nod to signify you have understood me."

Kastner could only bring himself to bat his eyelids but Brand removed the gag anyway. Kastner waited for his arms to be released and then addressed Brand as he removed the ankle ligatures himself.

"Herr Brand, your conduct of this mission has been compromised by personal considerations, chiefly your relationships with this female prisoner and her cohorts," Kastner said.

"You have shunned successive opportunities to bring the mission to a swift conclusion and incurred unnecessary risk. It is you who should face a firing squad and I will be happy to sue for that outcome. For now though I will continue to serve the Fatherland by assisting your flawed efforts in the hope we can both face justice and see who is judged to have been of more faithful service to the Fuhrer."

Brand felt like applauding this grandiose soliloquy which could have graced Freisler's Kangaroo Court. But time was wasting.

"Tidy yourself up and let's get going," Brand said.

"You made the 4U transmitter lock inoperable Trager?" Brand asked as they rowed over to the submarine.

"I did," Trager said.

"Very well. With these two valves from the VHF transmitter also removed, the ferry will be staying silent for a while," Brand said as he tossed the valves overboard. "And you Lady Brown, have you ever sailed in a submarine?"

Kiki looked askance at the silly question.

"You will find the conditions cramped, damp and, at times, oppressive. You will be confined to the Captain's quarters, and I will insist on you doing nothing to interfere with the orderly operation of the vessel," Brand said.

"How much longer will you have me tag along on this odyssey Brand?" Kiki asked.

"For as long as it suits us!" Kastner chimed in.

"Uncertain," Brand said. "The captain's quarters are close to our entry point, and I am counting on you to proceed there swiftly and without fuss when we board."

The Beau's steep climb encouraged Dahlmer to call his crew to battle stations and finally roused Corbin from his Scopolamine induced slumber.

"What have I missed," Corbin asked Vera.

Vera tugged on Duke's trouser leg and passed the speaking tube over to Corbin. Duke gave him a quick update including a bald assessment of the danger Kiki might find herself in once Gertrude set the Browning machine guns blazing.

"I think Kiki would prefer that bet to her chances with Brand and whoever carved up that boy in Fleet Street," Corbin said.

"I think so too but we're going try very hard not to endanger her," Duke said. "Buckle up!"

Gertrude came on the intercom to report she'd heard back from the XO of a frigate some ten miles distant who was closing in on their position to provide aid.

"But I think we need to engage now. Brace yourselves," she said calmly.

Gertrude approached the submarine head on hoping to nullify the flak gun on the sub's deck. On her first pass she had difficulty getting the timing of her firing synched up with coming out of her dive and she overshot the target harmlessly.

She was getting her first, immersive lesson in staying calm under fire. She figured out a flatter angle of attack would make the flak gunner's task more difficult. She banked and lined up for her second run all the while trying to control her breathing. Her next pass laid a neat line of fire parallel the sub's starboard flank opposite where Brand and his crew were scrambling out of the lifeboat. Kastner had attempted to be first out, but Brand had held him back while Trager bore Kiki to safety.

Avoiding the lifeboat crew was deliberate though Gertrude hoped she might still have helped their cause. But the attempt hadn't come free of charge. Duke told her the flak had sheared off the tip of the starboard wing, mercifully missing the auxiliary fuel tank which would have surely caught fire if hit.

With the raider's marksmanship improving and the threat of arriving surface vessels growing ever greater, Dahlmer ordered an emergency dive. While his gunners raced back to the tower he took one last look through the binnies. Dead astern he saw a tall mast, harbinger of a deadly threat approaching. He followed his gunners down below leaving Brand and Kastner to fend for themselves. His first duty was to his ship, and he'd already risked enough for these foisted guests.

Gertrude sensed she could cope with the change in the Beau's handling and was shaping up for another attack curve when she was called off by the approaching frigate. She banked sharply left and climbed as the frigate's captain weighed the risk of firing four-inch shells in the general direction of a neutral merchant vessel.

Corbin helped Vera clamber off him and asked Duke what he'd seen.

"Kiki reached safety and, sadly, so did Brand," Duke reported. "But not before he'd kicked one of his Nazi chums into the drink."

———————

With a loud thwack the bridge hatch slammed shut.

"Flood!" ordered the torpedo operator who had risen from his seat to aid Brand.

"Flood!" echoed the Chief Engineer having checked all lights on his lamp board were illuminated.

"Take us down to thirty metres," Dahlmer commanded.

"Dive tanks open," the Chief Engineer reported.

"What's the status of the Irish ferry?" Dahlmer asked his XO.

"On heading 270. 10 knots," the XO said. "And we have what's sounds like a River-Class frigate range eleven thousand metres astern."

"Very well," said Dahlmer. "Get us below the ferry and maintain that position. We'll put that frigate's skipper on the horns of a dilemma."

The noisy thrum of the diesel motors had been replaced by the hum of the electric propulsion and the din of compressors managing the precise balance of water and air in the sub's buoyancy tanks.

"I wouldn't do that Oberleutnant," Brand said.

"Herr Brand I presume? Why not?" Dahlmer asked.

"Obersturmführer Kastner insisted on returning to the merchant vessel with the intention of scuttling it," Brand replied.

Dahlmer's expression turned quizzical, but he had more pressing matters to attend to. A game of peekaboo with a River-Class was high risk anyway. His crew were ripe for some action after the monotony of drills, checks and cleaning. Some skippers bolstered morale with stunts like allowing their crewmen to water ski off the back of the vessel in warmer latitudes.

Dahlmer wasn't that kind of naval officer. Nevertheless weeks of hot bunking and drudgery could dull a man's appetite for combat and that edge had to be kept honed somehow. He preferred to keep them sharp with the sting of battle when a sensible opportunity arose.

"Belay that. Emergency dive to one hundred metres," Dahlmer said. "We'll give that frigate a taste of his own medicine once his depth charges have failed."

"What did the SS Obersturmführer hope to gain by sinking a neutral merchant vessel" an officer behind Brand asked.

"Herr Brand, allow me to introduce Hauptsturmführer Kramer, our SS Liaison Officer," the XO said as Brand turned to face his inquisitor.

"You'd have to ask him. I'm afraid Herr Kastner didn't always obey my orders," Brand said.

"Didn't?" Kramer asked, momentarily losing his footing as the sub continued its sixty-degree nosedive. Brand caught the SS officer's fall and replied calmly.

"In the sense he won't have reason to now."

Having lodged Kiki in the Captain's quarters and buttoned the heavy curtain that served for a door, Trager had returned to his appointed position near the center line where he caught the tail end of this exchange. Brand looked over at him for corroboration, perhaps his largest gamble since leaving London. Trager didn't disappoint and gave no sign of offering a contradictory account.

"Enemy vessel closing to six thousand metres," the sonar operator reported.

"Gentlemen, I'll thank you to pipe down. I need my crew razor focused. No distractions," Dahlmer said.

"All hands prepare for depth charges," the XO announced over the tannoy.

Five long, silent minutes later the distant boom of depth charges began and continued for thirty minutes more, getting ever closer but never presenting a serious threat to the hull's integrity.

Dahlmer took a perverse pleasure in the explosions. The men would benefit from this reminder of the danger they faced. He needed them alert to threat from every quadrant and, even down to never allowing more than one cup of coffee in the control room at any one time, he used every technique at his disposal to nurture that acuity.

After thirty-five minutes submerged he made his next move.

"Go to periscope depth," Dahlmer ordered.

"Go to periscope depth, half ahead both," the XO ordered the Chief.

"Both hydroplanes hard rise. Flood 50 liters," the Chief said while making the mental calculations that would bring the boat up without oscillating. Figuring in local salinity and currents he would trim the boat to fourteen metres and run the motors so neither the scope nor the props would create any swirl. He punctuated the rise into phases so men could reposition themselves to maintain the boat's desired attitude. A good engineer became a part of his boat, attuned to its every movement like a champion jockey aboard a thoroughbred.

Dahlmer knew he had less than an hour of darkness left before the odds would start to tip back in his target's favor. At 20 metres he entered the conning tower and sat on the leather seat anchored to the scope's column. Pedals allowed him to scope left or right and a mirror adjusted his sight seventy degrees up and fifteen degrees down. Every movement, even depressing the torpedo firing button, was made silently.

The torpedo fire-control table alongside the periscope was, perhaps, the sub's most telling advantage. Its logic processor took inputs directly from the periscope and allowed the operator to fire a spread at multiple targets in rapid succession. Dahlmer began his search from a mental picture of where he expected to find the frigate. True enough. He brought the crew back to battle stations and began figuring out his best approach.

"Starboard 20," Dahlmer ordered. There was no need to raise his voice, the conning tower's acoustics were excellent and there were several microphones on its interior walls.

The torpedo officer reported tubes one to four ready and outer doors open, the Chief compensating for the extra water flooding in and readying to adjust again once the torpedoes were launched. The boat was now running parallel to the frigate and Dahlmer had the target locked in the periscope's crosshairs. The torpedo officer continued his deadly instructions for the control table operators.

"Enemy red 90, enemy speed 15 knots, range 5000 metres, torpedo speed 30, running depth 5 metres," he said with menacing calm.

Once these values were entered the control table calculated the desired firing angles and lateral deflection. The torpedoes could bear up to ninety degrees away from the boat's course and once under the target a magnetic pistol would detonate the main charge exacting the maximum damage on the target's keel.

With everything lined up the operator threw the switch linking the periscope to the table and the tubes below. Cogwheels began whirring and the operators waited anxiously for the lights signaling successful synchronization. When the final light came on, the death trap was set. The system would automatically compensate for any course deviation between the sub and the frigate providing the torpedoes' ninety-degree turning arc wasn't exceeded. The system even allowed the boat's turn to safety to be commenced before firing.

"Fire at four thousand metres," Dahlmer ordered.

"Tubes one, three and four ready to fire," reported the torpedo officer.

"Permission to fire," Dahlmer said.

"Away," the torpedo officer said on pressing the firing button. A torpedo mate down by the tubes stood ready to press the auxiliary buttons if the primary failed but it rarely did.

Shells began raining down above the sub as she turned away but that was the last act of a doomed fighting ship. No lifeboat, raft or other sign of life from the frigate was detected.

Every hand aboard the sub was allowed a quick look through the periscope to witness the destruction they had brought about.

Brand found this ritual barbaric, but he was not about to criticize Dahlmer. He was a handsome young man, little more than twenty years of age Brand thought, with a rakish goatee and keen blue eyes. Decked out in his grey overalls there were no visible signs of the distinctions already in his service record, but command of this boat in and of itself stood testament to his caliber.

After months of grueling mental and physical training someone in the Kriegsmarine had seen fit to entrust this young fellow with a four million Reichsmark component at the tip of the Fatherland's fighting machine.

And he had just demonstrated with fearlessness his deserving of that trust.

————————

As celebrations aboard the sub subsided Brand turned to a task he'd had in mind since leaving Bath in a hurry – developing Corbin's fourth film.

He'd wanted to bring along enough chemicals to finish the job on the road, but their abrupt departure had stymied that. However Brand knew of ways in which film could be developed using improvised materials, notably organic liquids like wine and coffee. Though he'd never had reason to try these techniques before, he had good cause now.

If the film had been exposed during battle Corbin would have been pushing the film beyond its ISO rating to capture crisp, fast exposure shots. The Contax camera was built for action photography and permitted speeds up to f1250. But if he'd exposed the film at night he would have had the shutter wide open over a longer exposure to collect sufficient ambient light. A caffeine-based mixture might work with the 'slower' film but not if the film had been pushed.

The news value of Corbin's images from the beaches had already expired. Now all Brand was interested in was proof of Kastner's story about Churchill and Rommel. He would give the caffenol mixture a go. Brand made his way aft to the galley and asked the cook for a flask of coffee to help stay awake and some washing soda to give his underwear a rub through. The cook thought the laundry idea stupid because they would never dry but he kept the wisdom to himself.

"And would you happen to have some Vitamin C tablets," Brand added.

"Yes sir. They're part of our daily ration. The skipper insists on us being ready for extended underwater running," the cook said.

While the cook was fetching the tablets from the proviant store Brand scoped around for a developing vessel. Bizarrely he espied a cocktail shaker on a top shelf.

"What in heavens name is that doing aboard a submarine," Brand asked the cook.

"Oh that belonged to the previous commander. He didn't like to take his schnapps neat. By all accounts there was nothing neat about him," the cook said with a wry smile. "Herr Kramer had him replaced."

"Might I borrow it," Brand asked expecting a question in return.

"Mine not to reason why," the cook said assuming this stranger had exotic tastes too.

Brand turned to return to the Captain's quarters to find Kramer in the gangway between the storage lockers.

"Planning a party?" Kramer enquired.

"Hardly, our female passenger needs to wash her underclothes and rinse her contact lenses," Brand explained.

"I see. Every luxury extended," Kramer said.

"Compliance isn't always achieved under duress, Herr Kramer."

Kramer forced a smile, squeezed past and continued on to christen the head.

Gertrude had remained in the vicinity of the attacking frigate hoping the ship would get lucky and force the sub to surface. With great sadness they witnessed the frigate's demise and her mournful SOS. The track of the torpedoes had alerted Duke to the sub's periscope but that had soon disappeared.

"Where to now, Alastair?" Gertrude asked.

"My orders are to proceed to Rosslare and attempt to intercept Brand and his cadre.

"Although the U-Boat could be taking them anywhere within its remaining range, we have to assume he's still heading for the Republic" Duke said. Trouble is he won't surface until he's well clear of this area, especially in this daylight."

"Take a look portside," Gertrude said as she went into a low bank. "Do you see what I see?" she asked.

"An oil slick!" Duke exclaimed. "You did it Aunt Gertie," he said.

Gertrude was in no mood to gloat. As she tracked the sub's tell-tale Gertrude reflected on what might have been had she not radioed for assistance. How many lives and sorrows could have been spared? She lamented the futility of war – the litany of dashed hopes, broken dreams and could have beens.

"All good skipper?" Duke said over the intercom.

"All good," she lied.

Brand's recollection of the caffenol recipe combined two tablespoons of washing soda and a tablespoon of powdered Vitamin C with a litre of brewed coffee. Once the solids were fully suspended six top to bottom turns of the receptacle followed by three gentle inversions fifteen minutes later would allow the mixture to coat the film fully and react with the silver oxide thereon. This was going to be a hit or miss affair but Brand wanted to see what, if anything, was on this infernal film.

The Captain's quarters having only a curtain for privacy, Brand had asked Schaffer's permission to use the typewriter in the radio room to draft a report for Berlin. He locked the door and laid out the film canister and the flask of caffenol solution on the desk and readied a bulldog clip from which to hang the developed strip of film. He extinguished the lights and was about to open the film canister when Kramer paid a house call.

"Herr Brand, the captain requests your presence in the control room. We must discuss our next destination," Kramer said.

Brand wanted to contest the need for any discussion, but he refrained and replied through the locked door.

"Yes Hauptsturmführer Kramer, I will join you as soon as I've completed my report for Berlin," he said.

This fiction was enough to curtail further badgering but, judging by the lack of footfall, not enough to send Kramer back to the control room. Brand had the sense the agent was lingering in the gangway, perhaps hoping to observe some incriminating movement between quarters.

Regardless Brand pressed on, clacking on the typewriter randomly between twirling the cocktail shaker. In twenty minutes the developing process was complete and, after checking for all clear, Brand took the film over to the Captain's locker where he hung it up to dry before proceeding aft to the control room. Kiki had slept through the whole procedure.

"Ah thank you for joining us," Dahlmer said in a tone suggesting Kramer hadn't bothered sharing the purported reason for the delay. No matter.

"My orders are to transport you and your party to a destination of your choosing Herr Brand. I am at your service," Dahlmer said.

"Dublin please Captain," Brand said without hesitation. He'd been ruminating on his next best steps while rotating the developing flask and had decided to take Rosslare out of the equation. His primary contacts were in the capital city and the change of destination would throw Corbin and his meddlesome colleagues off the scent.

"May I ask the purpose of your mission, Herr Brand," Kramer said.

"Classified," Brand said with a degree of truth.

"I see," said Kramer. "We were informed your destination was Rosslare. Why the change? The rose fields protecting Dublin Bay represent much more risk for the Captain and his vessel," Kramer argued, referring to the minefields common place in the approaches to all major ports.

"To improve our combined chances of success. This mission is of crucial importance to the Reich," Brand said.

The last time Brand had checked he was a Gruppenführer which put him exactly four ranks above Kramer. He'd indulge this odious fellow in the interests of on-board harmony. But only so far.

Dahlmer was on the verge of acceding to Brand's request when the Chief Engineer spoke up.

"Captain, we're detecting a minor leak from the starboard fuel bunker. Suggest we surface immediately and put down a diver," the Chief said.

"Scope up," Dahlmer ordered. "Sonar report," he added.

With the coast clear Dahlmer gave the order to surface and deploy a diver to assess the damage and the FuMB aerial to detect whatever radar it could register. The news wasn't good. A bullet had ruptured both skins minimally, but the tear would only grow larger if they should dive again.

"I'm afraid you're going to have to take your chances at our nearest landing point, Herr Brand. Or you can stay aboard for a surface voyage to Brest?" Dahlmer said.

Gertrude had landed the Beau perfectly adjacent RNS Wexford, and Vera and Corbin had escaped, inelegant but jubilant, from their cruelly extended incarceration.

The Garda Inspector met them at the edge of the airstrip and assumed Corbin was running the show.

"Oh no, my friend. He's the man you need to talk to," Corbin said gesturing to Duke as he clambered down.

"We appreciate your help Superintendent," Duke said deliberately inflating the officer's rank.

"It's Inspector Cushmer," the officer said. "At your service, Agent Duke?"

"Yes sir," Duke confirmed. Our targets were collected by a U-Boat mid channel and, based on our last contact, we expect them to be making landfall on the beach near Carne Pier."

"Righto, that's about twenty minutes away" the Inspector said. "Pile in!"

In his attempts to find a weakness in Brand's story Kramer had shifted his attention to Trager.

"How long had you been operational with Obersturmführer Kastner," he asked Trager as they were eating in the mess area.

"Just over a year," Trager replied, determined not to venture more than required.

"Were you surprised when Kastner decided to return to the ferry without you," Kramer probed.

"Not really. Kastner is forever headstrong, and he doesn't take easily to orders he disagrees with."

"Did you agree with Herr Brand's plan?" Kramer asked.

"Sir, I understand Herr Brand, or Schroeder if you will, is a decorated General of the Schutzstaffel. I don't see it as my place to question his authority. Regardless, I've found his conduct exemplary in the short time I've been under his command," Trager said.

Kramer was getting nowhere with this direct attack, so he tried a different line.

"Do you think Lady Brown represents any value for your mission," he ventured.

"Again sir, well above my pay grade," Trager said, spooning another generous helping of sauerkraut. Rations on the U-Boats were double other ships and since he didn't know where his next square meal was coming from, Trager was taking full advantage.

"Prepare the landing party," Dahlmer announced on the tannoy.

In the control room Dahlmer drew Brand aside.

"I have received a Commander signal from Berlin with your new orders. I would like you to be with me in the radio room when I decrypt it," Dahlmer said.

Part Seven – 8th June 1944

47. County Wexford, Eire

The Commander designation on Berlin's signal had prevented other eyes, notably Kramer's, from seeing the content. After decrypting it Dahlmer had handed it straight to Brand, so he too remained oblivious to Brand's orders. Aloft in the bridge Brand addressed the Captain for the last time.

"Captain, your crew and your devotion to duty are a credit to the Kriegsmarine. Thank you for your hospitality and God's speed," Brand said.

"You're welcome Herr Brand," Dahlmer said. "I took a sneak peek at that film you hung in my locker. Please make it count," he added in a whisper.

Brand descended into the inflatable dinghy to join Trager, Lady Brown and the two sailors assigned to row them ashore. With Trager positioned in the bow, the others counterbalanced the inflatable dinghy sufficiently for it to make decent headway. A daytime disembarkation was not an operation you wanted to dilly-dally with.

Two IRA soldiers were waiting on the stubby pier, another three stood alongside their lorry on the coast road, forty yards away. The surf was pounding in, salt spraying the boat's occupants as the sailors steadied the dinghy alongside the rusty, barnacled pylons. Sensing the crew's urgency to push off Trager lifted Kiki, then himself, out of the boat and onto the pier. Brand was given a boost by one of the sailors while the other got ready to row.

The bedraggled threesome started walking towards land just as a black maria came careering down the coast road towards the IRA's lorry. Without waiting for an invitation the IRA soldiers started firing on the van as soon as it came into effective range. The Garda vehicle screeched to halt, turning broadside to shield the incoming fire.

Alert to what they were likely to face the Garda Inspector had his men issued with two revolvers and two WWI Enfield rifles with which they began to return fire. They were a poor match for the IRA's automatic weaponry now vectoring in from the lorry and the head of the pier. However the van and the sea wall provided good cover and the IRA men at the lorry seemed overanxious to get the fight finished. Two of them started walking towards the black maria, guns blazing, making easy targets of themselves with predictable results. The odds got better still when one of the IRA soldiers on the pier was taken out.

Vera, terrified but determined to bear witness, was ducking in and out of view from behind the police van. Curiously neither Duke nor Brand were firing even though she suspected them both armed. Fear of hitting Lady Amelia had been taken out of the equation when Kiki took cover behind a massive concrete bollard. Trager on the other hand had hit one of the Garda men before running out of ammunition.

Against all odds the Garda were gaining the upper hand when fate tipped the table against them. Fate personified by Duke. Vera saw him raise his pistol and begin firing - not towards the assailants but at the backs of the Garda officers. Corbin flung himself towards Duke and was hit straightway. Duke dispatched the last policeman standing and then levelled his gun at Vera's trembling forehead.

Before the war the likelihood of a British bobby bearing or facing a firearm was virtually nil. But she'd heard tales of what it was like to look down the barrel of a gun from her father. Nothing prepared you for the actuality of facing a shooter who had just almost emptied a cold-blooded clip into four fellow human beings.

The pause in the firing was punctuated by a single shot from a P45 that spun Duke around, knocking the gun from his grip. Vera looked across to see Brand striding towards her position, while keeping a sharp eye on Duke who was clutching his left arm and making no effort to retrieve his pistol. Now it was Duke's turn to inspect a hot gun barrel at close quarters, but the ordeal wasn't phasing him. No tremor, no sweat just a half smile.

"Is that the reward I get for saving your bacon?" Duke asked as Brand kicked Duke's pistol well out of reach.

"Please make your way to the other vehicle," Brand replied.

"And you young lady, please radio for emergency assistance, it looks like my photographer friend is still alive," Brand said before joining the others. The lorry sped away leaving Vera devastated and Corbin hanging on to dear life.

48. The Houses of Parliament, London

After a robust debate about the failure to appoint a new Chief Constable for Wolverhampton, business in the House ranged over the span of life: from primary school education to privately owned cemeteries. The Prime Minister then made his entrance and was called upon to make assurances about the status of the Belgian Government exiled in London.

Assurances swiftly given he went on to a question about his Government's policy on post war reparations which some in the chamber found presumptive, both in terms of the war ending anytime soon, and regarding the chances of Churchill's Government surviving into peacetime. Bedell-Smith may have accepted another one of Montgomery's bets on the war being over by Christmas but not everyone shared the American general's optimism. And there were those who, while willing to concede Churchill was the right man to win a war, remained convinced he'd be a patent liability in its aftermath.

As to the reparations question, Churchill recalled mistakes made after WWI, chiefly their severity and their unintended consequences. The British had sequestered not only the Kaiser's navy but also its mercantile fleet, at a value far below the cost per ton British shipyards could achieve. Orders were cancelled and shipwrights returning from the horrors of France were left jobless.

"I am sure that the mistakes of that time will not be repeated; we shall probably make another set of mistakes," Churchill told the MP whose constituency spanned the Scottish shipyards on the banks of the River Clyde.

Before getting drawn into speculations about the postwar use of German labor or, heaven forbid, any indiscretions about progress in Normandy, Churchill left the chamber to whet his whistle.

When time permitted, and he often made it do so, Churchill would repair to the bar adjoining the Member's dining room to mop up useful scuttlebutt. As he crossed the Central Lobby, accompanied by his confidante, Brendan Bracken, Churchill was approached by a man he barely recognized. Bracken leaned in to whisper a cue, but Churchill brushed away Bracken's hand from his sleeve as though he'd never needed the prompt.

As an hereditary peer Viscount Brown rarely felt obliged to attend the House, bar when the socialists were pushing for increased taxes on inherited wealth. Lung cancer had kept him even more absent of late and was threatening to gather him in before his father, the Earl, met his maker.

Churchill had little time for Brown and his ilk, but he respected his father whose forbears had fought with his own at the Battle of Blenheim. And, scarred by the loss of his beloved daughter Marigold and the more recent loss of Thompson's pilot son, he could be moved to tears by the prospect of a parent surviving a child. He stopped dutifully and nodded.

"Forgive me Prime Minister," Brown said returning the nod. "I believe you may be aware of the continuing plight of my wife, Lady Amelia?"

Thanks to Dorothy Paget, Churchill was being reminded of Lady Brown's predicament to the cusp of irritation. How one life could be deemed so important when so many were surrendering theirs by the hour eluded him. And, in Lady Clementine's view, that was a sentiment probably shared by Lady Brown herself.

Notwithstanding, Churchill nodded again respectfully.

"The momentous happenings across the Channel must monopolize your attention sir, but I implore you to do whatever possible to rescue my wife from the fiends who have her captive," Brown pleaded.

"You may rest assured Lord Brown that we shall not rest content until the Viscountess is returned safely to these shores," Churchill told him with a detail which let Brown know he was up to date with developments.

They nodded once more, and Brown turned away unsteadily. With heavy reliance on a gold-tipped, Malacca cane which connected sonorously with the marble flooring, the Viscount made his way back to the Peers Smoking Room.

Churchill lingered a while then addressed Bracken.

"Tell Gubbins I want a full report with recommendations pdq."

49. The Ordenspalais, Berlin

Goebbels had an interest in chess to the extent it brought together clever people: some worth cultivating; others ripe for removal. The titular President of the German Chess Federation saw the world in four dimensions and the fourth was information. The Reichsminister for Propaganda and National Enlightenment was a Grand Master of data acquisition and assimilation.

"Please place a call to Dönitz immediately," Goebbels requested. "Ask State Secretary Naumann to join the call."

Werner Naumann had been Goebbel's most true and trusted sounding board since hostilities began. They debated the merits of everything from grand plots to turns of phrase together.

"Grand Admiral Dönitz is on the line for you, Herr Reichsminister," Goebbels's secretary said with a gesture to say Naumann was listening in, as he frequently did.

"Good Morning Grand Admiral, I hope this is a convenient moment," Goebbels asked in perfunctory style.

It wasn't. Dönitz had adjourned the daily meeting at which he reviewed his U-Boat commanders' signals to take the call. He considered these reports his most reliable source of intelligence and was pained to have to relegate it to Goebbel's humbuggery. But he was altogether familiar with the Reichsminister's self-importance and the barrage of calls he would face until the call was taken.

"Yes of course, Reichsminister, how can I help you?" Dönitz said.

"What is the latest report from U-491," Goebbels asked.

"No significant change. Schroeder is in possession of the package and he and his party were successfully landed in Eire early evening yesterday," Dönitz said.

"Our Irish sources report enemy action in that vicinity at around the same time. Did your commandant refer to any difficulty?" Goebbels asked.

"He did not but then he was eager, rightfully, to clear the area during daylight. His vessel is damaged and surface running only," Dönitz said.

"Providing his mission was complete, Grand Admiral," Goebbels asserted.

Dönitz didn't expect someone disqualified by disability from any kind of military service to comprehend the fear riven deep into a submariner's psyche. But to conjure that somehow into a dereliction of duty was unforgiveable.

"My commandant's paramount duty is to his vessel and her crew," Dönitz retorted.

"And our Fuhrer! Please keep me appraised personally should any further detail come to light. Good day, Grand Admiral," Goebbels said, replacing the receiver before his interlocutor could reply.

Naumann entered the room to soothe his boss, if necessary, and inform per his job description. The latest dispatch from their source in the Irish Garda indicated the police action had been repulsed with the help of a squad of the Irish Republican Army.

Goebbels next move was a call to Joachim von Ribbentrop, former German Ambassador to the United Kingdom, now Reichsminister of Foreign Affairs. Ribbentrop had acquired wealth through marriage, his hint of nobility through adoption and, according to Goebbels, his position through misrepresentation. But from that position he bathed in Hitler's confidence and had to be kept onside.

"Good Morning, Herr Reichsminister, may I prevail upon you for a report of the ailments currently afflicting the Allied Powers' leadership, political and military?" Goebbels asked.

"Good Morning Goebbels," von Ribbentrop replied, with a Patrician informality intended to vex. "That will be quite a long report. Are you writing get well cards or selling life insurance?" he quipped.

"Neither, Herr Reichsminister," Goebbels said with a forced laugh. "It's material we may include in the Führer's next major speech," he continued, introducing the specter of the serious parent into Ribbentrop's mind before drawing the call to a close.

Goebbels was accumulating data from sources Hitler trusted to add credibility to his own intrigues. With the incriminating images secured, he was game playing the impact of the other element of Brand's mission on an epic scale. Goebbels needed a much larger smoke screen than Churchill's apparent peacemaking to divert the German Peoples' attention from Northern France. Ideally one which might change the course of history.

Reports from Washington suggested Roosevelt's health was deteriorating rapidly owing to a shared love of cigarettes, while nicotine and the stress of war were also taking their toll on King George VI. Stalin was the poster boy for chain smoking but appeared healthy enough, while Churchill's lungs seemed impervious to carcinogens and his liver resistant to daily marination in diluted scotch and Pol Roger.

If Churchill could be knocked over, other dominoes could fall. Roosevelt would give way to Truman. The King to his eighteen-year-old daughter or, better yet, his prodigal brother who had already demonstrated some support for the regime. Finally Churchill would give way to Anthony Eden, whose constitution was much weaker.

Stalin's territorial ambitions would galvanize these understudies into an alliance with the Third Reich to save allied lives and repel Russian advances. Diversionary noise could be generated by various peace entreaties via Franco's government and by pandering to Emperor Hirohito's inclination to sue for peace with Stalin.

This bewildering concoction was riddled with ifs, buts and maybes but Goebbels believed it could be the perfect cure for his Führer's pickle of persecution and paranoia. At least to the extent of endorsing his order to have Churchill assassinated.

50. Wicklow Mountains, Eire

After the battle at Carne, Brand, Trager, Duke and Kiki were taken blindfolded to a location further north, Kiki's hood soaking up her tears as they journeyed. Once the hoods were off Brand readily identified their beautiful surroundings as the shores of Lough Dan. After the rigors of recent days he welcomed the calm of the place, but he remained anxious to meet with his senior IRA contacts, and deeply skeptical of Duke's damascene allegiance to the Fatherland.

"When will your boss be joining us?" Brand asked the IRA soldier who appeared to be in charge of the six-strong security detail.

"When he's good and ready," came the unhelpful reply.

Brand had visited the locale some seven years previous, putatively fly fishing for brown trout and capturing large format landscapes, and surreptitiously forging links with the hierarchy of the Irish Republican Army. The atmosphere at the nearby manor house had been as dour as the architecture at first, but it became borderline raucous when the whisky flowed and the céilí dancing got going.

He'd declined successive invitations to join in and learn the routines until a disarming woman in her early twenties and swathed in Limerick green linen had made her request. Fewer landscapes and some unexpected life studies made it back to his darkroom as a consequence.

Not knowing when the IRA big wigs would show, Brand decided to bide the time actively and get one-on-one with Trager. There'd been no opportunity to plumb Trager's true feelings about Kastner's demise, and Brand wanted to get a better gauge of the man before Duke set about befriending him.

"You know Trager this lake has a mermaid, a Dublin Bay Mermaid to be precise. Can you sail?" Brand asked, pointing to a seventeen-foot dinghy moored at the end of the jetty.

Trager nodded that he could. Brand drew aside the chief minder and part asked, part informed him about taking the boat out. The minder acceded provided one of his men accompanied them. Perfect for Brand's purposes as it precluded any possibility of Duke joining them in the three-hander.

"Please pick me a slight third crewmember," Brand said, alluding to the substantial ballast Trager represented. The boat had been designed for the more expansive and choppy waters of Dublin Bay and Brand was confident its buoyancy would keep them all three of them dry and afloat on the calmer waters of Lough Dan.

With Trager at the helm and himself and their guard as far forward as the half-deck would allow, they set off on a gentle run upwind. Before long Trager was twitching the good ship "Tuano" ever closer to the wind direction, reprising handling skills learnt on the Schwansee and the Alpsee during bygone summers.

After a tack and a commendable gybe, Brand complimented his skipper in German before adding a ribald criticism of their sailing companion's contribution to the maneuvers. Trager knew what Brand was about and responded with a disparaging assessment of the Irishman's manhood. Satisfied they could not be understood they continued to talk at full volume.

"I've not had an opportunity to thank you for bearing me out when we boarded the U-Boat, Herr Trager," Brand ventured.

"And I don't recall having had an opportunity to talk about your unilateral action prior you taking it, Herr Brand," Trager replied.

A hundred meters off their port beam a peregrine falcon swooped to glance the water's surface and rise majestically with a three-pound trout in its talons. It was a fitting metaphor for the guile in Trager's response and they both smiled. Trager resumed the conversation after another of his graceful tacks.

"I don't condone what you did but bloodlust reaps its own reward eventually. In truth my departed colleague is not much lamented. I don't expect many, or any of us, to come out of this war with much honor due, in large part, to officers like Kastner and our new friend, Mr. Duke."

Brand let a slow blink and some silence signal acquiescence before sounding Trager out further.

"And what do you make of our new ally," he asked.

"Ah that's a level of discernment only granted to those of great rank like yourself, Herr Brand. But if you want some advice from a humble tanker?" Trager said. "Watch your rear."

In the gathering gloom a cormorant croaked its woeful call, before diving to forage the bottom of the lake. They shared another wry smile and headed back to the jetty.

51. The Old Hospital, Wexford

After being triaged by a general practitioner in Carne village, Corbin was rushed to Wexford for specialist surgery. Corbin's luck was holding out. A bullet had entered his left ribcage, apparently grazing his spleen as it pierced its way through and through the intercostal muscles. Less than inch in any direction and either splintered bone or the lead itself would have decimated his spleen and been the death of him.

Vera tended to him in the back of the Garda's black maria and was impressed by how well Corbin endured the journey. The doctor said he would be in great pain and had given her a generous vial of morphine and a syringe to keep him as comfortable as possible. Corbin was semi-delirious for most of the journey, but his pulse never faltered. Neither did his smile whenever he came round. At least until he remembered recent events.

"Is Kiki, I mean Lady Brown, is she safe? Did she escape?" he asked.

Vera shook her head and he grimaced.

"She's safe, but Brand still has her," she said.

"I'm responsible for getting her into this bloody mess Vera, he said. "Please save her for me and tell her she was the love of my life," he said as the anesthetic took him under again.

At the hospital he had just enough time to tell Vera where he'd kept his will before going under the knife for over three hours. When Vera returned to the waiting room she was approached by a stranger in civilian clothes. He introduced himself as an attaché from the British Representative's Office in Dublin sent to debrief herself and Mr. Corbin.

All Vera wanted right now was a mug of strong, black tea and somewhere to curl up and weep for a while. He was happy to oblige with the beverage, but he was insistent about pushing through with his interrogation.

He was nowhere near as handsome as his fellow spook, Duke and, from the quality of his questions, Vera soon perceived he wasn't the sharpest knife in the draw either. But, there again, he was piloting a desk out of this outpost while a real war was being fought not a hundred miles away. Once he'd exhausted all the commonplace he had on his pad, he revealed Vera's next challenge.

"You're going to be flown to London to meet with my superiors," he said.

"When?" Vera asked.

"Tonight," he said. "May I top up your tea before we leave?"

52. Wicklow Mountains, Eire

"How was the wind?" Duke asked as Trager and Brand re-entered the house.

"Predictable, just how we like it," Brand said.

Kiki was sitting at the opposite end of the massive kitchen table, keeping well away from Duke. The erstwhile British agent had tried several times to tice her into conversation, but she had no stomach for discourse with this murdering Judas.

"Had I known we were going on a jolly Brand, I'd have packed my flies," Kiki said. There was truth in her sarcasm - she was a gifted and avid angler. She could quickly assess what insects the fish were rising for and, if she didn't have something similar in her tackle box, she could tie a facsimile in a matter of minutes.

Brand smirked as he sat down while Trager made a B-line for the pantry. He re-emerged with a loaf of soda bread and a tub of the tastiest, creamiest, freshly churned butter he would ever eat. Brand sufficed himself with a half-pint glass of stout from a bottle one of the guards had just sampled.

"No appetite?" Duke asked.

"Depends what for," Brand replied with a smile.

"How long are you boys going to dance around the ring?" Kiki asked. "Isn't it time to land some punches? I'll happily referee," she said, releasing some of her own frustration and hoping to goad them into an indiscretion.

Brand stood up and went over to the window.

"Excuse me while I go and revel in the dying of the light," he said as his shadow rose to join him outside. After five minutes Duke followed.

"Some company?" he asked.

"If you must," Brand said.

"Lady Brown has a point," Duke said. "We do need to reach a rapprochement somehow. I'm willing to bury the hatchet. As long as it doesn't end up in my good arm."

"Not sure I crave any scheming with a man who shoots men in the back to prove where his loyalties lie," Brand said. "Loyalties like that might prove ephemeral."

"Look here we're more akin than you think, Brand. Or should I say Schroeder? I've been living a double life too, ever since Oxford. I'd have preferred to cast off my chrysalis and serve the Fuhrer without all the subterfuge, but I wasn't given the choice. Regardless I will serve the Fatherland to my dying breath."

"Very touching but you'll have to back up those words with deeds when called upon, preferably ones not so repugnant," Brand said and began walking back to the house.

Duke grabbed him by the arm and the minder made to intervene.

"Stay calm soldier," Brand said. "My friend here is just trying to make his point."

While speaking Brand decided against grabbing his wounded wing and, instead, calmly lifted Duke's right hand with a vice like grip and let it fall.

Back inside the chief minder was getting off the phone.

"You'll be taken to another location in the morning, he said and turning to Brand he continued. "You'll get to see the brass tomorrow."

53. SOE HQ, Baker Street, London

Vera was ushered into a wood paneled room at the top of the building and offered yet more tea, this time from Fortnum and Mason's and served in bone china. She was famished and about to ask if anything more substantial than Edinburgh shortbread might be on offer when another door opened, and the charlady beat a hasty retreat.

"WPC Wright, thank you for making yourself available. I'm Major General Gubbins and I'd like to ask you some questions about recent events in Bath and Eire," the bemedaled officer said as Vera stood and saluted.

"It's an honor sir," Vera said, taking out her notebook. Gubbins motioned her to sit back down and crack on.

Referring to her contemporaneous notes as she'd been taught, Vera took Gubbins through a chronology of events starting with the shout at the Royal Crescent in Bath. Gubbins interjected with the odd call for clarification but stored up most of his questions until she'd finished.

"The photographer, Corbin, what did you make of him? We have evidence he was on friendly terms with the German agent, Brand" Gubbins said as he offered to refresh Vera's teacup. Vera's bladder bade her decline.

"He told me they were acquainted sir, but I think all amity ended when Brand kidnapped Lady Brown. After that Corbin was rifle-focused on rescuing her," Vera said.

"The IRA soldiers who turned up to rescue Brand and his party, did you get a good look at the survivors?" Gubbins asked.

"I didn't recognize any of them, as you might expect sir, but I could take a look at photos if you have any?" Vera volunteered.

"Oh we have plenty for you to look at, though it's likely they were only foot soldiers. Their senior personnel tend to stay in the shadows," Gubbins said, speaking from personal experience of the Anglo-Irish War. Having dealt with the smaller stuff he was getting to what concerned him most.

"Now, during your journey how well did you get to know the man who identified himself as Alastair Duke?" Gubbins asked.

"Agent Duke, yes sir. Is Duke not his real name?" Vera said.

Gubbins had no answer that wouldn't make his own blood boil, so he ignored the question.

"Did you pick up on any sign he might not be loyal to the Crown?" he asked.

"No sir, until Ireland he seemed straight as an arrow. Though there was one thing that bugged me."

"Go on," Gubbins said.

"I couldn't figure out why he didn't smell Lady Brown's perfume when we were in Brand's cellar the first time. If he had, we'd likely have nabbed them there and then," Vera said.

"But you didn't see him collude with Brand or the German agents prior to the massacre on the beach in County Wexford?" Gubbins asked.

"Not to my knowledge sir," she said.

"Is there any possibility Duke's shooting of the three Garda officers could have been accidental?"

Vera shook her head ruefully.

"No sir, it was cold blooded murder," she confirmed.

"Then he'll hang for that and his treachery," Gubbins vowed.

Gubbins had been impressed with what he'd heard about this constable's sang froid throughout this mission. Now her composure and her words were underpinning his high regard and adding to the evidence of Duke's psychosis.

"Young lady your conduct in this whole affair has been exemplary and this organisation owes you a debt of gratitude," Gubbins said. "When was the last time you enjoyed afternoon tea at a swanky London hotel?"

Vera accepted the invitation graciously but hoped it would be for another day. Right now all she could think about was a plate of cod and chips with sufficient salt and lashings of malt vinegar.

54. A Dublin Safe House

"Welcome back to the Irish Free State," a familiar voice said as Brand's blindfold was removed. Members of the Irish Republican Army refused to refer to their country as Éire.

"Thank you Michael, it's good to be back. Allow me to introduce my colleagues, Agents Trager and Duke, and Lady Amelia Brown" Brand said as their hoods were removed.

"A Lady *and* a Duke! My goodness Brand, how well you've insinuated yourself into British society," Hollins said

Michael Hollins was a senior IRA officer who Brand had tipped to be the organisation's Chief of Staff by now. But as Officer in charge of Overseas Operations he was precisely the right man to be negotiating with.

"And your agent friends, would that be agents of the Abwehr or the SS?" Hollins said, picking at an old scab he knew irritated some German intelligence officers.

"We all serve the will of our Führer," Duke interjected.

Hollins smiled, invited the others to sit and took Brand into an adjoining room before continuing with his questions.

"And that wills the death of Churchill does it now?" Hollins asked.

"Ardently," Brand said.

"Sorry but we've walked down this garden path with you lads before, only to see it trail off to nothing," Hollins said.

Brand nodded, "I come with a token of our earnest Michael, may I" he asked, gesturing to reach into his jacket pocket.

All four visitors had been searched thoroughly and their weapons remained confiscated, but Brand was standing on ceremony. Hollins nodded back and Brand took out a canister of developed film.

"Here you'll find evidence of the British Prime Minister plying for peace through the good offices of a Field Marshal of the Third Reich," Brand said.

"Which Field Marshall?" Hollins asked.

"*The* Field Marshall," Brand replied.

"If that's on the level why would you want to kill Churchill now," Hollins asked.

"To stir the pot even thicker," Brand said, returning the film canister to his pocket.

Hollins thought long and hard while offering Brand a seat he accepted and a whiskey he declined.

"I won't pretend it wouldn't suit our purposes too," Hollins said eventually. "We've lost some good men lately and doing away with the Cry Baby would do wonders for morale and our coffers. But things are a lot tighter now than they were of yore."

"Can you still get to him," Brand asked.

"Where there's a will but such resources don't come cheap" Hollins said.

"I'm sure an accommodation can be made. Do you have a unit in place?" Brand asked.

"I have a very capable cell awaiting activation in London and an opportunity beckons. We don't see the Prime Peacock ducking Parliamentary Question Time now things are going his way over there in France," Hollins conjectured. "He was preening himself in the Commons on Thursday and we hear he's going to insist on going over to Normandy any day now with his buddy Smuts.

"If he comes back alive wild horses won't keep him away from the House next Wednesday," Hollins said. "And we have it on very good authority he'll be bidding farewell to the General at his favourite hostelry afterwards."

Brand needed no clues as to the restaurant in question. Churchill favored London's Savoy Hotel which owed its culinary credentials to Auguste Escoffier and his pragmatic distillation of the genius of Marie-Antoine Carême. Some dishes were dedicated to celebrities like Nellie Melba and Sarah Bernhardt and others, like the Turtle Soup and the Petite Marmite, had become firm favorites of Churchill whose palate had never found issue with cholesterol.

Brand wouldn't admit it in this company, but he'd tried that consommé with its rich garnish of bone marrow toast and had come to love it too, in moderation. Perhaps he had been sucked too far into British society.

"Will my companions and I be welcome to tag along," Brand asked.

"Providing you mind your Ps & Qs," Hollins said.

Part Eight

55. Montgomery's HQ, Cruelly – June 12th

Churchill believed his military experience, as combatant and non-combatant, made him uniquely qualified to lead a country at war. It bolstered his willingness to challenge his commanders, sometimes stringently, and gave them cause to reconsider their plans in the round. Churchill's own challenge was in knowing where the hazy line between scrutiny and meddling lay.

He'd eventually been dissuaded from joining the British forces on D-Day itself. In part for his own safety, and because introducing the distraction of a prominent civilian into the thick of a modern battle was preposterous. Even Elizabeth I had managed to assert her warrior credentials from the relative safety of Tilbury.

Churchill continued agitating to get over there and on DD+6 he got his wish, boarding a British destroyer, the HMS Kelvin, for the trip to the Normandy beaches and Montgomery's HQ just beyond. He was accompanied by his great friend Field Marshall Jan Smuts, Prime Minister of South Africa. Smut's presence lent weight to the mission's military value and would, it was hoped, temper Churchill's tendency to overreach into military tactics.

Smuts was uniquely placed to talk sense into Churchill. Like F.E. Smith, Churchill's other great friend and confidante, Smuts had a legally schooled brain: a brilliant one that took an unprecedented double first at Cambridge. As an influential military and political leader he had his detractors, but Churchill could empathize with the vicissitudes of statesmanship. And, as with Smith, their friendship went back decades and only grew deeper after Smith's death in 1930.

Because he was travelling by ship Churchill wore his Royal Yacht Squadron uniform which was much less showy than the army or air force uniforms he was entitled to wear. Smuts' fatigues were similarly understated, reflecting the notion this was a working trip, not a publicity stunt. Meetings were held in Monty's caravan, avoiding the grandiose backdrop of the Chateau and the majestic nearby tower where the press corp had been billeted.

Plans were reviewed and photographs taken, mostly by Smuts who was happy to stay out of the limelight. His extended presence in Europe since the recent Commonwealth Minister's conference was drawing criticism back home.

Churchill was greeted enthusiastically by the troops who caught sight of him and his trademark V for Victory encouragement. And for the British and American generals present the main objective of the exercise was achieved: they had left the PM in no doubt about the grave risk of any of their confidences being leaked to the press or Parliament.

56. En Route to Kilburn, North London – June 12th

Brand and his crew were too conspicuous to travel back to the mainland ensemble so diverse routes were taken. Trager and Duke were given the keys to a Foden DG box truck together with tickets for the overnight sailing from Dublin to Holyhead. They were hauling barrels of Guinness, which British and American Forces massed on the mainland could not get enough of. This high demand and the banter about the Black Stuff which usually distracted the on-duty guards, meant they sailed through the checkpoints they couldn't circumnavigate.

Decked out in his olive-green overalls Trager was in his element behind the wheel of the diesel eight-wheeler and was happy to do all the driving down to North London from where another driver would take the stout on to a base in Essex. The 387th Bomb Group of the Mighty Eighth Airforce were planning a celebration before rebasing their B-26s in Hampshire.

During the journey Trager regressed into his successful strong and silent persona and Duke was left to carry off an Irish accent as though he'd kissed the Blarney Stone often and recently. All had gone swimmingly until a stop at a transport café on the A5 in Staffordshire. Trager hadn't eaten since the slim pickings on the ferry and was in dire need of a refueling.

The bill of fayre was, as Duke expected, cheap and calorific. For Trager he ordered a full English breakfast with blood pudding and kidneys standing in for pork chops and bacon, and, for himself, a sandwich of tinned corned beef on white bread. He wanted Trager satiated so they wouldn't have to pit stop again but he hadn't factored in the need to speak another foreign tongue in England's Black Country, so called for the soot which had cloaked the buildings during the Industrial Revolution.

"Am yow sure abart that cock?" asked the woman behind the counter, an inch of ash hanging precariously from a Woodbine cigarette stuck by tarry saliva to her bottom lip. "Weave gorra spesh on faggots un gray pays, one un six!"

The daily special was proving to be a slow mover in the summer heat, and she was determined to see the back of it. She'd warned her chief cook and bottle washer spouse it wouldn't sell, but he knew better, as usual. Offal was easier to come by than prime cuts and his main poacher-come-spiv had recently been detained at His Majesty's pleasure.

Unable to understand a word of it but not wishing to appear rude, Duke asked her to repeat the question by means of a quizzical tilt of his head. The reprise proved no more illuminating, and he stood bamboozled until a lorry driver queuing behind him butted in.

"Stop yer ivverin' an' ovverin' mate un' get on wi'it woll yow! Wif awl gorra a wum ter gooto," he urged, adding to Duke's unease.

To the proprietress' dismay Duke reiterated his original order and made to pay.

"Un howabart a puddin'?" she asked. "Summa Bert's jam roly-poly wool put 'airs on yer mate's chest. Bostin' wiv a dollop a Bird's Custard."

Duke caught enough of that to revive best forgotten memories of suet puddings from his boarding schooldays, and he politely shook off the offer and thrust a one pound note towards his tormentor.

Resigning herself to how much change she would have to return she told them their food would be ready in two shakes of a lamb's tail. As her head motioned them to a table by the window the cigarette's ash succumbed to gravity and landed in the serving chafer containing the unpopular faggots. Without missing a beat she worked the ash into the gravy with a ladle before ringing up the sale.

Both of them got the gist from her head movement and did as she said. There was some xenophobic chuntering back at the till about bloody micks and average Irish intelligence which Trager couldn't comprehend, and Duke chose to ignore.

The food arrived and Trager tucked in with gusto. He had impeccable table manners, but the sheer volume and the lingering image of the gravy thickening had turned Duke's stomach. He wrapped up the other half of his sandwich for later and repaired to the outside lavatory while Trager ploughed on. Before leaving the table he reminded Trager, in whispered German, to keep his head down. This was the first time Trager had heard his travelling companion speak German and he'd nodded his agreement before realizing what had just happened. Duke's German was very good.

Less than a minute after entering, Duke was followed into the lavatory by the irascible gent from the counter. He stood at the adjacent stall and proceeded to build on the bigotry he'd exchanged with the proprietor. Duke ignored him in a manner consistent with his earlier bewilderment, but the insults went on.

Duke shook himself off and buttoned up as he took a step back. Grabbing the trucker by the nape of his neck with his good right arm he drove his nose into the porcelain divider between the urinals and then frogmarched his victim into the toilet cubicle.

The Armitage Shanks ceramic pedestal was a new wide-throat model Bert the cook come owner had installed after successive blockages had augmented his plumbing duties. It proved a mite less than head sized and would require fracture to free the trucker's head when he was discovered unconscious thirty minutes later, his todger still hanging limply from his open flies.

Duke closed the cubicle door and smiled at the humor inscribed there.

"Who's Armitage, and what's shanking," the graffitist had asked.

After Trager and Duke left the safe house Brand gave Kiki the choice of dyeing her hair brunette herself, or having it done for her.

"I'll dye my own hair thank you," she said. "On condition that damned chloroform bottle stays firmly trousered on the next leg our journey."

"Very well," Brand said handing her the bottle of hair dye.

Brand killed time by cleaning the recent discharge from Kastner's P45 which Collins had handed back after their conversation. The guards had consistently kept their balaclavas down since the transfer, so it wasn't easy to discern their state of mind. To be on the safe side Brand sought permission before unholstering his weapon. The taller one of the pair then obliged with some cotton wadding, a ball of sweet string and a small can of machine oil. Twenty minutes later the pistol was back in its pristine state.

Kiki emerged from the bathroom without her blouse and her hair wrapped in a white towel. She sat at the table opposite Brand.

"Why didn't you kill Duke with that when you had a chance," Kiki asked, continuing her search for some daylight between her captors.

Brand found her niggling amateurish, but he indulged her for the sake of sustaining her hopefulness. If despair set in she'd become even more obstreperous and might have to be dispensed with after all.

"Agent Duke has convinced me of his allegiance to the Third Reich and he will prove to be a useful member of our team, I have no doubt," Brand lied.

"Like he proved himself capable of shooting three men from behind," Kiki said. "Don't you worry your back will be next?"

"I'll concede that was overzealous, but these are desperate times," Brand said.

Kiki unraveled her terry towel turban and leaned in, shaking a musk of perfume and freshly washed hair towards his senses.

"You're a better man than that Brand," she said in a lowered voice. "All this phony indifference doesn't pull the wool over my eyes."

"And my eyes aren't blind to your considerable charms, Lady Amelia," he said keeping his gaze resolutely away from her torso. "But you'll find me immune to them."

"I wasn't trying to appeal to your libido Brand," she purred. "You'd know if I did. I'm trying to appeal to your sense of decency."

"Then I'll admit you had me confused," he said. "But unaffected."

"Now I suggest you get dressed and look through the clothes in that dresser for a few extra layers," Brand said. "You'll be glad of the warmth tonight."

As they were leaving the shorter, younger guard put the finishing touches to a love spoon he'd been whittling from a fallen branch of bird cherry. He handed it to Kiki. She'd found the smell of the damp bark unpleasant as he stripped it, but the finished piece was anything but.

"A souvenir of the old country for yers," he said. "Be sure to come see us again."

She accepted the gift but had no idea whether or how to thank him. From down deep she found the magnanimity to smile.

Late afternoon they set off for the harbor at Bray in a Bedford QLD truck which wasn't built for human comfort. Kiki rode shotgun alongside a guy brandishing one. Brand drew the short straw and rode in the back with another guard.

He'd prevailed upon Hollins to sanction a minor detour to a small village cemetery en route. He wished to pay his respects at the grave of his treasured nephew, SS-Untersturmfuhrer Klaus Dörmer.

Klaus had been a member of the elite 1st SS Panzer Division Leibstandarte and was captured by retreating Allied forces at Dunkirk amidst the confusion caused by Hitler's bewildering no advance order. He barely survived a reprisal beating and after a hasty, unyielding interrogation was put on a train to Liverpool to meet the SS Arandora Star bound for St. John's in Newfoundland and the internment camps beyond.

During the night of July 2nd, 1940, the Arandora became the latest trophy to grace the record of U-47 under the command of the Kriegsmarine ace, Günther Prien. Klaus perished along with eight hundred other souls, the majority of whom were Italian civilians living in England when Mussolini through in his lot with Hitler. For Klaus death came slowly and painfully clinging to flotsam that drifted for days before being chanced upon by a trawler operating out of Bray. A cruel death Brand attributed directly to the Führer's infamous, ill-informed meddling.

The grave was shaded by an oak which had grown to twenty feet since Hollins had it planted there. A sparce Celtic cross bore the young soldier's name, date of birth and the approximate date of his demise. One half of his dog tag had been nailed into the granite adding his service number and blood group; Brand took the other half from his pocket as he approached the grave.

Kiki had followed to the drywall of the graveyard and watched as Brand knelt and, as best she could make out, began using a knife to tend to the ground at the foot of the cross. As Brand rejoined her at the truck Kiki could see his eyes were still teary. Without doubt this man had a soul and she would tap into it before this adventure was over, for good or ill.

After the Black Country pit stop the beer delivery proved pedestrian in terms of encounters and blistering in terms of progress. Duke was no stranger to speed but Trager's willingness to test the roadholding of the loaded Foden unnerved him. Not being at liberty to protect his wounded left arm with a sling added to his discomfort whenever it nudged the passenger door.

Heavy goods vehicles were subject to daytime speed limits to conserve fuel, but they weren't strictly enforced, especially when urgently needed beer was involved. Trager took full advantage of the laxity to pelt along.

Fortunately the weather was dry, so they stayed both on the surface and the route of the historic A5 until reaching a transport café at Staples Corner. The prospect of spectating another he-man meal was grinding on Duke until they pulled up next to a temporary structure which had already closed for the day. The bombed-out ruins of the original premises lay nearby.

"This used to be a grand place before the bombing," said a stocky fellow with a tweed flat cap and a frying pan face as he walked up to the truck. "Well, let's be having you. I need to be across town. A car'll be here to collect you in no time," he said as he climbed into the Foden's cab and drove away.

Trager and Duke didn't have long to wait before a black Humber Super Snipe saloon pulled up beside them. Trager was happy to see it was considerably larger than the Austin he'd been shoehorned into a week previous. He sat next to the juvenile driver and Duke joined another, older man in the back.

With night falling and with no desire to attract attention, the pace down the Edgware Road to Kilburn was a glacial 20mph and much to Duke's liking. Trager was taken with the grumble of the four-litre inline six and would have liked to put it through its paces.

The Humber's wheels crunched the gravel as they pulled into a private driveway. This detached safe house was grander than Duke had anticipated, secluded by the perimeter trees of Kilburn Grange Park on one border and dense, tall conifers on all others. The IRA's fundraising efforts must be paying dividends, Duke thought.

The interior, however, was dilapidated and there was a faint but pervasive smell of damp. The elaborately embossed tin ceiling and the Calacatta-marbled fireplace of the main receiving room gave hints of the home's former pomp. But your eye was dragged back to repainted anaglypta wallpaper struggling to defy gravity, and alcove shelves still sagging though long vacated of books.

"Ah, she must have been a beauty until some shyster of a slum landlord got hold of her," the elder IRA man said. "The war took the wind out of his sails, and we stepped in."

He ushered them downstairs to the kitchen and offered them food and drink. Duke was still digesting the second half of the corned beef sandwich he'd taken away from the inhospitable café whereas Trager was more than happy to accept the Irishman's hospitality. Never knowingly taken in by affability, Duke remained cagey as the Irishman continued to ladle on the Gaelic charm.

"I'm Patrick, Paddy if you will," he said. "And who might you be?"

"Duke, Alastair Duke. And this is my colleague, Herr Trager," he said causing Trager to look up from a bowl of beef and barley soup and smile.

"And this here is Dermot," Patrick said indicating his younger colleague. Dermot grunted and sidled out of the kitchen.

"I understand we're expecting two more friends of yours to join us this evening?" Patrick said offering to refill Duke's tot of Tullamore D.E.W..

"All being well," Duke said, declining. "Do you have a working telephone?"

"We do not," Patrick said. "Once us boys are activated, further contact is, as Herr Trager here might say, verboten. That way we all stay nice and safe."

Duke knew all about the protocol of active cells, but he doubted Patrick lacked a lifeline. The GPO junction box on the outside of the house looked like its newest feature.

"Well there's no point of us getting into any game plans until your boss turns up, so I'm going to run a few errands. Dermot can help you out if needs be," Patrick said jangling the keys to the Humber as he began climbing the stairs.

Duke hadn't thought of Brand as his 'boss' but, perhaps, Hollins had styled him so. Or Patrick had just assumed he couldn't be running the show from their side. It didn't much matter. Time would tell who was calling the shots.

A moon moving into its last quarter was rising as the German S-Boat stole into Bray harbor and moored against the southern wall. Its three, twenty-cylinder Daimler engines were idled while Brand and Kiki made their way along the harbor wall.

As soon as they clambered down the Captain gave the order to cast off and the motors were gently engaged. Corbin had told Kiki about these extraordinary boats he'd seen in Spain during the Civil War, and of the rumored havoc they'd caused recently off the Dorset coast. But, at first sight for herself, she couldn't see what all the fuss was about.

They exited the harbor entrance, pointed south-east and all six thousand horsepower took the vessel up onto a plane. The only basis for comparison in Kiki's experience belonged in a fairground. Brand had warned her to take a firm grip, but she hadn't heeded him well enough and stumbled back into his right arm. It arrested her fall and she looked up into his face trying to put a nonchalant smile on. It didn't fool anyone; she was plainly terrified. She thanked goodness for having had the sense to follow his advice about a few extra layers because even on a mild night the displaced air could chill to the bone.

Conversation was out of the question, so she gritted her chattering teeth and prayed for it to be over soon. It was a little over two hours till her wish was granted, and the boat came off the plane well before they slunk into New Quay harbor in Wales.

There was to be nothing as comfortable as the Alvis waiting to retrace their trek across the Principality. Hollins fully appreciated Brand's standing with the Nazi regime and didn't want him captured on his watch. He'd arranged more elaborate transportation.

An Austin KY/2 ambulance had been stolen to order from an Army base in Powys, together with three, full-size resuscitation dummies. The dummies were to play the part of corpses while Brand assumed the role of a high-ranking living casualty complete with saline drip and reams of crepe bandage. Kiki was to play nurse, Brand warning her to look like she cared if challenged at a checkpoint.

Kiki had reached tether's end with being thrown around in the back of the truck by the time they reached Swindon and tried a hissy fit to affect a transfer into the cab. Brand was feeling fatigued too and was having none of it. He brought the P45 up from under the blanket and let it rest on his abdomen, safety on.

"My dear Lady, you are tettering on the verge of becoming a pure liability," he said. "Either stop this infernal moaning or prepare for the worst!"

"You wouldn't dare Brand! Your life would not be worth living if you ended mine," she said and then lunged for the pistol.

Brand was waiting to see if she'd try. He grabbed her wrist and twisted her onto the parallel stretcher. With a flurry of bedding, mannequins and medical trappings, he rounded on her and pinned her flailing limbs to the canvas.

Somehow she managed to nip his left ear lobe with her teeth, and it bled down profusely. The blood only seemed to enrage her more and she continued to buck beneath him. But after another brace of convulsions her strength gave out and she was reduced to finishing her struggle by spitting at him.

Brand reciprocated with a more intimate exchange.

"I've got you now," Kiki thought and returned the kiss with interest. Brand licked the blood from her cheek and the next forty miles flew by.

After re-establishing order in the back of the ambulance, Brand was ruing his weakness and Kiki was finding it hard to keep a self-satisfied grin off her face. An awkward silence prevailed until they reached Wembley. The vehicle stopped and one of the crew came round to tell them to ditch the costumes and transfer to a saloon car parked further down the lay-by.

Brand was given the keys and an address and asked if he needed directions.

"No need. I know the area well," Brand said.

"Well it's good to see you're both none the worse for wear, Colonel," the ambulance driver said. "We thought you'd gone into a fit around Newbury," he added with a grin.

Brand ignored the impertinence and asserted some reference dignity.

"Be sure to relay my thanks to General Hollins," he said. The young comedian saluted involuntarily at the mere mention of the fabled fighter.

Compared to an Austin truck and precious little else, the Austin 12 was luxurious, and it made light work of the 20mph crawl to the Kilburn safe house. Brand tried to adjust some perceptions along the way.

"It would be foolish to think the intimacy back there marks a turn in our relationship, Lady Amelia," Brand said.

"If you mean neither of us yet trusts the other further than we can spit, I'll sign up to that," Kiki said. "But you must admit that was an interesting turn of events?"

"Insignificant and inconclusive I assure you," Brand said. "When we reach the safe house there'll be another cell of soldiers waiting. Please put your Machiavellian schemes out of mind and behave yourself. These Irishmen are a kill squad, and they won't put up with any of your nonsense."

"Jawohl, mein Herr!" she replied.

———————————

Brand pulled into the safe house drive just as Patrick returned from his errands, which gave Brand pause for a moment.

"Herr Brand, I'm Patrick," the affable Irishman said as he rushed over to the Austin.

"Good evening, Patrick. Allow me to introduce Lady Amelia Brown," Brand said as they exited the saloon. Pleasantries exchanged they entered the house and descended to the kitchen. Trager rose to greet them good heartedly; Duke made do with a half-hearted wave. Dermot was in a corner and didn't look up from an edition of The Daily Sketch newspaper trumpeting the joining of US and British forces outside Caen.

"Is everyone here?" Brand asked, certain he'd seen a curtain twitch in a dormer window as they were by the cars.

"That's right," said Patrick. "And we can get down to brass tacks as soon as you like?"

"That gets my vote," Duke interjected.

"Well we're not fighting for a democracy," Brand retorted. "We'll rest up Patrick and get to things fresh in the morning. We have time enough."

That left Patrick in no doubt who was calling the shots amongst the visiting crew, and after some brief orientation he excused himself and Dermot.

"What makes you so confident this pair of Micks can assassinate the British Prime Minister?" Duke quizzed Brand once his hosts were well out of earshot.

"You've been here how long Duke and you haven't gathered there's at least two other operatives holed up here?" Brand shot back. "I've caught a glimpse of one in the attic and the Republicans habitually allot four men to a cell. Typically a sniper and/or an explosive specialist, an armorer, a goffer/driver and a commander. I'd say Paddy and Dermot do the logistics and the driving, so we haven't met the meat in this sandwich yet."

Kiki was lapping this up and she gave Duke a Cheshire grin that did nothing for his mood.

"How's the arm Herr Duke," she asked him.

"As if you care," Duke replied and poured himself another glass of whiskey.

"If you're going to be effective you should slow down with the alcohol and keep your wits about you," Brand said.

"That's my second," Duke said. "And it's taking my mind off the perforation you put in my wing last week."

"Trager, anything to report," Brand asked.

"Nothing remarkable," Trager said. "Judging by the empty milk and whisky bottles they've been here one or two weeks even if there are more of them."

"Good. Anything else," Brand asked.

"I haven't heard the boy speak yet," Trager said.

"I'll join you in that nightcap now Duke," Brand said. "Would you care to join us Lady Amelia?"

"Only if the Irish are bottling sparkling wine these days," she said.

———————————

Brand was weary but his mind wasn't ready to sleep. He found his way to Patrick's room and informed him he'd be going for a walk.

"You can have young Dermot tail me if you wish," Brand said.

"Oh that won't be necessary," Patrick said. "Just be sure not to draw attention to yourself."

Brand ignored the impertinent superfluity and left the building. The mercury had been inching down all afternoon and the air was heavier now, waiting for a storm to leaven it. A bed of peonies still censed the garden generously despite all the neglect and an owl hooted a warning to any mouse smart enough to listen. The park gate had been padlocked but its height was no obstacle and Brand began his perambulation.

He wanted to sift through the inconsistencies Hollins was presenting: the escort for him versus nil for headstrong Duke; the timing of the activation; the cloaking of the cell's size. Hollins was probably marching to more than one drum; Brand needed to discern which beat would dictate the dance.

In contrast with the ramshackle house, the adjacent park was immaculate. The preponderance of perennials was driven by cost and the arthritic knees of the WWI veterans who tended the gardens. Gladiolas, roses and all manner of lilies were pitting their fragrance against beds of rosemary and eucalyptus. Brand stooped down to isolate the damask from a show of Baronne Prévost roses and mused fleetingly about taking a bloom back for Lady Amelia. He straightened back up and told himself to get a grip.

He headed back to the safe house. The rain was coming, and he didn't want poor Dermot to catch a summer cold.

57. Kilburn, North London – June 13th

By 7am the safe house was being infused bottom to top with the smell of a Bauernomelett Trager was preparing in a vast cast iron pan. The simple combination of eggs, potatoes, onions, parsley and milk was missing the authenticity of some bacon, but an ancient bottle of HP sauce bequeathed by a previous occupant lent a substitute layer of flavor.

With no ceremony the other two members of the cell joined the breakfast table. Trager scoffed down the rest of his slice and set two more places. He then began making a second omelet, leaving Duke and Brand to size up the new diners, and vice versa.

The slender one brushed aside the knife and fork as though he'd been unhabituated to flatware even before losing two of the fingers on his left hand. His leery right eye danced around the room whereas his left one was immobile, as if of glass.

The other fellow bore more than a passing resemblance to Hollins and carried himself with as much poise and menace.

"If you don't mind me saying you bear an uncanny resemblance to my comrade, Michael Hollins, Are you related?" Brand asked.

"Just first names here. I'm Ryan, and this is Shane," the urbane one replied.

"A king and a chieftain," Brand said with reference to the Gaelic meaning of their names.

Ryan breezed past the small talk as easily as he had Brand's first feeler.

"No doubt you'll be anxious to review our plans and…." Ryan broke off as Kiki entered.

"Ah good morning Lady Amelia," Ryan said. "Please enjoy your breakfast with us this morning but I will have to insist you confine yourself to your bedroom for the rest of your stay here."

"Kidnapping and unlawful imprisonment," Kiki responded.

"Just two of our many timeworn specialties," Ryan said.

Kiki sat down demurely and allowed Trager to serve her a sliver of omelet and a mug of black coffee. She took a whiff of the brown sauce he proffered and winced. Shane's good eye had stopped roving and was channeling between Kiki and his empty plate. Until Ryan brought his knife hand to rest on the tabletop.

Ryan gathered up his coffee mug and with two more hand signals instructed Dermot to stay put in the corner and Patrick and Shane to follow him upstairs. Shane's timid ascent presaged the bollocking he was about to get. Brand invited Trager and Duke to join him in whispered congress at the table, positioning themselves so Kiki blocked Dermot's line of sight. Shane wasn't the only one who couldn't take an eye off Kiki and Dermot was so distracted he didn't rumble the reason for Brand's stage management.

"Safe bet explosives will feature in this attack," Duke observed. "I wonder if Shane has a device ready built?"

"I hope so," Brand said. "I wouldn't like to hurry him into making one."

"And Ryan likely knows his way around a long gun judging by his military training," Trager said.

"So that gives us the foursome we expected?" Duke asked, as though he had.

"Plus a few operatives on the inside of the target venue no doubt," Brand said.

Trager and Duke cleared the table and Trager assumed washing duty at the sink. Still smarting from Ryan's isolation order, Kiki had another dig as Duke took up the teacloth to dry.

"What a touching scene of domestication Brand," she said. "You must be immensely proud of your brood?"

"You just won't let up will you?" Duke said. "I pray you find a way to temper your petulance, before it becomes the death of you."

"Do you pray at an altar or from within a circle of blood?" Kiki fired back.

"Trager, please take Lady Amelia to her room when she's finished her coffee, and lock the door," Brand said. "Then join Duke and I in the dining room. And thank you for a first-class Bavarian breakfast."

———————————

Ryan had laid out a four-foot square diagram of the Savoy Hotel and its environs on the dining room table. It detailed the ground floor amenities and all ingress and egress of the hotel and adjoining buildings together with the rights of way and major obstructions beyond.

Brand cast his eye over it and said:

"I think you'll find there's a gate between that alleyway and the steps below which is locked shut on feast days."

"Well we can thank the Blessed Virgin and all the Saints they'll be no such celebrations tomorrow," Ryan said, attempting to make light of the omission.

"Let's dive into the detail and see what else we find," Brand said. "In case we need to do a reccy this afternoon."

"Always possible," said the ever-affable Patrick, earning a piercing look from his commander.

"Neither necessary nor prudent," Ryan said, trying to regain face before continuing.

"Churchill's favorite table is here," he said pointing to a blue cross.

"How can we know Churchill will be there?" Duke said, impatient to get to what he considered the plan's many flawed assumptions. It was Brand's turn to get his ducklings back in a row.

"We'll get to that, said Brand. "Please carry on Ryan."

"Churchill will be dining with General Smuts. Churchill's bodyguard, Walter Thompson, invariably positions himself here and, if Smuts does attend, his aide de camp will be there too.

"An incendiary device will be secreted here, and its blast pattern will radiate out here. Its blast is not intended to kill but to force Churchill and his protection out into Savoy Court here. From there he'll be drawn away from his bodyguard, and over to the other side of the street putting him in the field of fire of a sniper positioned on the top floor here. This turret structure has 270-degree windows onto the street below."

"Why not just blow them to smithereens in the restaurant?" Duke said, unable to bear any more elaboration.

"A device of the necessary power to do the job conclusively would be too big to hide and keep stable?" Brand ventured.

"Correct," said Shane, speaking from bitter experience.

"And a wounded Churchill would be even more intolerable than a healthy one," Ryan added.

"Why not just have someone on the street ready to spray the evacuees with machine gun fire," Duke pressed on.

"Is your boy here always so cantankerous Brand?" Ryan said, not waiting for an answer.

"We're not wanting to conduct a massacre on mainland soil in the midst of the Normandy campaign," he said. "Public opinion across the pond is vital to us and, whereas the loss of one egoistical British politician can be reasoned away, indiscriminate killing of civilians, particularly visiting Yanks, would be strategic suicide for us.

As a failsafe there will be another handgun shooter in the street here in case the sniper misses," Ryan added. "But I shan't."

"And how will you exit the tower, Ryan?" Brand asked.

"It's good of you to ask," Ryan said. "There's an escape route through here that'll get me out into Savoy Way and down the hill before the bobbies get everything cordoned off."

"And how will the PM be lured over to the other side of the street?" Brand continued.

"Ah that's where your fair Lady comes in," Ryan said ominously.

———————————

Drilling the plan had continued up to and beyond a lunch of cheddar cheese and onion sandwiches and dandelion and burdock pop. Duke had continued to find fault wherever he saw fit but none of his misgivings resulted in material amendments.

Brand, on the other hand, had made several more telling observations and Ryan had stopped trying to minimize their importance. He'd even come round to the view that the benefits of a reconnaissance trip that afternoon outweighed the risks. Although he would not concede that any of the details of the hotel's interior warranted scrutiny. Well embedded operatives could be contacted to iron out those few wrinkles. The afternoon trip would focus on the hotel's surroundings and would be made by Brand with Patrick as driver.

Patrick stayed off the A roads and weaved his way around Regent's Park and past the British Museum to the Aldwych. Turning right onto the Strand he then made to turn left into Savoy Court and drop Brand off in the turning circle. They had played with the idea of Brand sitting in the back for the journey so he would look like some big wig being chauffeured. As Patrick lined up for his final turn Brand was glad he'd decided to sit up front.

He reached over and gently pushed Patrick's steering into the right-hand lane. Brand knew the traffic direction of Savoy Court was a throwback to hackney carriage days when drivers could reach down and open the suicide doors of their cabs for their disembarking passengers without dismounting. Patrick colored up and sweat broke out on his upper lip while Brand continued to worry about what else might have been overlooked for want of local savvy. He decided limiting his recce to the outdoors was a bad idea.

Brand acknowledged the doorman's tip of the hat.

"Don't worry sir," he said. "Catches everybody out. Your driver can wait over there if you'll only be short while? Otherwise 'fraid he'll have to clear the precinct."

"That's very helpful. It is just a flying visit," Brand said, slipping a pound note into the doorman's white gloved palm. The largesse was just enough to stretch the permitted wait time to the limit, while not encouraging curiosity.

Brand's concerns centered on the aftermath of the blast so he tracked back from the restaurant exit and began envisaging the options Churchill's bodyguard would encounter in the ensuing mêlée. True enough there was a pivot point where, unless one route could be made non-viable, the odds of Churchill exiting onto Savoy Court were halved. And, if Churchill was shepherded south, two alternative escape paths came into play.

As he re-entered the lobby he scanned a woman he vaguely remembered coming through the revolving doors. He ducked behind a Chinoiserie screen to his left and retrieved a napkin an elderly lady had let fall from her lap.

"Why thank you, young man, so gallant," the old lady said, not sure whether a thank you was sufficient, or a tip was called for. She opted for generosity and began reaching for her handbag. Brand stayed her hand. The combination of his kind smile and gentle touch made the Dowager's day and gave time for the young lady to traverse the lobby with her handsome escort en route to the Riverside Room.

Brand followed them down to the Thames Room, ready to veer off towards the cloakrooms if spotted, while his memory went into overdrive.

"Ah yes," he thought. "The policewoman from the pier."

Back at the safe house all hell had broken loose in Brand's absence. A bloodied Dermot was lying on the dining room floor while Ryan was sat at the table, a damp towel bound around his right hand.

Ever helpful Duke offered to explain events and congratulate himself in the process.

"I did say keeping that woman around was a liability," he said.

It was Brand's turn to request silence with his knife hand and he turned to Trager for an unbiased account.

"Dermot was taking tea to Lady Brown and got into an argument somehow. Herr Ryan heard the commotion before I did and dragged him down here for some schooling. I'm glad he got there before me, Lady Brown has been through enough," Trager reported succinctly.

Patrick had knelt to tend to Dermot, and it was clear the young man had taken quite a beating.

"All very chivalrous Ryan," Brand said. "But is our friend here still fit for duty?"

"It's of no consequence," Ryan said. "What matters is I appear to have cracked my hand on him. I should've shot the firkin eejit."

Ryan unwrapped the binding to reveal his hand, puce and painful looking.

"That looks like a pair of fractured metacarpals. Your trigger hand?" Brand asked. Ryan nodded ruefully and Duke added a dose of sarcasm.

"As an American friend of mine would say, "Just Peachy"."

"I told you I wouldn't assist in your treachery, Brand, and if you think this further affront has persuaded me otherwise you're richly mistaken," Kiki said, winding up to a tirade.

"Don't even think about telling me again how this isn't what you intended and all that horse manure. You're no better than the rest of these animals and I hope you all rot in Hell."

She was in no mood to be physically examined so, while she ranted, Brand gave her a visual check-up. Evidently Dermot didn't have Kastner's talent for cruelty and, as Trager had added discreetly before Brand came upstairs, Kiki had done a number on Dermot's groin before he could do her any real damage. Trager could still recall the searing pain her sharp knee was able to inflict.

"Well I'm sure you did nothing to incite or confuse the young man," Brand said. "Unless there's anything requiring urgent attention I'll come back when you've had an opportunity to compose yourself."

A china mug broke into pieces on the inside of the bedroom door as Brand exited and locked it.

Brand went into conclave with Ryan on coming downstairs.

"If you are Hollins' brother you must have been way behind him in the queue when they were handing out common sense," Brand said. He was running out of patience with the immaturity of the senior operatives around him.

Ryan was feeling contrite and offered no defense for the beating.

"Michael's my elder brother and when he hears about this he's going to disown me, or worse" he said. "I think we have to scratch this mission."

"Negative and maybe he doesn't have to," Brand countered.

"How so?" Ryan asked.

"What type of sniper rifle do you use?" Brand said.

"Lee-Enfield Mark 4," Ryan said.

"SAL or Holland and Holland?" Brand asked.

"I've no idea," said Ryan.

"It doesn't matter, the question was only meant to impress upon you that I'm familiar with that weapon," Brand said. "And to support my intention to substitute for you as sniper on this mission."

"Michael will never agree to that," Ryan said.

"He doesn't need to know – unless you'd prefer one of your brother's henchmen to crack your kneecaps?" Brand said. "Think it over – but quickly – while I tell you about a few more things we need to revise to get Mr. Churchill into my sights."

The remainder of the evening passed calmly with a few hands of gin rummy for those still able to hold a hand of cards, minor plan adjustments for Ryan and Patrick and final priming of the device by Shane.

"One of our inside men will make sure that alternative escape route is headed off as soon as the bomb goes off," Patrick reported, coming off the phone which, apparently, no longer needed to be kept a secret.

Trager had made a vegetable soup and had taken a cup and some buttered toast up for Kiki's supper.

"She wants to speak to you," he told Brand on his return.

"Not while there's loose crockery in that room," Brand said. He finished his supper and then attended to her.

"You've hardly touched your food," he said. "Our chef will be offended."

"I want to make one last appeal to your better nature," she said. "Abandon this crazed mission and let me go."

"I don't know what you think my mission is, but rest assured it's rational and will help hasten the end of hostilities," Brand said.

"I know it involves the Prime Minister and, given the caliber of the company you keep, I doubt you're planning to decorate him. Besides which, I really don't see how I can help you."

"You, my Lady, are going to help keep the Prime Minister safe while we dispose of our real target. If you refuse to cooperate you will have his blood, and that of your paramour Corbin, on your hands," Brand said.

"He's going to be there too?" Kiki asked anxiously.

"Touching but no," Brand said. "Though he won't be hard to track down in a war zone and a stray bullet will finish the job Duke started, if you choose to act irresponsibly."

58. House of Commons, Westminster – June 14th

The Prime Minister was on his feet putting a straight bat to a plethora of questions laid down in search of news about France. His old adversary Mannie Shinwell, MP for Easington in County Durham was there, and had just taken his customary pot shot. In unlikely league with The Earl Winterton, another patriotic critic of Churchill, Mannie was reinforcing his reputation as the poison in Parliament's "Arsenic and Old Lace".

But it was the Celtic loquacity of Aneurin 'Nye' Bevan, the member for Ebbw Vale, which was taking up most of the oxygen in the Chamber this evening, provoking one the PM's popular put-downs.

"I am afraid the honourable Gentleman's question was so long that I have forgotten what was the point of it," Churchill said.

The admonitions of his generals at Cruelly remained top of his mind. They still worried Churchill might, even inadvertently, betray details of their battle plans either to the press or Parliament if he was drawn into a debate. So Churchill soldiered on with a few more parries, refusing to be drawn on the War's conduct, and then left his lieutenant, Anthony Eden, Leader of the House of Commons, to mop up questions concerning the Dodecanese Islands and Egypt.

There was some cheering and waving of order papers as Churchill left the chamber. The mood in the country was equally buoyant. The last time Northern France had featured so heavily in the British Press had been coverage of the ignominious retreat from Dunkirk.

Now tabloids and broadsheets alike were trumpeting the breaches of Rommel's Atlantic Wall and the incursions into the hedge country beyond. In the Far East, American Marines and Seabees were establishing air bases in the Marianas Islands and the bombing campaign against mainland Japan was in full flight.

But it wasn't all plain sailing and Churchill was accustomed to the inevitable reversals of war. Earlier that day Monty had called off Operation Perch, the taking of Caen, just as Patton had forecast he would. If the Speaker opened the floor to debate the rough would come out with the smooth.

In the Commons lobby Smuts was chewing over a thorny Privy Council matter with the Liberal Chief Whip, Sir Percy Harris, when Churchill exited the chamber.

"Grooming my successor Percy?" he said in a stage whisper.

Smuts eyes narrowed as he turned to see Churchill in motion, as always, and in jest, as was most welcome. Churchill was referring to an old chestnut promoting General Smuts as the PM's best replacement should anything ill befall him. Since the idea had been originally floated by Churchill's Parliamentary Private Secretary it was suspected to have had Churchill's blessing, once upon a time. But, while a great compliment to Smuts' credentials, it was both impractical and unconstitutional.

"While I have the utmost admiration for the General's qualifications, I could not bear the thought of losing your steady hand on the tiller of State, Prime Minister," Harris said.

"Well if you are to fill my shoes Smuts, we better fatten you up a smidgeon," Churchill said. "You'll excuse us Percy, we have matters of the graviest importance to pour over."

59. Kilburn, North London – June 14th

The daytime passed uneventfully with Kiki locked away and everyone else trying their utmost to maintain an air of calm. More plan drilling, repetitive weapon cleaning and card playing whiled away the hours. No alcohol, at least not in company.

Although he did the best job concealing it, Brand's anxiety was at its highest pitch. There was too much about this jape which didn't sit right. On the Irish side: the grand, though faded, property; the conspicuous car; a careless bomber and an intemperate commander. It felt like failure by design and to this he was adding a loose homicidal cannon, a well-meaning ex-tanker and an unpredictable aristocrat.

Assassination attempts although seemingly simple were notoriously difficult to pull off. Killing was never easy and when the merest whim of a myriad of players could change the arc of a mission in a moment, the odds were never good. Brand decided he needed to tweak the odds in his favor and called Ryan aside.

"I'm going to need Trager alongside me in the tower," Brand said.

"Who's going to drive the second getaway vehicle?" Ryan asked.

"That Humber shouldn't be deployed, it's too grand. Trager and I can make our escape on foot," Brand said.

"Why do you need Trager anyway, he's not a sniper is he?" Ryan said.

"He is actually but that's not it. There's only one feasible exit from that position as you know and, if we have to fight our way out, Trager's the man for that detail," Brand said emphatically.

Ryan wasn't comfortable with this late change, but he couldn't see that it made much difference to their chances of success. And, in the event of failure, he didn't want to give Brand any excuse to present to his elder brother.

"As you wish," he said. "But make that your last alteration Brand. Good butter only gets churned so much."

Coming from this deeply flawed chef the culinary image was risible, but he maintained his façade of respect, nodding his agreement. Rejoining the troops Brand tried to put some pep in their step.

"What gastronomic delights do you have in store today, Trager?" he asked. "Or have you handed the chef's apron back to Patrick here?"

"Right you are," Patrick said. "I'm pitching in today and a finer bubble and squeak you'll never have tasted. Why I've even managed to lay hands on some pork hock to go with"

Trager's ears pricked up at the mention of pork hock; memories of his Aunt Greta's crispy Schweinshaxe flooded back. He was going to ask Patrick if he'd be frying or roasting the meat when Duke cut across.

"Bathed in that brown sauce of yours Paddy I'm sure it'll be almost palatable," Duke said.

"Well there's nothing to say you have to eat it young fella," Patrick said. "No reason to spoil that lean and hungry look of yours."

Brand marveled at the pace with which his intended motivator had subverted into a Shakespearian flash point. Tensions really were rising.

"Well Patrick those hocks won't cook themselves so why don't you and Trager set to," Ryan intervened.

The chefs went downstairs to join Dermot and Shane who'd been keeping out of the firing line in the kitchen.

"Proof a toff education can't instill leadership qualities if there's nothing there in the first place. Eton was it, old chap?" Ryan asked Duke.

"Winchester actually. And you, Clonmel Borstal?" Duke asked.

"Good grief gentlemen! From the foot soldiers perhaps, but not from the officers," Brand interceded. "If you won't help me bolster morale, keep your mouths shut. Now I suggest, make that insist, that we go to neutral corners and regain some focus!"

60. The Savoy Hotel – the Evening of June 14th

The consistent meetings of The Other Club had fascinated the IRA since the club's foundation thirty years since. Churchill and his close friend, F. E. Smith had decreed its purpose in the second of its succinct rules: to dine. And dine they did, at the Savoy every fortnight. The club's broader purpose was to bring together an eclectic group of men of all political leanings and interests to discuss everything from affairs of state to the price of peas.

Perhaps out of respect for his late friend, Churchill had determinedly attended the club's gatherings throughout the war, and it was that metronomic regularity, and the other prime targets amongst the membership, that beguiled the IRA's planners

The authorities had urged hotel management to stop hiring Irish staff. But, over time, it had proved relatively easy for the IRA to maintain a presence in the Savoy's kitchens and front of house. Providing the Irish brogue wasn't too thick and Protestant beliefs were asserted, it wasn't hard to secure a position especially since so many mainland hospitality staff had been conscripted or hired away by the factories. A welter of intelligence was relentlessly collected from these insiders and, whenever preparation of certain ingredients was made in quantity, it lent added credence to who would be dining that night or the next.

One thing the security service did insist upon was no ceremony whenever the PM's Humber rolled up. He and his guests were to be ushered out of the car, never use the revolving doors and move onto their destination without delay. This objective was often thwarted when Churchill lingered over instructions to his driver or encountered someone worth talking to in the lobby. But not for want of trying.

This evening the Prime Minister and General Smuts were lickety-split and jovial as they entered and made their way to their table, Walter Thompson and the General's aide-de-camp in close attendance.

As soon as Dermot and Shane returned from delivering the device, Patrick, Trager, Brand and Kiki piled into the Austin. The plan called for Duke to join them, but he insisted on going alone. Brand didn't like the last-minute alteration but there was adequate time for him to make it, even by public transport. And packing the Austin with five was a mite conspicuous.

With no good reason to be there, other than getting directly involved in any mistakes Brand might make, Hollins stayed back.

"Be sure to keep me updated on the radio," he said as Patrick let out the clutch and got underway.

Hollins went back inside and began supervising the boys' clean-up work, Dermot copping for all the nasties.

Thompson was recounting how many assassination attempts had occurred on his watch while, at the Prime Minister's table, Smuts was sharing a report he'd received earlier.

"Do you remember me saying I could smell Nazis nearby when we were at Monty's camp the other day?" he said.

"Yes, stuff and nonsense, what of it?" Churchill asked.

"Two well-armed German soldiers came out of the nearby bushes and surrendered today. They'd been cut off from their unit and were hiding there throughout our visit," Smuts said, tapping his nose.

"It is a very fine nose you have Smuts," Churchill said, tilting his head. "For both the Hun and the Stellenbosch. Tell me, what do you make of this Rioja?"

Their banter continued through the consommé and on to the main course. Pre-war that might have entailed a Sole Alice prepared tableside for Smuts, aromas of thyme and flash fried oysters priming the palate. In perfect unison Churchill's Dover Sole would come to table, fried, wrapped in smoked salmon, and garnished with scampi.

Tonight they both "made do" with a classic Sole Doré, lightly dusted in seasoned flour and shallow fried in a modicum of clarified butter. Not a huge sacrifice admittedly but a deserved treat now the end had begun.

Before they could tuck into a modest cheese plate of gruyere, cheddar and Wensleydale paired with a Six Grapes Port, the incendiary device detonated. A blast far less impressive than many Churchill and Smuts had experienced sent shockwaves through the room and fire began feeding on drapes, table linen and Wilton carpet.

In a trice Thompson had his long arms around his boss and was guiding him towards the exit. Smuts had eschewed his a-d-c's help and was coaxing a screaming woman who had been literally petrified by the blast. The crack of a mirror dispelled her inertia, and they followed hard on the heels of the Prime Minister and his bodyguard.

Thompson had wanted to head down to the Thames Room and the riverside exits but an officious fellow in black jacket and striped trousers barred their way, insisting in a plummy accent the path to safety lay in the other direction towards Savoy Court. Thompson hesitated, suspicious of this chap's calm demeanor. Why was a fellow like him not in the war? But Churchill took the advice and made his way to the street with Thompson playing catch up and shaking his head as Smuts came alongside.

"What's wrong Walter?" Smuts asked, hacking some smoke out of his lungs.

"Keep your eyes peeled sir," Thompson said. "Something's fishy."

Out in Savoy Court, Thompson got to assessing next best actions. The crowd of evacuees was beginning to fill the street. He didn't want to traipse Churchill out onto the Strand but neither did he feel secure kettled in this cul-de-sac. It was exactly why he'd wanted to head towards the river.

Before he could reject both bad options and head back, he heard "Prime Minister!" being shouted by a woman, and saw Churchill begin striding towards the call. A Knight in all respects, he had recognized Lady Amelia Brown across the street and felt compelled to go to her aid.

The shout alerted the gathering crowd to the Prime Minister's presence and a wave of admirers began to track in his wake, impeding Thompson as he tried to get back on Churchill's hip. As Churchill approached, Kiki saw where Duke had been all this time. He was exiting a door of the adjacent theatre and closing in on the Prime Minister.

In the turret above Savoy Court Brand had adjusted the rifle's telescopic sight for the optimal magnification and put a round into the chamber. Trager stood ready to open the southerly window as soon as the bomb blast was heard. On hearing it, Brand settled into his firing position, regulated his breathing and moved the rifle's safety lever to fire.

He put Kiki into the crosshairs and waited for his target to come into view. Brand always kept his other eye open when sighting to maximize his field of vision. It paid unexpected dividends when he saw Duke exiting the theatre earlier than planned, looking like he intended to intercept the Prime Minister.

Kiki darted forward into Churchill's arms as Duke fired his pistol.

In the same instant a rifle crack reverberated between the buildings and a bullet tore a gaping hole in Duke's skull.

"Did you hit him?" Trager asked. Brand nodded as he calmly withdrew his weapon and closed the window, shutting out the ringing bells coming along the Strand and the screams from the Court below.

"Time for us to make tracks," Brand said.

———————————

Down below a kneeling, weeping Churchill was cradling Kiki in his arms, ignoring Thompson's insistent calls for them to get out of harm's way. Smuts, pistol drawn, was standing over his old friend and casting around for further threats. None came.

"There's a handsome, young photographer I'm fond of," Kiki breathed hoarsely. "I'd be very grateful Sir, if you could let him know I was thinking of him…"

Churchill said he would, and she breathed her last. His tears moistened her forehead as he kissed it and then lowered her eyelids.

"There's nothing more we can do here sir," Thompson implored again, anxious to be gone before photographers arrived.

"He's right Winston," Smuts added. "Best we get out of here."

They helped Churchill up and out onto the Strand. A waiting police car whisked them away.

———————————

As Trager and Brand came out into Savoy Way, pistols in hand, they were confronted by Ryan standing in front of the Humber – his damaged hand cupping a radio handset to his ear and a revolver in the other.

"Patrick here tells me he's just seen Churchill being bundled into a police car on the Strand. Right as rain," Ryan shouted. "Are ya that bad a shot Brand or just a durty lyin' Fascist?"

"If you can shoot so well with your left hand you should've stuck to the task, Ryan," Brand replied, closing the distance between them. "If not, perhaps you shouldn't be so free with your insults."

Ryan lifted his pistol but not as fast or steady as Brand. A .45 round drove a lethal path right between the Irishman's eyes and he crumpled to the ground.

Brand lay the sniper rifle alongside Ryan's body and joined Trager in the Humber. They drove down Savoy Hill at a sedate pace and out onto the Embankment.

"I'm not one to question your actions Herr Brand," Trager said. "But was that wise?"

"Perhaps not, Trager," Brand said. "I'll have to confine my fly fishing to Scotland from now on."

Epilogue

A light south-westerly breeze was rustling the oaks of Kensal Rise Cemetery and the odd cloud kept pace with the cortège as it processed to a double gravesite. Lady Brown's sudden demise had been too much for her husband's frail condition and he had succumbed one week after hearing of her murder.

The Commons wasn't sitting and, even if it had been, The Prime Minister would have insisted on paying his last respects, especially in the graveyard where his own daughter was lain. Given the debt owed to Lady Brown, Thompson had expected nothing less.

Having rushed back from Eire too soon Corbin had suffered a relapse and was confined to a wheelchair, pushed by WPC Vera Wright and accompanied by Major General Colin Gubbins.

After a brief committal the mourners began to slake away. Churchill paused before Corbin who tried to stand. The Prime Minister gestured for him to remain seated and shook his hand.

"Lady Amelia would have wanted you to have this token of my Government's gratitude for her bravery," he said, and placed a velvet covered case on Corbin's lap. He nodded and left Corbin to read the words 'For Gallantry' engraved on the silver cross therein.

Corbin and Vera lingered a while longer before rolling slowly back down the hill. It was taking all of Vera's will not to join in Corbin's sobbing and the unwelcome sight of tall man coming out from behind a tree to bar their path triggered a reaction.

"Get out of our way!" she ordered, assuming him to be a journalist.

Corbin put his hand on hers to becalm her.

"I thought we might see you here," Corbin said. "Especially skulking in the bushes."

Brand accepted the gybe and waited a moment before speaking.

"Lady Amelia was a courageous woman, and I am deeply saddened by her death," he said.

Finally Vera felt the penny drop. This was no journalist. She reached for her whistle. Brand patted his chest holster and shook his head to discourage her.

"I doubt our paths will cross again Corbin, but I'm glad they did," Brand said. "Some very bad actors got their comeuppance, and the British bulldog gets to fight another day."

"You saved my life, I owe you that," Corbin said. "But you should have spared Amelia, and I'll never forgive you that."

Brand blinked and strode past them while they resumed their descent.

He tossed two Baronne Prévost roses down onto Kiki's coffin, one for himself and one for Trager, before making his escape.

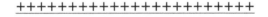

Printed in Great Britain
by Amazon

64837859R00142